"And then she mouthed a word at me—an unmistakable word that told me everything I needed to know. *Checkmate.*"

❖

*E*valine Stoker and Mina Holmes have reluctantly agreed to act as social chaperones and undercover bodyguards for Princess Lurelia of Betrovia, who has arrived in London to deliver a letter with the location of an ancient chess queen that's been missing for centuries. But when the letter—which will heal a centuries-old rift between England and the Betrovians—is stolen out from under Evaline and Mina's watchful eyes, the two girls are forced into a high stakes race to ensure they find the chess queen before anyone else does . . . including their foe, the Ankh. For the chess queen is not only a historic symbol of a woman's political power, but it has literal power as well—the queen will unlock the chessboard, revealing both treasures and ancient secrets the Ankh would kill to possess. It will take Mina's smarts and Evaline's strength to beat the thief and untangle this mystery before it is too late.

MORE PRAISE FOR THE STOKER & HOLMES NOVELS

The Clockwork Scarab

"With its fog-shrouded setting, its heart-racing and clever plot and, most of all, its two completely delightful, kick-butt heroines, *The Clockwork Scarab* is pure, delicious fun from beginning to end."

—Rachel Hawkins, *New York Times* bestselling author of the Hex Hall series

"Thank you, Colleen Gleason, for giving the world the teenage female equivalent of Sherlock Holmes! Where has she been all these years?"

—Sophie Jordan, author of the Forgotten Princesses and the Firelight series

"Two strong, intelligent heroines, who establish themselves as worthy of the legends that surround each of their families, come together to solve a most dangerous mystery. Gleason's writing is witty, humorous, tense, and beautifully Victorian."

—Kady Cross, author of *The Girl in the Steel Corset*

The Spiritglass Charade

"If Buffy the Vampire Slayer and Sherlock Holmes ever met, this book would be the result. If you loved 'Nancy Drew' or 'The Hardy Boys' as a kid, you're going to love this sci-fi/fantasy mystery series."

—*SLJ Teen*

"Well written, fun, and a clever mix of new story with historical and contemporary references that just kept the pages turning."

—*Nerd Girl*

The
Chess Queen
Enigma

A STOKER & HOLMES NOVEL

*T*HE *C*HESS *Q*UEEN *E*NIGMA

COLLEEN GLEASON

CHRONICLE BOOKS
SAN FRANCISCO

To

Darlene Domanik March
Talented artist,
Inspiring teacher,
Dear friend

First Chronicle Books LLC paperback edition, published in 2016.
Originally published in hardcover in 2015 by Chronicle Books LLC.

ISBN 978-1-4521-5649-1

The Library of Congress has cataloged the original edition as follows:
Gleason, Colleen, author.
  The chess queen enigma: a Stoker & Holmes novel / by Colleen Gleason.
    pages cm
  Summary: In 1889 London, vampire-hunter Evaline Stoker and investigator Mina Holmes once again join forces at the request of the Princess of Wales—this time their mission is to escort and protect a princess who is part of a trade mission from Betrovia, a country which has had a rocky relationship with England, starting with a four hundred-year-old dispute over a valuable Byzantine chessboard.
  ISBN 978-1-4521-4317-0
  1. Detective and mystery stories. 2. Vampires—Juvenile fiction. 3. Princesses—Juvenile fiction. 4. Chessboards—Juvenile fiction. 5. London (England)—History—19th century—Juvenile fiction. [1. Mystery and detective stories. 2. Vampires—Fiction. 3. Princesses—Fiction. 4. Chessboards—Fiction. 5. London (England)—History—19th century—Fiction. 6. Great Britain—History—Victoria, 1837-1901—Fiction.] I. Title.

PZ7.G481449Ch 2015
813.6—dc23
[Fic]

                    2014047273

Manufactured in China.

Cover photograph by Marc Olivier Le Blanc.
Design by Jennifer Tolo Pierce.

10 9 8 7 6 5 4 3 2 1

Chronicle Books LLC
680 Second Street, San Francisco, California 94107

Chronicle Books—we see things differently.
Become part of our community at www.chroniclebooks.com/teen.

London, 1889

Miss Stoker

An Astonishing Request

Y*ou killed him. You killed my brother!*
I woke with a start and my eyes bolted open.

My heart was pounding and the sheets covering my skin were damp. Darkness pressed into me. I fought to shake off the dream, but awful visions of blood and darkness, fangs and glowing red eyes, still danced in my mind.

You killed my brother! The shrieking accusation echoed in my head. *How could you kill him?*

I flung off the bedcovers and stumbled to the window with shaky knees. Silvery moonlight filtered over the tree looming just outside, but there was no flash of evil red eyes to be seen.

As I drew in deep breaths of dank, gloomy London air, my pulse slowed. Surrounding me was the constant undercurrent of steam—the breath of our city, flowing and hissing like that of a massive being.

In the distance, Big Ben's round face glowed dully behind strands of heavy night clouds. Pikes, pipes, and the pitches of rooftops, along with the unmistakable spire of the Oligary Building, jutted upward in an infinite black jumble.

I'd done the right thing, staking the vampire.

I was a vampire hunter. That was my calling, my legacy. I couldn't second-guess my duty.

But Willa Ashton's accusations and her enraged expression still haunted me, both during the day and in my nightmares. *You killed Robby! You murdered my brother!*

A shadow across the street, sleek and catlike, caught my attention. All thoughts of Miss Ashton and her brother fled, along with the last bit of sleepiness.

I recognized that shadow.

It took only a moment to whip off my nightdress and yank on a pair of boots, a chemise, and a short, simple gown (in that order). I was still buckling my new front-fastening over-corset when I climbed out the window.

While I dressed, I'd watched the shadow slip across the empty road and into the darkness spawned by our neighbor's hedge. So when I landed on the ground, light and soundless, I knew where he would be waiting.

But before I could open my mouth, a dusky voice spoke in my ear, "That was a righ' quick change o' duds, luv. Unless ye were sleepin' in yer boots."

I managed to control my startled reaction. How did he move so fast? "Perhaps someday you'll learn not to underestimate me, Pix."

He laughed softly, and the sound traveled down my spine as if he'd traced it with a finger. "Evaline, luv, yer the one person I would never underestimate."

My knees felt trembly again, and I decided it would be best to put some distance between myself and the disreputable, annoying, *sneaky* pickpocket. "What are you doing here?"

"Thought ye migh' want some company on yer patrols." Pix remained in the shadow of the tree, but I could still make out the pale shape of his eyes, a sliver of light along one side of his jaw, and the messy cloud of dark hair. I'd also come to know him well enough to recognize the exaggerated nonchalance in his voice.

"Is that so?" I asked, realizing I sounded uncomfortably like my cohort, Mina Holmes. If she were here, she'd probably already have deduced how Pix had gotten to my neighborhood, why he was present, and what he'd last eaten. I pushed away the thoughts of my know-it-all partner—who claimed her unnatural ability was merely a practice of observation and deduction—and shifted to get a better look at him. "How many nights have you been lurking here, waiting for me to go out?"

I felt a little exposed, and I don't mean because I was hardly dressed (at least by my sister-in-law's standards).

The truth was, despite the fact that three weeks ago I'd slain nearly a dozen vampires in the space of seven days, I *hadn't* been out on the streets, looking for more UnDead. Not since that awful episode with Willa Ashton. And if Pix had been watching and waiting for me each night, he would know I had been shirking my duty.

I pushed away a niggle of guilt.

"Now, luv, don' yet get yer corset lacings all mollied up. I jus' happened t'be in th' vicinity and thought I might find ye climbin' down yer tree."

A Night-Illuminator trundled by, burping steam and sending a small circle of golden yellow light around in its wake. Pix and I shifted as one, moving out of the edge of its glow.

"I haven't seen any UnDead since that night in Smithfield," I said, which, strictly speaking, was the truth—mainly because I hadn't been looking for them. I was certain there weren't any left in the city anyway. Or so I'd been telling myself. "Have you?"

"Nay, luv. Nary a red eye nor a fang t'be seen—at least in Whitechapel and thereabouts."

I relaxed slightly. After all, it had been Pix who'd warned me the vampires had returned to London for the first time in decades. "So what brings you to this 'vicinity'"—I'd noticed the inconsistency of his Cockney before—"that made it convenient for you to be calling on me?"

His shadowed expression changed, and for a moment, I thought he wasn't going to answer. His lips flattened, his gaze shifted away . . . then came to focus, sharp and dark, on me. "I need yer 'elp, Evaline."

I blinked and closed my mouth, which had fallen open. Then I grinned. "Of course you do. So . . . what's the problem? You said you haven't seen any vampires around, so it can't be my stake you need. . . . Is Big Marv giving you a difficult time? You need someone to put him in his place again? Break another finger? Or—wait, I know—you want me to be your arm-wrestling champion for some big competition. No worry, there, Pix, *luv* . . . I'm happy to stand in for you." I could hardly control my glee. "Or are you looking for pointers about your wardrobe? You could stand to replace that overcoat. It's a bit shabby, and there are some fine Betrovian wool—"

"Evaline." His voice shook, as if he too were fighting to keep from laughing. "Be still. And I do believe that's the first time ye've ever called me luv." He ducked closer to me as he spoke, and the last few words wafted over my cheek. His breath was warm and pleasantly scented with tobacco and some other pungent spice that Mina Holmes could probably identify, but I couldn't. Pix's hand—ungloved as usual—brushed against mine, and I wasn't certain whether it was an accident.

"Oh, you needn't read anything into it—that's how I address all the young men I know."

"Including your Mr. Dancy?"

"Of course," I responded—even though I'd hardly given a thought to the handsome, charming, and well-dressed Mr. Richard Dancy in weeks. "Now, about that overcoat . . ."

"We can discuss overcoats and sundries later, luv. Righ' now I'm on to more pressin' concerns." He hesitated, and I got the impression he was steeling himself to make his big request—whatever it was. "I need ye t'find out somethin'."

My interest faded. "I'm not the one who *finds out* things, Pix. I'm the one who *does* things. I'm sure Mina would be delighted to assist you, after she lectured your ears off—*are* those your real ears, or are you wearing fake ones again?—about her techniques and observation skills and how she's as brilliant as her Uncle Sherlock, which I think is stretching things quite a bit."

"I've a new customer," Pix said. "A partic'larly large and lucrative client, and I need to find out who—"

"Customer? For what?" I had a fairly good idea what he was talking about, despite my question. I still didn't know what that small, palm-sized device was I'd pickpocketed from him a few weeks ago, but I'd come to the conclusion it wasn't the only one of its kind.

Approximately the size of a pound note folded in half, the object had been flat and sleek, with an intricate array of copper, bronze, and silver wheels, cogs, and dials on one slender end. It also had two small, stiff wires protruding from it. I couldn't begin to guess what it was or what it did, and I hadn't had the chance to ask Mina to take a look at it before Pix blackmailed me into giving it back. But I was fairly certain the little machine had something to do with what he called his "affairs."

"Evaline." His voice had gone sharp. "I've tol' ye before, there are things ye don' need t'know."

"Right then. How can I find out who your new customer is—that's what you want from me, isn't it?—if you won't tell me what they are buying." That was a reasonable question.

Something crinkled softly, and he pressed a paper into my hand. I was bringing it up to examine in the drassy light when he stiffened.

"Hush." He shoved me into the darkest shadow—and though *I* hadn't heard anything, I closed my mouth and listened.

Nothing. I heard nothing but the normal, mechanical sounds of the city at night, saw nothing but the random golden circles of gas lamp streetlights, felt nothing but the normal shift in the air . . . and the strong, silent power of his grip.

After a moment I started to speak, but Pix lifted a hand sharply.

Then, without a word, he curled his fingers around my arm and tugged me after him. I pulled easily out of his grip, but continued to follow as he darted from the shadows of tree to hedge to alley to fenceline.

"Look." He pointed abruptly into the sky.

Several blocks away in the narrow space between buildings, brushing past the sky-anchors that floated above a fog-enveloped cluster of roofs, was a slender, elegant vessel, cruising through the sky. Of a long, elliptical shape, it had a bulge at the bottom and batlike wings on the sides.

It was an airship, the likes of which I'd only seen once before: the night I met Pix.

I was aware of a sense of déjà-vu, standing in the darkness with his lean, muscular body brushing against mine, looking up at the eerie object as it made its way silently through the sky.

A beam of light winked on from the airship. The pale stream aimed straight down, riding over the peak of a roof, bumping down the side of the building, and then up the side of the next building as the ship continued to glide over the city. Another beam flashed out, scoring over more buildings in the same choppy way. The ship was coming closer, and the very sight made all the hair on my body prickle and lift as if I'd been dunked into an icy river.

Pix's breathing had become more shallow. His normal easy stance tensed.

"What is it?" I asked. I'd done so before, several times, with no response—so I had little hope he'd actually answer. "Is it the same one we saw . . . before? At the British Museum?"

His chin brushed my forehead. "Aye. I'd hoped they'd gone, but no."

"They? Who?" I realized he hadn't dropped the 'h' in 'hoped,' but for once I was smart enough not to be distracted. I was more interested in finding out about the airship than calling him on his inconsistent accent.

"They're watching the city. All of us. Stay out of the light, Evaline," he said, his words warm against my hair. "Mark m'words, luv, things are about to be changin'." He groped for my hand, and the paper crinkled as he closed my fingers around it. "I gander this might 'elp. Find out what ye can, and let me know. Ye know where t'find me."

And with that, he melted into the shadows.

Miss Holmes

In Which Our Heroines Take on Two Tasks

Though I was certain my colleague, Miss Stoker, spent all her mornings lazing in bed, I had adopted the daily habit of perusing a range of newspapers and other noteworthy publications whilst in Miss Irene Adler's office at the British Museum.

Happily, this process removed me from underfoot of Mrs. Raskill as she attended to her daily tasks in our household, which more often than not included multiple and varied expressions of her opinions. Most of them were regarding the work I did in the back room, which was outfitted as a laboratory. Her range of emotions—from disgust to irritation to shock and horror and back again—were so common as to be predictable (not to mention loud, as in the time a scorpion scuttled over the counter she was dusting—I had been attempting to collect its poison, for obvious reasons), and thus I seized the opportunity to be absent as much as possible.

Therefore, whether or not Miss Adler was present in her office as the Keeper of Antiquities, and whether or not I had some other reason to be there, by eight o'clock nearly every morning I could be found sitting at a massive desk, drinking her excellent Darjeeling tea, and using the Proffitt's Dandy Paper-Peruser to turn the pages as I scanned the *Times*, the *Voice*, and the *Herald* . . . as well as numerous publications from the Continent and America.

I was engrossed in this process when the impetuous, bold, and—one must admit—brave Miss Evaline Stoker found me one Wednesday morning precisely twenty-three days after we concluded the Case of the Spiritglass Charade. It had been a dull three weeks, and I was eager to find something of interest to occupy my brain.

My colleague burst in, as was her own habit, in a flurry of skirts, umbrella, and cloak, bringing in a gust of musty museum air tinged with the coal smoke of outdoors. The papers on my desk puffed up and shifted as she slammed the door closed, and the top of Miss Adler's teapot rattled in its brand-new brasswork Pouring Station.

"What can you tell me about who wrote this?" Miss Stoker said without preamble.

I confess I wasn't disappointed to be distracted from the uninteresting article about an imminent State Visit involving representatives from the Kingdom of Betrovia. Political and foreign maneuvering are my father's expertise, not mine.

I accepted the scrap of paper from Miss Stoker, noticing she'd eaten a glazed cherry tart whilst wearing gloves and had once again neglected to put money in her tiny handbag. Rather than ask for further information, I turned my attention to the note, which read:

Two dozen this week.
Two dozen next week.
The usual location.
Don't be late, or you'll know the consequences.

Cryptic wording, but there was so much more to be deduced about the sender merely by observation.

Expensive, thick, crème paper . . . yet not exceptional or unique and without monogram—*the individual has wealth and taste but wishes to remain anonymous.*

Very little slant to the penmanship, letters formed nearly upright, with the left margin growing wider as the message went on—*an assertive individual who is logical and practical but deeply invested in some future goal.*

Tall, spiky letters, particularly the "s"—*the individual is intellectual and confident. Most likely a male, and very ambitious.*

Then I looked more closely, frowning. Curious. I lifted the paper to my nose and sniffed.

Faint floral scent, a dusting of powder clung to the edge of the paper—no . . . *a woman wrote this.*

I looked at Evaline. "From where did you obtain this?"

"Pix gave it to me. He wants to know who wrote it."

"And . . . no, I suppose I shouldn't be surprised he doesn't know who it is. When one is dealing in illegal trade, whatever it is, one certainly doesn't want one's identity known."

I sniffed with disdain for Mr. Pix and his business dealings. "Whomever this individual is, my first inclination is that it's an intelligent, confident, and powerful female, who likely has some sort of objective on which she is focused. A business perhaps. She is clearly determined to remain anonymous, and is attempting to disguise her gender by appearing to be a male—" I stopped abruptly, staring at the partial note. My lungs felt as if mummy wrappings were binding them so tightly I could hardly draw a breath.

"Like . . . the Ankh?" Miss Stoker's voice dropped to an uncharacteristically modulated tone.

I didn't respond. My palms had become damp and my pulse kicked up faster as a thrill of excitement rushed through me, followed by a prickle of apprehension.

Scotland Yard was under the assumption—an exceedingly shortsighted and false assumption—that the individual known as the Ankh was dead. I, however, knew that could not be the case. For the last three months, I had waited for some proof I was correct—which was part of the reason I read every publication I could get my hands on and forced myself to go about in public as much as possible while watching for signs she had returned.

This meant I paid particular attention to the activities of Lady Isabella Cosgrove-Pitt, wife of the esteemed leader of Parliament and distant relative of my nemesis, Scotland Yard Inspector Ambrose Grayling. Though I'd never publicly stated my opinion, I was certain she was the Ankh.

And, in fact, I had once looked directly into the eyes of the Ankh and informed her I was aware of her true identity.

"Everything we know about the Ankh fits the description of the individual who wrote this note." I spoke slowly and deliberately as I tried to imagine what this development might portend . . . and if I was merely indulging in wishful thinking so as to prove everyone wrong. "How is Mr. Pix involved?"

I couldn't keep a hint of distaste from my tone as I asked about Evaline's particular acquaintance. Aside from having a ridiculous appellation (although having been christened Alvermina, I suppose I should refrain from judgment; one truly has no control over one's parents' decisions), the disreputable young man was doubtless a thief, most certainly involved in illicit and illegal activities, and had no sense of propriety. Every time I recalled the sight of him in the Ankh's opium den sporting an open vest that revealed tanned, muscular arms and a *bare chest*, I felt uncomfortably hot and a little breathless.

No other male I knew would don something so scandalous—not even my friend Dylan Eckhert, who was from the future, where, I understood, things were quite a bit more lax when it came to propriety.

And certainly the very last person I could imagine wearing such clothing—or lack thereof—would be the stiffly proper Inspector Grayling. Surely the swath of freckles that dusted his capable hands didn't extend to the breadth of his shoulders . . . did it?

"Your cheeks are turning pink, Mina. Are you feeling all right?"

"Of course I am." I lifted my teacup. "I'm merely waiting for you to tell me how your shady acquaintance is involved."

"He came to me for help." Miss Stoker sounded supremely pleased with herself. "It seems the person who sent the note is a . . . well, a client of his. An anonymous client."

"Client?" Warning bells began to jangle in my mind. "One can only imagine what sort of business in which the likes of Mr. Pix is involved. And he wants your *assistance*? Are you addled?"

"Might I remind you, Mina Holmes, that Pix saved your life on at least one occasion—two, if you count him bringing me to find you in the vampire lair at Smithfield, where *I* saved your life. The least we can do is try to repay the favor."

"I refuse to do anything even remotely illegal."

Miss Stoker rolled her hazel eyes. "He just wants us to find out who wrote the note. And if it is the Ankh . . ." Her voice trailed off suggestively.

I sighed. "Very well. I shall keep this note and perform a thorough examination. But it would be quite helpful to know what it is this *client*—who does appear rather threatening—wants from Mr. Pix. At one point, you repeated to me his assertion that he deals with information—collecting it and selling it or otherwise using it to his advantage. It's clearly not the case here, for it sounds as if he—she—is ordering a supply of something. And if she doesn't get it, I wonder what the consequences will be."

"I'm not sure about any of it. Pix had this device . . . he seemed very protective of it. He was selling it or trading it with a vampire when I interrupted the exchange—this was just before the night you and I were in Smithfield. I think the mechanism might have something to do with his business, but he wouldn't tell me anything about it. And he's obviously concerned about her threat, or he wouldn't have asked for assistance."

"Do you suspect he is manufacturing it? Or was that the only one of its kind?"

"I think there are more of them. If I had to guess—"

"Guessing is a futile effort, Miss Stoker. How many times must I remind you that valid *theories* are borne of *observation* and *analysis*? One doesn't *guess*. One deduces."

She rolled her eyes again, and I deduced (based on the observation of her tightening lips, narrowing eyes, and shifting jaw, combined with my knowledge of her character) she was about to say something irritable, but then the office door opened.

My heart did a funny little skip every time that happened, for there was always the chance the newcomer would be Dylan Eckhert.

In this case, however, my base physical reaction to the hoped-for arrival was in vain, for it was Miss Adler who breezed into the chamber . . . followed, quite astonishingly, by none other than Her Royal Highness, Princess Alexandra herself.

Miss Stoker and I bolted to our feet as I dropped the teacup back onto the edge of its saucer. It tipped with a loud clatter and slopped the floral-scented tea all over a stack of papers on the desk. My cheeks burned as I tugged a handkerchief from the cuff of my sleeve.

"Excellent. You are already here," Miss Adler said. "That will make our task much more expedient." Her eyes strayed to the puddle of tea, but she made no comment.

"Good morning, Your Highness." Miss Stoker curtsied with perfect grace.

I hastened to follow suit while trying to surreptitiously mop up the spilt tea and save the papers from their ink running.

The princess, who employed a topaz-and-emerald-encrusted walking stick, made her way to the most comfortable seat in the chamber: a large, barrel-shaped armchair with generously thick cushions. She pushed a button on its arm and the seat rose silently to just beneath her bustle. She angled back onto the cushion, and the seat lowered her to a more comfortable level. "You may be seated," she told us as the chair puffed to a halt.

With one last dab at the wet papers, I vacated the desk chair for Miss Adler's use and selected a place next to Evaline. My brain ticked through its checklist of observations about the princess (she'd recently acquired a small copper-furred dog, selected her own jewelry today, had breakfasted on kippers and blueberry scones, her coach had brought her via the Strand) and my mentor (she'd had her hair trimmed, burned her hand pulling a bread pan from the oven, and appeared particularly well-rested and lively) when the conversation began.

"Ah, I see you've been reading up on the Betrovian visit, Mina," Miss Adler commented. With spare, graceful movements, she extricated the current *London Times* from its moorings, taking care not to set it in the damp spot on her desk, and closed the Proffitt's Dandy Paper-Peruser with a neat click.

"It's rather impossible to avoid doing so. It's been the lead story in every periodical to which I subscribe." With the exception of the *Ladies' Tattle-Tale*, but I wasn't about to admit I knew about that rag, let alone read it. Which, of course, I did. One can never be too informed, even through sensational gossip and fashion stories. I found the latest *on dits* about the comings and goings from a new gentlemen's club called the Goose & the Pearl unaccountably fascinating.

"As well it should be, for it's an important—and sensitive—event. In fact, that's precisely why Princess Alix is here this morning. Madame the Queen has commanded her to be personally involved in all aspects of the visit, including finalizing the details for the event tomorrow." Miss Adler turned to the other woman.

"Indeed. There hasn't been a diplomatic visit between Betrovia and England for more than fifty years. The last time a Betrovian contingent arrived in London, it was a disaster. The young Betrovian prince, who'd been engaged to marry a Russian princess, decided he preferred an English girl—a maid, no less—and the two ran off to Gretna Green in Scotland and eloped. The scandal nearly ended our trade agreement with the Betrovians. As it was, you may be aware that our current arrangement for the importation of their wool, cotton, and internationally prized silk is laden with tax surcharges and limitations."

Miss Adler took up the narrative, a smile curving her lips. "In fact, there have been comparisons to the unfair Stamp Act and Tea Act that England imposed upon my country last century, causing the Americans to revolt. Of course it is an utterly different circumstance—Betrovia is not and never will be a governing body over England and vice versa—but there will, of course, be complaints and unfair, inaccurate comparisons as prices go up. In fact, the trade agreement is in jeopardy of being renewed at even worse terms. And it is all due to a centuries-old dispute revolving around an ancient chess set. But we shall get to that shortly."

I cast a glance at Miss Stoker and wasn't the least bit surprised to see her eyes glazed over with either boredom or confusion. I confess, in this instance we were both of the same mind (although I assure you, Dear Reader, I might be bored, but I wasn't the least bit confused).

"Right then." Miss Adler seemed to recognize our polite disinterest and, thankfully, moved from politics to more relevant information. "The Lord Regent Mikalo Terrence will be the Betrovian official in attendance. He has been charged with delivering a gift to England—a long-lost letter from the Great Queen Elizabeth—along with negotiating a new trade agreement between England and Betrovia. Most importantly, the Princess Lurelia will be accompanying the Lord Regent. It is because of this young lady's attendance that Her Royal Highness requires your involvement. Princess Lurelia must not only be entertained and amused during her visit, but she must also be kept safe and her reputation spotless. Who better to fulfill both requirements than the two of you." Miss Adler bestowed a pleased smile upon each of us in turn. "You are of an age with her, and I trust you will show her the delights of London Society as well as ensure nothing untoward happens."

I dared not look at Miss Stoker, for I suspected the same horror I was feeling would be reflected in her eyes. Society? Entertainment? Did Miss Adler truly expect Evaline and me to be the princess's chaperone to musicales, teas, and soirées? Rides in the park? And whatever else young royals did for amusement?

I could think of few things I would *less* like to spend my time doing.

"How long will the princess be in London?" ventured Miss Stoker. I noticed she wasn't looking at me either.

"No more than a month, I daresay," our mentor replied. "And as it is Second High Season from now until the end of October, there will be plenty of opportunity for you to show her a varied and exciting time."

A month?

"Is the princess in danger? I mean to say, do you expect anything untoward to happen?" I asked.

"Not at all," replied Princess Alix. "But Lurelia is engaged to be married in six months, and it is incumbent upon us to ensure that she returns to Betrovia fully prepared to be wed, and with absolutely no hint of a scandal attached to her. Anything other than a continued spotless reputation could put her marriage at risk. I need not say we do not want a repeat of the previous debacle."

This time I did exchange looks with Miss Stoker. Considering the fact that during our brief acquaintance we'd visited an opium den, encountered two dead bodies, allied ourselves with a pickpocket, and been held captive in a vampire's hideaway—not to mention nearly died at the hands of the Ankh—I wasn't certain we could guarantee Princess Lurelia's reputation would remain spotless if she were encouraged into our company.

"Right then," Evaline said. "When are they due to arrive?"

"Tomorrow," I replied, feeling as if I'd just announced a death sentence.

"*Tomorrow?*"

"Indeed," said Miss Adler. "Princess Lurelia decided to join the trip at the last minute, hence the urgency of our meeting today. There will be an official Welcome Event at the museum late tomorrow afternoon. Of course the two of you will be in attendance." Her voice was smooth and assertive, but her gaze was sharp and unyielding.

Evaline and I exchanged glances once more, but the die was cast. We were to be babysitting a princess for the next month. I could only imagine what the girl would be like: spoilt, fairy-headed, and interested only in shopping, dancing, and her forthcoming nuptials. I wasn't certain which would be worse: listening to the girl prattle on about wedding plans already in place, or having to offer advice and suggestion in order to help her make them.

As we left Miss Adler's office, the note Mr. Pix had given Evaline crinkled in my skirt pocket. At least I had something interesting to look forward to.

Miss Holmes

Wherein the Importance of a Matter Is Argued

Since I would be at the mercy of a princess and her social whims for the next month, I decided it would be to my benefit to find out as much as I could about the Betrovians and their visit.

I remembered reading something about the chessboard Miss Adler mentioned. It was ancient and of Byzantine origin, but other than that, I knew little detail about the situation that had nearly caused our two countries to go to war. Whatever the event, it had happened three centuries ago and was hardly pertinent to my daily work.

Miss Stoker wasn't convinced about the necessity of spending time on such research, but she had no choice but to receive (though likely not fully comprehend the implications of) the information I'd gathered as we rode to the Welcome Event late the next afternoon.

Unsurprisingly, Evaline's first concern was about that disreputable pickpocket's client, rather than the Betrovians. It was six o'clock when I climbed into her carriage, and she immediately began to pester me.

"I've been waiting to hear from you since yesterday, and not a word. Not even a brief note. I thought you were a Holmes! I thought you knew everything! What did you find out about Pix's client?"

It had been dark and blustery all day, and, already being damp and cold, I had hardly settled my bustle and skirts into place on the carriage seat (which is a task easier spoken about than accomplished, considering the numerous layers of fabric involved, and the awkward bump of the bustle low on my spine). My thick hair was turning into bric-a-brac kinks, and I was in no mood to be lectured. "Miss Stoker. One doesn't 'find out' things when one is investigating. One observes, then analyzes and dedu—"

"*Mina.*" Her eyes blazed and I thought she might lunge across the carriage at me. I believe I also heard the sound of her teeth grinding. Apparently, she was in no better mood than I. "What have you *deduced* about Pix's client? Is it the Ankh?"

I resisted the urge to hush her; we were, after all, in her private carriage, and Middy, the driver, couldn't hear anything we said. "I shall tell you all about that later. I have had limited time to spend on the scrap of paper, due to the more pressing matter of the Betrovian visit."

"The Betrovian visit is more important than knowing if the Ankh has returned? Blooming Pete, are you *mad*?"

"I did not say it was more *important*. I said it was more *pressing*. Of course it is of the utmost importance to determine whether the Ankh has returned. But, unlike others in this vehicle, I have no intention of blazing off on a trail without a plan, or at the very least, solid information. I, for one, won't be standing up in the middle of a meeting and shouting accusations and jeopardizing our investigation—not to mention ourselves."

This was, of course, a reference to the time Miss Stoker had announced our uninvited presence at a secret meeting led by the Ankh. We were there anonymously until my companion stood up in the back of the chamber and demanded answers from the villainess. We barely escaped with our lives, and that was only the first time Miss Stoker's impetuousness had endangered a case.

Miss Stoker's face turned pink, and then red, and I was uncertain whether its cause was shame or fury. I didn't care; we weren't far from the museum and I had information to share.

"I've done some research about the Betrovians—"

"I don't *care* about the Betrovians. Blooming fish, Mina, what's wrong with you? Are you *afraid* the Ankh has returned? Is that it? You don't want to face her again? You're avoiding the investigation because—"

"I am not avoiding—don't be *absurd*. That's ridic—"

"Well, you nearly died. No one would blame you if you didn't want to get involved again." Her voice had become quieter. Almost sympathetic.

I struggled to keep my temper and expression under control. I wasn't about to admit I'd clawed myself out of a nightmare early this morning in which I was reliving those terrifying moments of being strapped to a statue, preparing to be electrofied by the villainess herself. Aside from that, I'd felt that same sort of underlying sympathy coming from Evaline more than once in the last few weeks—since we'd realized my mother had been Miss Stoker's vampire-hunter mentor. Neither of us had attempted to discuss this discovery; it had been a strange and unsettling moment, leaving us both silent and uncertain. Even I had no desire to talk about it. And so the knowledge hung there between us like a puffy black cloud.

"Make no mistake, Miss Stoker. I fully intend to find and bring the Ankh to justice. But for now, we really must focus our attentions on the matter at hand. The museum is just two blocks away, and—"

My companion gave a derisive snort and slumped back into her corner. I took this as invitation for me to commence with educating her about the history between England and Betrovia. "The relationship between our nation and that of Betrovia is long and varied, and fraught with upheaval, mistrust, and competition—but it comes down to two important things: we British have become great consumers of the unique and beautiful Betrovian fabric, and the Betrovians wish to supersede Paris as the center of fashion in the civilized world. Therefore, the Betrovians wish to have open trade and excellent diplomatic relations with England because of the reaches of our Empire, and our deep pockets. But it's only been fifty years since the Betrovians returned the Theophanine Chess Table and we've reinstated a working trade agreement."

"What on earth does a chessboard have to do with anything?" Evaline asked rudely.

That was my opportunity to launch into the explanation I'd been trying to give. "The chessboard and pieces were separated centuries ago during a war in Byzantium. The chessboard was promised to Queen Elizabeth as a gift—she had, at some point, acquired the pieces of the chess set—but the King of Betrovia refused to let her have it. That is what caused the great rift between our countries, and it was only fifty years ago that the chessboard was finally delivered to Her Majesty here in London. I'm certain you recall seeing it—it's a massive piece built into a table—and it's displayed in the Third Graeco-Roman Saloon. Surely you—"

The carriage gave a great jolt, nearly throwing me off my seat as the vehicle slammed to a halt. Evaline and I looked at each other, then swung to look out our respective windows.

The last time we'd experienced such an event, that scoundrel Mr. Pix had engineered the cessation of traffic merely so he could deliver a message to my companion. Apparently, flair and dramatics were his *modus operandi*. But this time, it appeared he had no hand in the mess on the lower street level . . . for the thoroughfare was filled with people celebrating the arrival of the Betrovians.

Flags of purple and gold, emblazoned with the Betrovian seal, fluttered from extendable rods from whence they were waved by a great number of spectators at every street level. I wondered whether the flags were made from Betrovian silk or plain old British cotton. There were a great number of them, as if someone had distributed the pennants and gathered the bystanders into place to ensure a celebratory welcome for our foreign guests.

I chafed at the delay as our carriage wended its way through the throngs of people on the street and then turned into the drive of the museum. At last it was our turn to alight, and as one of the guards assisted me to step down, I spied several people making their way up the long, low staircase to the side entrance of the museum.

The gentleman who caught my eye wasn't particularly tall, but he carried himself with such authority that he appeared to tower over everyone near him. Dressed in the most regal and up-to-date fashion, the man moved smoothly and gracefully despite the copper-knobbed cane he employed to climb the steps. I knew the necessity of the cane was due to an accident he'd suffered at the hands of a business rival several years ago, which had resulted in the death of his business partner.

The gentleman wore a tall hat with a particularly curly brim, but I had seen pictures indicating he had a full, thick head of dark hair just beginning to thread with gray at the temples. He sported long sideburns and was otherwise clean-shaven. His handsome features might have been carved from marble. The press reported his age to be approximately forty, but based on what the man had accomplished, I suspected he could be a year or two older.

"Is that Mr. Oligary?" asked Miss Stoker in an undertone.

However, her circumspection wasn't needed in this particular situation, for the crowds were loud (now they were singing the Betrovian National Anthem), and the sound of a loud motor above us (a small dirigible pulling a welcome sign behind it) would have drowned out her question for anyone but me.

"Yes, it is," I replied, my eyes still fastened on the man who had been nicknamed the Genius of Modern Times. I have no idea who would have dubbed him with such a simplistic and exaggerated appellation, but the press had taken hold of the phrase and that was the end of that. "I've never actually met the man, but of course he is very recognizable from the photographs which appear weekly in the papers."

"And there are Lord and Lady Cosgrove-Pitt," my companion pointed out.

Her comment was unnecessary, for it was just as impossible to miss the Parliamentary leader and his wife as it would have been not to notice the Queen herself. He was short and muscular, but very distinguished and with a voice that carried easily over the crowds (and, one presumes, through the walls of Westminster). He was speaking emphatically to a companion as he guided his wife by the arm. Lord Cosgrove-Pitt doffed his hat just as they stepped into the museum, and I saw the silver of his hair and muttonchop sideburns.

For once, I paid little attention to Lady Cosgrove-Pitt other than sparing a moment of admiration for her fashionable magenta dress and the matching handleless parasol that hovered mechanically above her head, for my attention had been drawn to a broad-shouldered, ginger-haired figure who climbed nimbly up the steps in the wake of his distant relatives.

"Isn't that Inspector Grayling over there?" There was a definite smirk in Miss Stoker's tone. "He is a remarkably tall man, isn't he?"

"I'm perfectly capable of observing and identifying the attendees of today's event all on my own," I told her primly as I did my best to keep from looking for that abominable steamcycle Grayling insisted on driving. I had no idea where he would have parked the monstrosity. "You needn't point out every individual walking up the steps."

Evaline didn't respond, but I noticed the curve of her cheeks and the way she ducked her head to hide the sparkle in her eyes. "I wonder if he's here in an official capacity, or as an escort to the Cosgrove-Pitts."

I sniffed and sailed through the open door into the museum, leaving Miss Stoker to follow with her shorter strides. I had nothing further to say on the subject of Inspector Grayling, and I sincerely hoped we would not cross paths during this event.

Fortunately, Miss Stoker and I had been given our directions yesterday during a brief tour with Princess Alix and Miss Adler, so we were able to avoid the throng of people that milled about the Roman Galley. Instead, we turned to the right and walked through the Grenville Library to the Assistant Keeper's Room, where we were to meet the Betrovian princess.

"Miss Evaline Stoker and Miss Alvermina Holmes," announced a guard as he opened the door to a private parlor with a flourish.

I managed not to wince at the use of my full name and stepped into the small chamber. There were only three other people in attendance, but the place was filled with an abundance of antiquities. Unlike in other areas of the museum, where the valuable artifacts were kept in glass cases and far out of the reach of inquisitive fingers, here was a display meant to be examined with not only the eye, but the touch and perhaps even smell.

Small golden Egyptian statues, jade and onyx beaded jewelry, glass mosaic vases and platters, plate-sized paintings, and numerous other ancient *objets d'art* sat on tables, open shelves, and on the floor. I could only imagine what they were worth—more than the Crown Jewels of England, I surmised.

I would have looked at them all day, but my attention was drawn to Princess Alix. Fortunately, I hadn't forgotten my manners, for I'd dropped into a fairly graceful curtsy as my name was intoned a second time—in this instance by the princess herself.

"Her Royal Highness Lurelia Gertillia Vasvenne, I am pleased to present Miss Mina Holmes and Miss Evaline Stoker. They have offered to be your companions during your visit, and I am quite certain you will enjoy their company immensely."

As I rose from my curtsy, I looked up with no small curiosity into the face of the young woman who would be my charge for the next few weeks.

Miss Stoker

Coincidence or Conspiracy?

I have no idea of Mina's initial impression of the princess—though it was surely more detailed than mine. For me, the first word that came to *my* mind when I saw Princess Lurelia was "colorless."

She wasn't unattractive. She was merely bland. Drab. From head to toe. She had mousy blond hair, gray eyes with blond, invisible lashes, pale lips, and fair skin. Even her dress, though made of the coveted Betrovian silk, was colorless—neither white nor cream, nor even ivory.

"I'm pleased to meet you," said Princess Lurelia. In a colorless voice.

Her eyes held no spark of interest or enthusiasm. Her expression was merely polite. Her movements, when she inclined her head to accept our introduction, were stiff and practiced. She didn't appear dumbstruck, or unintelligent, or even nervous or befuddled. She was simply *there*.

I couldn't help but glance at Mina.

The same dismay I felt was reflected in her eyes. We were to be saddled with this girl for four weeks?

I sighed. Maybe she'd relax a bit once we got to know her.

"Mina and I are looking forward to showing you around London," I forced myself to say brightly. My companion, for once, didn't seem to have any wisdom to offer. "There will be parties and theater and picnics, or riding in the park if you like. And of course, we must go shopping and visit New Vauxhall Gardens."

"I will look forward to it." Princess Lurelia's words were well-modulated and as smooth as if rehearsed. Her lips curved up ever so slightly at the corners.

"There is also to be the Official Welcome Ball at the Midnight Palace, hosted by Mr. Oligary," Princess Alix said. "Tomorrow night." She flickered a meaningful glance at me. Somehow I managed to keep from grimacing. Blooming fish, so soon?

"I look forward to it as well," intoned the princess.

I cast another look at Mina, one that was a little more desperate. Then a thought struck me. Maybe Princess Lurelia didn't speak English very well, and that was why she seemed so . . . dull.

Just then, the door of a curio cabinet next to me opened to reveal the inner workings of a clock. A small shelf burst forth, and on top of it were two mechanical men with sledgehammers. They took turns pounding on a tiny anvil in between them. *One . . . two . . . three . . .* , all the way to *six*.

And then a mechanized young woman trundled out onto the shelf and slammed her own hammer into the anvil. Once, twice.

It was half-past six. The ceremony was to begin promptly at seven o'clock.

"We must go," said Princess Alix, gesturing to the door.

The Welcome Event and Exchange of National Gifts was to occur in the elegant Arched Room. Mina and I had walked through the large corridor-like library many times during our visits to the museum, but this time it was filled with people, streamers, and, to my delight, tables of refreshments. Although we had walked over with Princess Lurelia and the others, Mina and I didn't have to make a grand entrance with them. Instead, we slipped past the stage where the ceremony was to be held, and into the small crowd.

"I see they've moved the Theophanine Chess Table into this chamber for the Welcome Event. That was an excellent decision and will emphasize the improved diplomatic relations between our nations," Mina said.

I glanced over to see a massive stone table. It had a wide pedestal base and a thick round top. Presumably, that was what had caused the upset between England and Betrovia. I couldn't imagine why anyone would care about a chess table enough to start a war.

While Mina tripped over Lord Bentley-Hughes's overly large shoes, I headed straight for a table groaning with miniature sandwiches and some colorful liquid in rows of crystal cups. The egg-and-bacon-salad sandwich on tomato-toast was excellent, and I was reaching for another thumb-sized piece when a clock struck seven.

Trumpets sounded, echoing throughout the chamber. I looked up to see four of the long brass horns shining from one of the small balconies that overlooked the hall.

Someone used a large, mechanized funnel to announce in a tinny voice: "Her Royal Highness, Princess Alexandra."

Everyone clapped and cheered, including me. The princess was very popular with the people. She emerged from a paper-festooned entryway and warmly greeted some of the attendees. I recognized most of them as being of the peerage—they were rich, powerful, and important people.

Speaking of rich, powerful, and important people—the next introductions were no surprise to me, for they included such important British personages as Lord Cosgrove-Pitt and Mr. Emmet Oligary.

But it was the last announcement that had me gaping in shock. "And finally, the esteemed Sir Mycroft Holmes."

I spun to look at Mina, whose expression had gone blank, and then stood on my tiptoes to try and see what her father looked like. Why hadn't she mentioned he would be here? I'd heard about the man, who apparently was the Queen and Parliament's most trusted advisor, but never met him. I wasn't acquainted with his more famous brother, Sherlock, either, but at least I'd seen pictures of the detective in the papers.

Sir Mycroft Holmes was tall and slender just like his brother, and daughter for that matter. Unlike the other members of his family, he did sport the beginnings of a paunch beneath his well-tailored coat. He had a prominent, beak-like nose and gray-threaded brown hair that was beginning to thin at the temples. The word that came to mind for him was "stony." He seemed unapproachable, emotionless, and yet very gentlemanly. Even from where I stood, I saw cool calculation in his dark eyes as they swept the area.

I was fairly certain I saw him pause, eyes widening ever so slightly, when his attention skimmed over my companion. But Sir Mycroft gave no other indication he'd seen or recognized his daughter.

I tried to imagine why Desirée Holmes—or, as I'd known her when she was my vampire-hunting mentor, Siri—might have found the man marriageable. He exuded power, he certainly had some wealth, and he wasn't unattractive . . . but Sir Mycroft did not seem like a man who'd woo a woman or care for a wife. He certainly didn't care much for his motherless daughter.

"Announcing Her Royal Highness, Princess Lurelia Gertillia Vasvenne, and the Lord Regent of Betrovia, Mikalo Terrence!" cried the powerful voice.

More music began to play. Probably the Betrovian National Anthem, but I wasn't sure. I didn't find it very pleasant. It sounded more like a funeral march than anything meant to promote patriotism. Or maybe the point was to remind the Betrovians of those who'd died for their country?

Loud cheers erupted, and some tinny-sounding drums rolled as the two Betrovians stepped into view from beneath the arbor.

Since the Lord Regent had not been in the private chamber when Mina and I were presented to Princess Lurelia, my eyes were drawn to him. He was short and rotund and had an incredible blond mustache that extended far beyond his cheeks. It curled into black coils at the ends. What little hair he had was also straw-blond, tipped with black, and gathered into a tail at the nape of his neck.

He seemed to be making up for the princess's colorlessness, for his clothing was red, gold, purple, and blue. The bright hues made it hurt to look at him, so I turned to the young woman at his side.

Although she did gaze up and around, there was still no sign of interest or enthusiasm in her expression. She paced forward with her fingers on the arm of the Lord Regent, and stood as silent and still as a ghost while the ceremony proceeded.

There was a lot of talk—a *lot* of talk—about trade agreements and taxes and historical events that I didn't give two figs about. Lord Cosgrove-Pitt turned out to be very long-winded, Mr. Oligary was hardly any more brief but at least he told a few jokes, and Sir Mycroft didn't speak at all.

"Zhank you vor your most gracious welcome," said the Betrovian Lord Regent, when all of the British speeches were finished and he and Princess Lurelia stood alone on the stage with Princess Alix.

To my dismay, the Regent rambled on for a time as well, his black-tipped mustache dipping and swaying as he spoke. On and on and on. I wondered how the two princesses could stand there so still in their heavy layers of gowns. I was fidgeting, and I wasn't even wearing heavy court dress.

At last, the Regent seemed to wind down. "And so, as a token uff our esteem vor our English brethren, zhe Betrovian Royal Family is pleased to present Her Royal Highness Princess Alexandra with a letter—"

"A *letter*?" I muttered to no one but myself. "All this for a letter? That's it? No jewels or gold or a—a mechanized horse or something like that?"

I never heard the rest of his description, for Mina's sharp elbow jabbed me in the ribs. "The letter is from Queen Elizabeth, you dolt! I was attempting to give you its history in the carriage, but you had no interest. Perhaps now you will give me your complete attention, so you can be fully cognizant of the importance of the British-Betrovian relations."

I didn't care. And one would have thought she'd take the hint when I began to edge toward the food table again. All the speechifying made me hungry. I had seen some puffy delicacies that looked like little blue clouds and I wanted to make sure I got one before they were gone. And then there was that bright red beverage that fizzed so much little sprays shot out from the top of the punch bowl.

But to my dismay, Mina followed me, hissing in my ear about missing epistles—which I figured out were letters—

and Byzantine treasure (which did get my attention some-what) and finally something about Queen Elizabeth and a Betrovian duchess.

She would have continued until midnight, I'm certain, if she had the chance, whether I was listening or not. But I was just about to reach for one of the frothy blue clouds when I was rescued.

"Why, Miss Stoker. I cannot tell you how pleased I am to see you in attendance . . . and that you have found your way to my favorite part of the food table as well," a voice murmured in my ear. "If I may?"

I looked up to find Mr. Richard Dancy standing at my elbow. A curl of light brown hair had fallen over his forehead, and his sideburns were trimmed short and neat. He had a square jaw with a handsome cleft chin, and showed dimples when he smiled. Blue eyes twinkling with warmth, he offered me a tiny doily-covered plate holding a frothy blue cloud. I had remembered to remove my gloves for once, and I reached for the tiny puff of sweetness. "Why, thank you, Mr. Dancy."

My smile was warm, partly because he was one of the few—well, the only—young men I knew from London Society who was gracious and *wasn't* boring, and partly because Mina's lecture had been stopped in its tracks.

"Am I to assume that since you are in attendance here, you shall also be gracing the dance floor at the Official Welcome Ball tomorrow evening?" Our voices remained low so as not to disturb the Exchange of National Gifts, which appeared to be continuing without our attention. Fortunately.

Mr. Dancy stood close enough that I could feel the warmth of his arm near mine and smell a hint of something pleasant, while at the same time maintaining a proper distance.

At least he would never back me into a dark corner and steal a kiss.

"Indeed I shall," I managed to reply, irritated that the thought of Pix had broken into my concentration. He always managed to put me into a foul mood, blast him.

"Then I must make certain to find your pages—surely you must have two or three of them—in the dance album immediately upon arriving, for I fully intend to claim at least two waltzes. Perhaps three. And I must warn you, Miss Stoker . . . even spilt lemonade won't keep me from squiring you about the ballroom this time."

My heart skipped a little beat and I smiled up at him. "I shall endeavor to keep from wearing *eau de limone*, then, Mr. Dancy, for I should hate to see you disappointed."

He grinned and was reaching for another tiny plate when the room plunged into pitch black.

A woman screamed, and a chorus of surprised voices filled the air. I heard the sounds of people moving, of clunks and bumps and a heavy scraping noise. A male voice shouted for everyone to remain calm, and someone else directed people to remain in their places. That was a good suggestion, for I couldn't see my hand in front of my eyes. There was a distinct chill in the air, as if a drafty window had been opened. Someone floundered against me, flailing in the darkness (Mina, of course), and from the other side, a hand steadied my arm.

"Have no fear, Miss Stoker. I'm certain the lights will be fixed momentarily." Mr. Dancy probably meant well, but he would have been better off keeping Mina from stumbling into the food table than offering me assurances. I was the only female in the room—probably in all of London—who had no reason to be afraid of anything.

The hair on the back of my neck lifted and prickled. I wasn't sure whether it was because someone had opened a door and released a draft, or for some other reason.

A red-eyed, sharp-fanged reason.

Blast and blots. I hadn't thought to bring a stake.

Pulling from Mr. Dancy's grip, I slipped into the close throng of people. His "Miss Stoker? Where have you gone?" was lost in the chaos.

There was a dull clang and the sounds of scuffling. Someone bumped into me from behind, and that same person grappled with my sleeve and bodice to steady herself.

"Blast it, Mina, just stay where you are," I said from between gritted teeth, as she hissed, "The princess! Get to the princess!"

"What do you think I'm trying to *do*?"

Just as I pulled free of her death grip, the soft glow of a light beamed from a corner, illuminating the familiar face of

Inspector Grayling. Of course he'd have a light-up gadget on hand—he was such a cognoggin. After a moment, more and more circles of light began to fill the chamber. And finally, the full lights came on and everything was back to normal. The murmurings and strained exchanges settled into conversation, and the tension in the chamber relaxed.

I had pushed my way toward the stage and looked over the crowd to assure myself Princess Lurelia was still there. Yes, there she was—unharmed and just as drab as ever. I turned to point this out to Mina when someone exclaimed, "The letter! It's gone!"

This caused another surge of excited voices to rise. Some people shouted, others muttered and gasped. Most everyone seemed to spin around in place, looking for the missing letter.

"It vahs right here, in zhees case!" Lord Regent Terrence cried in Betrovian-accented English. His bi-colored mustache fairly quivered with indignation as he jabbed a finger at the small case standing next to the chess table. The case had been positioned conveniently near the edge of the stage. "Efferyone saw it! And now it's gone!"

I swallowed my own comment—which would have been along the lines of "Who cares?"—and caught Mina's eye. She was right behind me, fire in her eyes.

"Hurry!" My partner began pushing me toward the small dais.

What the blooming fish did she expect me to do? An old letter from Queen Elizabeth might be of interest to someone like Miss Adler or Sir Franks, the museum director, but I didn't care. As long as the princess was all right, and there weren't any UnDead in the vicinity, I had no reason to be involved. Thievery was a job for Scotland Yard.

But Miss Mina Holmes is a force all her own. She shoved me forward so firmly I stumbled from the crowd and nearly slammed into the platform.

Before I could turn and glare at her, I found myself looking up at Princess Lurelia. Our eyes met, and for a moment I thought I saw a flash of something there . . . Excitement? Interest? Or perhaps it was just a glint from the lights, for whatever I might have seen was gone. The princess's expression was the same blandly polite one of before. She seemed as stiff as her starched petticoats, which were so brittle they made a crinkling sound as she gave a nod and turned back to the Lord Regent.

Mina had brushed past me and made her way to Miss Adler, who'd come forward and was speaking with Princess Alix from below the stage. Our own royal's face was strained and set, but I couldn't hear what they were saying.

The only thing left for me to do was to ensure the chilly breeze that had filtered over me was nothing more than a drafty door or window, and not an UnDead. But I wasn't sure how to go about proving there *hadn't* been a vampire around.

I pushed my way through the crowd, which was still chattering about the missing letter, and headed toward the east end of the chamber. It led deeper into the museum, while the western end was an exterior wall. The southern side tucked up next to the main galleries and was where most visitors would have come. Eastward was the direction I supposed an UnDead—or anyone else, such as a thief—would have made an escape, for it would be easy to lose one's pursuers in the maze of halls, and an UnDead would not go outside, as it was an unusually sunny day in September.

I was looking for any sign of a shadowy figure—with or without red eyes—lurking in the alcoves or behind the tall, floor-to-ceiling bookshelves, or down other corridors—when I stubbed my foot on something that shouldn't have been there.

The large, heavy object made a soft grating sound across the hardwood floor. I looked down, intending to shove it out of the pathway, when I saw what it was.

A stone statue, as long as my forearm. It was supposed to be a person, I think. Mina would probably know what kind it was or what age, and probably who it depicted. Someone appeared to have knocked it over . . . or *placed it there*. I went cold.

But it wasn't the entity or the face that caught my attention and sent that chill down my spine. It was what the statue's stone hand was holding. Brandishing, like a shield or weapon.

Or a threat.

Surely it couldn't be a coincidence that the statue's fist was gripping an *ankh*.

Miss Holmes

Wherein Miss Stoker Serves as Lady's Maid

"*E*valine, *there are no coincidences.*" I glared at her reflection in the mirror behind me as one of the hairpins I was attempting to utilize slipped from my fingers. I muffled an unladylike exclamation and bent to pick it up, which is easier said than done whilst wearing a corset.

Miss Stoker had arrived unannounced at my home, ostensibly to provide transportation to the Official Betrovian Welcome Ball. But, though clearly dressed for the event, she was nearly an hour too early. And aside from that, Princess Alix had already arranged for a carriage to pick me up. Apparently, Her Royal Highness was determined I would attend, and in a timely manner.

"How many times must I remind you that coincidences simply don't happen?" I continued, jabbing the pin into place at the back of my head. If only my hair wasn't so thick and unmanageable . . . and if I had a lady's maid like Miss Stoker did. Mrs. Raskill was useless when it came to coiffures and fashion, and the one time she'd suggested my employment of her niece Kitty for such tasks had been an undisputed disaster. "It's utterly impossible that statue *fell* by accident. The Arched Room is a library, and there are only *small* artifacts in cases. An Eighteenth Egyptian Dynastic statue—especially one of that size—doesn't belong anywhere in a library, it belongs in the Egyptian Saloon! Someone put it there. *She* put it there." And Lady Cosgrove-Pitt had been present at the Welcome Event, further strengthening my belief.

"But why?"

"Why would the Ankh leave a message? It's a calling card, Miss Stoker. How can you not see that? It's a message, a taunt, a tease. She knew we would see it. She's sending us a message. It's a *challenge.*"

I had no doubt about this last statement, and I had even less doubt about to whom the Ankh was issuing her challenge: Holmes & Stoker. (Or, at least, Holmes. After all, it was I who had outsmarted her in the end, and I who had seen through her disguise.)

"Do you think the Ankh stole the letter? What would she want with an old message?" Miss Stoker wandered through my small, book-cluttered bedchamber, brushing past the Easy Un-Lacer I was obligated to use to extricate myself from corsets when Mrs. Raskill had retired for the evening, and peered into my wardrobe.

I followed my companion's progress in the mirror as I struggled with my dratted coiffure. It was hard enough to do my hair when I was alone, but while carrying on a conversation—especially one fraught with unnecessary and banal questions—while monitoring a guest's nosiness made it even more frustrating.

"I've been attempting to tell you precisely *why* the letter is important for two days now, Evaline," I snapped, bending awkwardly to pick up another hairpin. "It's from Queen Elizabeth—over three hundred years old—and in the letter it explains where she's hidden the Theophanine Chess Queen."

The bored look in her hazel eyes told me all I needed to know. "You don't understand the importance of the Theophanine Chess Set, do you? What *did* you learn in school, Evaline?"

"I got my education in other ways . . . from other *people*. And though I may not have as much book-learning as you, I've been taught other, more useful skills." Her eyes moved deliberately to the photograph of my mother, which I had recently moved into my chamber.

My cheeks warmed and I looked away. I still hadn't been able to come to terms with the realization that my mother, the beautiful, social, graceful Desirée Holmes, had secretly been a vampire-hunter trainer. (Less than a month ago, I hadn't even fully believed in the existence of the UnDead creatures, but recent events had proven otherwise.)

The knowledge that Evaline Stoker had known my mother—Siri, as she'd called her—in a way I couldn't comprehend, couldn't share or even imagine, caused an ugly combination of emotions to surge inside me every time I looked at her picture. I couldn't name the emotions; I didn't want to try. The very thought of the woman who'd birthed me caused my insides to twist and churn. And then left me feeling empty.

Mother had disappeared, leaving Father and me more than a year ago, with no explanation and very little communication since. The last I'd heard, she was in Paris—or so the letters and their postmarks had indicated. Three notes, the last of which had arrived more than ten months ago, and none of them gave a real clue as to her location or motive for leaving.

My eyes stung. I blinked rapidly, keeping my face averted as I pretended to search through my small jewel box for more hair adornments.

"Why don't you tell me why the Theoph—whatever—chess set is so important, and I'll finish the back of your hair. Otherwise we'll be here forever."

I sat rigid as Evaline moved in behind, taking up the heavy hanks of my chestnut brown hair and deftly pinning them into place. "What is known as the Theophanine Chess Set was created and designed for the Byzantine King Otto II, and his wife, Theophano. Scholars believe it was one of the first instances of the game in which the chess queen piece makes an appearance."

"Do you mean the queen wasn't always part of it? But chess is a very old game, isn't it?"

"Yes, indeed." I relaxed slightly and launched into my lecture; Miss Stoker seemed surprisingly well-versed in playing lady's maid. "The game we know of as chess was first played in India and Persia in the fifth century, although it resembled more of a war strategy exercise rather than a game of entertainment. Along with the king and his men, there were chariots and elephants as well as horses as pieces—all of which were common to Arabian armies.

"The earliest versions of the game that came West from the Far East included a piece that was called a vizier, which as surely you know, is the king's most trusted advisor and confidante. And that piece began to be replaced by a queen around the year 1000, or more specifically, in the 1030s . . . when King Otto was married to Theophano. The particular chess set of which I am speaking was commissioned with a chess queen replacing the vizier—for the white player only. Not only is it a unique set because of the mismatched pieces, but it could be the first one ever with a queen." I eyed Miss Stoker's work critically, but could generate no complaints. If anything, she made my hair look softer and more feminine than usual, which was fortunate, considering the size of my proboscis.

"Your hair is such a pretty color," Miss Stoker said as she jabbed—none-too-gently—a glittering sapphire and jet pin into the top of my coiffure. "It's brown, but looks auburn in some light. And it's got threads of gold in it, and even a little copper."

"Thank you," I replied, surprised by her compliment. But there was more to tell her. "The Theophanine Chess Table, as you have seen, is currently housed in the British Museum;

but for centuries it was in the custody of the Betrovians until it was brought to London fifty years ago during the last State Visit. However, the chess pieces themselves have been in the possession of the English since Eleanor of Aquitaine, the mother of Richard the Lionheart. The entire chess set, with the exception of the queen, has been on display in the museum since the return of the chess table. The queen has been missing for centuries, and the last person known to have had it was Queen Elizabeth."

"Right. So this letter—which has been stolen—supposedly tells where she hid the chess queen. I do not understand all this fuss about an old chess piece." She sounded bored.

"It's not just an old chess piece, Evaline." I rose impatiently from my chair. "It's part of a combination-like key that opens the bottom of the Theophanine Chess Table. Surely even you noticed it yesterday, and you can see how massive the base is. Legend claims a cache of Byzantine jewels, as well as some ancient writings, are hidden inside."

The mention of jewels seemed to perk up my companion. "Well, that's something. So if the chess queen is located, then the treasure is found."

"Naturally. And the Ankh is clearly after the treasure. Why else would she want the letter? Although," I mused, "I would suspect the Ankh's interest would lie more heavily toward the writings than jewels. Who knows what ancient secrets might be in those papers."

"Speaking of the Ankh." Evaline began pacing the chamber again. Her vehement steps made the glass jars on my dressing table clink. "What have you learned from the note Pix gave me? And don't tell me you haven't had time to look at it."

She was correct, of course. "I subjected the item to a number of vigorous tests and examinations. The penmanship has similarities to the two previous communications I received from the Ankh during your short-lived captivity at her hands. But I cannot be certain whether it—or any of the messages, for that matter—were actually scribed by the villainess in question. It is extremely likely, but not yet utterly provable, that all three were written by the same person. However, I did note several important factors about the origins of the scrap provided by Mr. Pix. I detected a scant bit of facial powder dusting the corner of the paper, which supports the supposition that it was a female correspondent. The brand of facial powder is lightly scented with vanilla and has a minute amount of gold dust mixed in, making it extremely unusual and expensive. Nevertheless, the ink is commonplace, and the paper easily obtained by anyone who frequents Mrs. Sofrit's Stationery."

"That hardly helps us at all! Wasn't there anything else? You're a Holmes, aren't you? If it were your uncle, *he'd* be able to tell me everything about who wrote it just by looking at it!" Miss Stoker's frustration was not the least bit becoming to a genteel young lady. I hoped she didn't demonstrate this sort of behavior while with Princess Lurelia.

The internal reminder of the Betrovian princess had me checking the small clock on my bureau. "Drat! It's nearly eight. You've put me off my toilette, Evaline, and now I am going to be late. The princess's carriage should be here any time."

"Right, then. I suppose I shall just have to continue this investigation on my own." Apparently Miss Stoker wasn't quite ready to give up her overt frustrations; but I had no energy or attention to spare her sensibilities.

She flounced out of the room. A moment later, I heard her carriage drive off, and I wondered if she would actually direct Middy to take her to the ball or whether she would indeed take investigative matters into her own hands. That could be quite entertaining, watching Miss Stoker attempt to observe and deduce and follow a trail of clues.

However, I would be greatly irked if she was absent from the ball and I was relegated to playing nursemaid to the drab, uninteresting Lurelia. We'd had very little interaction with the princess due to the events last evening, but Miss Adler had made it clear Evaline and I were to begin our chaperonage of the young woman tonight.

I was just pulling on fingerless gloves of midnight blue lace, which reached halfway up my forearms and matched my sparkling, diaphanous over-gown, when Mrs. Raskill appeared in the doorway. She wore an expression somewhere between astonishment and irritation (she hated being interrupted during her work). "There is a person here who claims he is to deliver you to a ball?" Her tone ended on a definite upswing, as if posing an inconceivable question to either me or herself.

I snatched up my wrap (also of delicate dark blue lace, but decorated with swashes of tiny copper- and topaz-colored gems) along with a small handbag and hurried from the room.

When I caught sight of the tall, broad-shouldered figure standing in the small vestibule, I jolted to a halt. "Inspector Grayling?"

At first I thought he must have come to discuss the case of the missing letter, but then I realized he was dressed formally in black coattails and a crisp white shirt. As if to attend a ball. He even held a top hat in one hand. And he was wearing spotless white *gloves*.

All thoughts seemed to leak from my brain and I could do nothing but stand there gaping. He looked rather . . . imposing, and . . . well, gentlemanly. One might even use the term "handsome."

"Miss Holmes." He folded his tall self into a brief, stilted bow.

"Inspector Grayling, what on earth are you doing here?" I was acutely aware of Mrs. Raskill hovering in the doorway between the kitchen and the parlor, close enough that she could see and hear the exchange happening in the foyer.

His freckled, pleasantly ruddy cheeks darkened slightly. He'd done an excellent job shaving this evening, except for a tiny nick near the left corner of his square jaw. "I am to be your escort to the Welcome Ball this evening. I thought . . . I was under the impression you had been informed."

"Right, then. Of course," I managed to say. My cheeks were warm. "Shall we proceed?"

"Indeed." He seemed as much at a loss for words as I.

But he did remember to offer me his arm, which I took after preceding him through the door. Grayling led me down the short walkway to a waiting carriage, which bore the crest of Her Royal Highness.

I walked gingerly, taking great care not to catch my slender heels on any layers of skirt, petticoat, or lace flounces. It seemed as if every time I encountered Inspector Grayling, I was either tripping, falling, or dripping wet from an unexpected swim. I was determined not to repeat any such mortifying activities tonight.

Especially if he was to be my escort.

Heavens. Did that mean we must stay in each other's presence *all evening*?

"What, no steamcycle tonight?" I attempted a jest as we approached our transportation.

Before Grayling could respond, the driver flung open the door. *Please don't let me trip.*

I clambered as gracefully as possible into the depths of the carriage, firmly gathering up my skirts to keep wayward hems away from spiky heels and clumsy toes.

Thanks in part to my corset's unyielding embrace, I was out of breath by the time I arranged my petticoats, skirt, bustle, wrap, and posterior on the plush velvet bench inside the carriage. Inspector Grayling, being a male and thus unencumbered by the travails of fashion, slipped in and settled himself with enviable ease.

The door closed and we were alone. The inside of the vehicle seemed to shrink. I could smell the faint scent of something lemony, tinged with peppermint and bergamot, wafting from the man across from me.

"It would have mussed up your hair and skirts," he said as the carriage rolled smoothly into action. Apparently, having a royal driver eliminated the sharp lurching and jolting of a less lofty vocation.

"I beg your pardon?"

Grayling shifted, and I noticed one of his arms rested along the back of the bench on which he sat, while the fingertips of the other hand curled around the brim of his hat. He appeared much more at ease than I felt. Light filtered through the carriage window and made his dark coppery curls gleam like the sunset, or a roaring fire. "The steamcycle. I feared it would be an impractical mode of transport dressed as you are. It would be a shame—er—right. Miss Holmes, that's a very nice dress. You look very—er—that is to say, one would hate to be the cause of it obtaining a streak of grease, or to become torn. Or—or wrinkled."

I was thankful for the uneven light of the carriage, knowing it would help disguise the sudden flush heating my cheeks. "Indeed. And—er—thank you."

I wanted to ask how he'd come to be assigned as my escort, but I couldn't find the proper words. I could only assume Miss Adler and the princess had had something to do with it, and possibly even Lord or Lady Cosgrove-Pitt. Perhaps it was simply a matter of convenience, if we were both to be attending the ball. Fewer carriages to be ordered, and so on.

"Aside from the state of your attire, I was under the distinct impression you never wished to clamber onto that vehicle again." His voice was wry.

"It is a rather . . . tenuous mode of transport." I tried, and failed, to banish the memory of having to cling to his waist, pressing my face against his broad, solid back as we careened through the streets and alleyways of London. The momentary exhilaration of speed and the blast of fresh air had been overtaken by my constant fear of crashing. Two wheels are hardly stable enough to instill confidence when one is zooming along at high speed. "Nevertheless, one must never rule out any future possibilities."

"I'm gratified you feel that way, Miss Holmes."

We lapsed into silence for a short while, and then both began to speak at the same time. My voice trailed off into an awkward laugh.

"Pardon me, Miss Holmes," he said, indicating I should continue.

"I confess, Inspector Grayling, I did not expect to find you in attendance at the Welcome Ball. Are you to be present in an official capacity, or as a guest of Lord Cosgrove-Pitt?" *And his wife, the most dangerous and cunning villainess of our time?* I could hardly imagine anything more awkward than encountering Inspector Grayling's murderous relative whilst on his arm.

"A bit of both. After all, a crime was committed yesterday at the British Museum, during which I was present—as well as yourself—and there is significant pressure on everyone involved that this visit by the Betrovians goes well. Lord Cosgrove-Pitt—and of course your father—neither of them want another national embarrassment."

I hadn't realized he'd noticed my presence at the museum. "I see. But since when does a homicide investigator such as yourself become involved in a bit of petty thievery?"

"When that bit of petty thievery—and you know as well as I do, Miss Holmes, that the robbery of the Queen Elizabeth letter is more than mere petty thievery—is also connected to a murder, then a homicide investigator is most certain to be involved."

"Murder?"

"Obviously you weren't aware of the circumstances under which one of the museum guards was discovered. My apologies. I assumed that if there was a dead body to be lying about, as usual you would be found in its vicinity."

The only reason I didn't respond with a sharp retort was because of course he'd known I was unaware of the murder . . . and because I *thought* I detected a bit of humor in his voice. Clearly, he had offered me the information for some reason known only to him. Likely in order to obtain my assistance in the investigation.

"I encountered no dead bodies during my examination of the area where the robbery took place. But with it being in the dark and in the midst of such a crush of people—all of whom have no common sense about trampling over possible clues or scant traces of residue—there was little to be gleaned, even with my thorough examination. The culprit must have come from either the crowd itself—"

"Or the balconies above, Miss Holmes," he interjected.

"I was just about to say that, hence my use of the word 'either,'" I returned. "The attendees were searched before being allowed to leave, but of course the letter wasn't found on anyone's person. Which means *either*," I said, giving him a quelling look, "the letter was hidden somewhere in the museum to be retrieved later, or—"

"Or the culprit left the way he—or she; let us be open-minded here, Miss Holmes—came. That is, from above."

"Such an obvious point hardly needs to be mentioned." I sniffed.

"Then I certainly need not point out the proximity of the location of the letter to the edge of the stage. And the fact that the lights surely were purposely extinguished—"

"—which means at least two individuals must have been involved."

"Of course. But there was also the fallen statue," he added smoothly.

My eyes narrowed at this unexpected comment. "Indeed. And what did you glean from the position and placement of that so-called *fallen* artifact, Inspector Grayling?"

"It wasn't so much the position and placement—both of which were obviously deliberate. It was the symbolism in the particular artifact itself." He held my gaze with purpose.

I saw no reason to respond and, in fact, had no opportunity to do so. The royal carriage pulled up to the entrance of the Midnight Palace, having obviously been given precedence over other, less important vehicles that still waited in queue to approach.

As the footman handed me out of the carriage, I realized Grayling had neatly redirected my attention from the details of the murder, while at the same time extracting from me all of the information I'd observed from the scene of the robbery. Drat him!

But since I was doomed to be in his company much of the evening, I was certain there would be opportunity to interrogate him about the murder.

Moments later, Grayling and I stood in a small trolley-like conveyance that was to transport us inside the social hall built by Mr. Oligary. I looked around with interest, noting a number of familiar faces—including Society's most eligible bachelor, Mr. Richard Dancy, along with Mr. Southerby and

Baron Leiflett. In the car ahead of Grayling and me was a man about the same age as my companion, and he seemed vaguely familiar. I couldn't place him, even though I stared at the back of his blond head and watched him for a few moments. He was accompanied by three young women and another man, none of whom struck any familiar chord.

But as we approached the entrance to the Midnight Palace my attention was diverted. The structure had been completed three years ago, and was adjacent to Mr. Oligary's more recent and modern project, New Vauxhall Gardens. While the Gardens were an outdoor pleasure park, the Midnight Palace was clearly meant to be a competitor to the Crystal Palace, which had been built for the Great Exhibition in 1851. Both locations were used for events, parties, and exhibitions, but the Midnight Palace was much smaller and more intimate—though no less grand and elegant.

Indeed, I had been inside the Crystal Palace and been stunned by the beauty of its glass roof and walls, but the Midnight was even more awe-inspiring. In fact, I was relieved to be transported along rather than attempting to ambulate under my own steam while taking in our surroundings.

The Midnight Palace glittered, from its outside walls—which were decorated with strategically placed sheets of glass, steel, and mirrors all designed to catch whatever meager sunlight might force its way through fog-shrouded London—to the inside. Our trolley car brought us smoothly and speedily through a grand entrance fettered with sparkling strips of fabric that acted as a waterfall-like curtain, and once inside my first impression was one of being delivered precisely where the structure's name promised: into a starlit world.

The interior was swathed in darkness. Lush midnight blue, deep gray, and black furnishings, floors, and walls draped the hall like a night sky. Yet, the palace wasn't dark, for sparkling lights glittered everywhere: on dusky canopies and curtains slung artfully overhead, on tapestries hanging from the walls at every height, and in the air on the same mechanical fireflies that darted and swooped through New Vauxhall Gardens.

Though the ceiling in the center of the large chamber loomed four stories over our heads, from all sides and in all corners were platforms—elevators, side-to-side trolleys, and even moving stairways—that raised, lowered, and transported guests on light-festooned conveyances. This had the effect of constantly moving, always twinkling bits of illumination.

"I've never seen anything so beautiful," I said, trying in vain to cease from gaping.

"It is the perfect setting for you."

I looked up at my escort, caught by the tone of his voice. It was hardly more than a murmur, as if he were speaking more to himself than to me.

He drew himself up stiffly when he saw my expression. "What I mean to say, Miss Holmes, is that your dress, and you—er—your—er—fripperies . . . that is to say, accoutrements are—"

"Ambrose, darling! Why, you look utterly *splendid* in those tails. The cut of that coat is *exquisite*; I've never seen you look so handsome. It quite shows off the breadth of your shoulders! We must get you spruced up more often, no? And Miss Holmes . . . what a glorious gown. Why, with all those jewels and sequins, you look like a night sprite who might have been spawned from this very glittery world. It suits you immensely."

I turned to meet the calm gray eyes of Lady Cosgrove-Pitt.

Miss Stoker

Wherein Our Heroine Plods About the Dance Floor

I hadn't had the chance to tell Mina there might have been an UnDead at the Welcome Event last night. She practically chased me out of her house. And after I'd done her hair so beautifully!

But that was fine with me. I hadn't seen any evidence of UnDead at the museum. That didn't mean there hadn't been any, though. I just wasn't perfect at being able to tell when there was a draft or when there was a vampire present. But it was clear I could no longer avoid patrolling the streets—because if the UnDead were back, I had to know.

And that was a fine excuse for leaving the Welcome Ball early.

Which I could do if Mina Holmes ever arrived and took my place entertaining Princess Lurelia. I cast a quick glance toward the long raised table, where Princess Alexandra and her husband, Prince Edward, sat conversing with the

Betrovian Lord Regent, Lord Cosgrove-Pitt, Mr. Oligary, and several other dignitaries.

Princess Lurelia and I had been sitting with them and making stilted conversation about the weather until Princess Alix suggested we prepare for the dancing to begin. I practically bolted away from the table. Fortunately, the princess followed me, saving me from looking foolish.

"And here is your dance album," I said to her, gesturing to the wall.

An array of thick copper slates hung in three rows. Each one was about the size of a small book. Because she was a guest of honor, hers had been assigned before she even arrived, and it was displayed prominently. I showed her mine, which was just where I wanted it—tucked in a low, corner slot where no one would notice. I had already scribbled my name on it, and now pulled down the album from its moorings. I thought I might "forget" to return it until the dancing was over.

"You see," I told my companion, "I've had to write my own name—with this special pencil on the copper sheet. And—inside is a list of all the dances to be played tonight. If a gentleman wishes to dance with you, he will write his name on the line next to the one he chooses. There are waltzes and quadrilles and . . . what is this? A *kelva*? I've not heard of that."

"The *kelva* is the national Betrovian dance," Lurelia said. Her English was nearly perfect, with only a slight accent on occasion—which put to bed my theory that she was shy speaking an unfamiliar language. She examined her dance album, turning it over in delicate, white hands, for the first time showing interest in something. "They are rather like the chalk-boards we use in the classroom. But heavier. And beautiful. The scrollwork and gears along the top are very pretty . . . oh, and the mechanisms work! Is that how the pages turn? And the pencil . . . is it engraving into the copper?"

"Yes, it's a steam-pencil. It must be returned to its slot, to keep the water inside hot and create steam when you press on it to write. And after each set of dances, the slate is erased so it can be used again."

"Oh. So we cannot keep them for a remembrance."

"I'm certain Mr. Oligary would present you with yours if you asked, Your Highness. You are the guest of honor."

"Please call me Lurelia. And I will call you Evaline, yes? I am sure we will become good friends while I am here."

"That would be very nice." At least she showed some sign of spirit and interest, but I still found her conversation mundane and her personality timid and colorless. Of course, I might be the same way if I was engaged to be married. I wondered what her fiancé was like; I hadn't had the opportunity to ask.

When I first arrived at the ball, I had reluctantly signed my own album. Now I flipped on the elegant little mechanism that turned the pages. "Oh," I said when I noticed nearly every dance was already filled in. Blast. I had hoped my penmanship too messy for anyone to read my name.

I recognized all but two names on the list—most of them were bachelors I'd been trying to avoid at balls ever since my debut. Ones with bad breath, boring conversation, dingy-tipped gloves, clumsy feet—or all of the above. The bright spot was that Mr. Dancy, as promised, had claimed two dances. Both waltzes. I couldn't help a *small* twinge of disappointment he'd only taken two, and not three as he'd threatened. Maybe that was because all the waltzes were taken and he didn't want to try a minuet—or the *kelva*—with me.

"Mr. Martin VanderBleeth. Mr. Richard Dancy. Baron Leiflett. Lord Feelbright." Lurelia was looking at her album, which was also nearly full. I wondered whether the men had added their names under duress or not. "Do you know any of them?" she asked after reading off the list.

"Most of them. Except Mr. VanderBleeth . . . but he is on my list as well," I said, peering at the nearly illegible name. It looked as if he'd scratched it out and written over it. "So we shall both become acquainted with the gentleman. And very soon, for the orchestra is just about to begin the first dance."

Tonight, Princess Lurelia was dressed in something that didn't make her look like a ghost . . . although not by much. Her gown tonight was a pale, water-silk (Betrovian of course) pink. Unlike current fashion in London and Paris, her skirts were wide and full and layered with two gathered-up over-skirts. It was a lovely dress, but with Lurelia, it was a case of the dress overpowering the woman inside it, rather than the woman wearing the dress.

Unlike Mina Holmes, who continued to surprise me with her acute fashion sense. Her gown tonight had made me more than a little envious, for it was stunning and elegant. A rich midnight blue gown with an ethereal overskirt and wrap made of fragile netting. Both were studded with glittering beads and sapphire gems. With her hair done up in a pile of soft curls and more sparkling jewels (thanks to me), Mina had looked quite fetching.

"At last I've found you! I was required to take three elevator rides, and one on those odd moving stairways in order to look down and locate you in the crowd."

As if I'd conjured her up, Mina Holmes appeared. Excellent. I couldn't wait to turn Lurelia over to her and slip out onto the streets, blast the waltzes. Although . . . perhaps I should stay for at least one with Mr. Dancy. He was rather charming and funny.

"Mr. VanderBleeth is the son of an American businessman," Mina informed us, obviously having overheard part of our conversation. "He was in the trolley ahead of us when we—er, I—came in tonight. There were a number of individuals discussing him in the ladies' salon. All of the young women are batty-eyed and simpering over the chance to meet him. Apparently he is very rich—something about window glass in New York City—and quite handsome. I happen to find mustaches, especially ones as large and thick as his, unappealing. But apparently that is the style in America. One can blame the author Mark Twain for that mode of fashion.

Or perhaps it was that General Custer, who met such an unpleasant fate on the American prairie."

"Mr. VanderBleeth has claimed a dance from me," Lurelia said, looking much too interested for a young woman who was engaged to be wed. Apparently, mustaches didn't put her off.

Mina gave me a meaningful look. "Indeed. Well, I'm certain he's to be only one of many."

"Where is your dance album, Mina—if I may call you that. May I? And I am Lurelia to you, if you please."

"Of course. And I never need to take a dance album, for dances with me are never in demand." Her words were blithe and easy. I was certain she actually believed them. "Evaline, if I could have a word with you. Your Highness—er, Lurelia, if you will excuse us for just one moment?"

I had no choice when Mina looked at me that way, even though it was rather rude to leave our charge standing by herself. But my partner cared little for social niceties. There was a table of food nearby. Perhaps Lurelia would find a distraction there.

"What?" I hissed.

"When I was in the ladies' salon—I had to search every-where for you, Evaline, it was quite a waste of time!—I overheard some of the young women talking about Mr. VanderBleeth. It seems he is here in London in search of a titled heiress . . . but I suspect a princess would be an even more attractive coup. Especially for an American. We cannot let Lurelia out of our sights, particularly with Mr. VanderBleeth. If they were found in a compromising position, it would be scandalous–"

"History repeating itself. I understand. My dance with him is after Lurelia's. I shall distract him from the princess." *Blast.* That meant I was going to need to stay longer than I planned.

"Excellent. I am confident you will handle him with the same skill with which you handled Mr. Treadwell during the spiritglass case." I turned to leave, but Mina grabbed my arm. "There are two more things. First, there was a murder at the museum yesterday. Grayling believes it's related to the robbery of the letter."

"A murder? Who? Where?"

Mina looked frustrated. "I didn't have the opportunity to get the details from Grayling, but I shall interrogate him about it as soon as possible. It sounded as if it was one of the museum guards. I'll offer my assistance with the investigation, of course." I barely managed to stifle a snort, but my companion didn't seem to notice. Instead, she barreled on. "But more importantly, at least for now, I found a trace of facial powder with a scant bit of gold dust near the dance albums." Her eyes were bright and determined.

"The same powder you found on the paper from Pix?"

"Almost certainly. Though there wasn't enough for me to tell whether it carried a vanilla scent, I am confident it is the same. I will have to test the sample to be certain, but I am confident in my ability to visually identify twenty different types of powder. I wrote an entire treatise on the differences in the scent, granularity, makeup, and flammability of face powder, including—"

"Right, then. So it's possible the person who wrote the note to Pix is here this evening."

"It's not only possible, it's nearly certain." Mina had a mutinous look in her eyes. "Yes, the individual who is Pix's client is present at this ball—that very same person whom we believe is the Ankh. I've known the identity of the Ankh for months, and that suspect is also here tonight."

"You know who the Ankh is?" This was news to me.

Mina seemed to shrink back. "I am fairly certain I know who it is. But I am not going to name the individual. Not yet."

"In case you're wrong?"

"I'm a Holmes. I'm never wrong."

"Then why won't you tell me—"

"Miss Stoker, we do not have time to discuss the veracity of my suspicions. At least, not at the moment. We are here to watch over Princess Lurelia, and, now that there is reason to believe she is here, to investigate the person who wrote the note to Mr. Pix. I have been doing the latter, and I merely wanted to share with you what I've found. And in the meanwhile, if you should encounter any female who carries the scent of vanilla in her face powder—"

"And how the blooming Pete should I know that? I would have to be close enough to embrace anyone to even have an inkling of what—"

"Miss Stoker, must you always argue my suggestions into the ground? I was merely suggesting that if you noticed any woman putting face powder on in the ladies' retiring room, you should attempt to determine if it is vanilla-scented. And then identify whether is has a bit of sparkle in it too. Perhaps you could ask to use some for your own nose. It is a bit shiny."

My jaw hurt, for my teeth were clamped tightly together. "Very well, then, Mina."

As we made our way back to Lurelia, who'd remained a discreet distance during our conversation, there was a loud trumpeting sound, and the three of us turned as one to see the orchestra's platform rise slowly from the ground across the dark-swathed floor. Celebratory music and an added array of sparkling lights accompanied it, announcing the beginning of the dancing. When the platform had lifted the musicians approximately five feet off the ground, the orchestra transitioned into the first dance: a minuet.

"I shall continue to pursue my investigations while the two of you dance," Mina said, looking beyond my shoulder. "I have no intention of wasting my time turning about the floor."

I pivoted. Two young men—neither of whom I found attractive, interesting, or otherwise worth spending my time with—were approaching. Blast it. I did not want to spend my first dance avoiding Baron Leiflett's oversized feet! It was nearly impossible to do so, and that meant the rest of the evening I would be dancing on injured feet. Evening slippers are so flimsy.

Nevertheless, I sighed, and when he offered it I took Leiflett's arm. This was going to be a most trying evening.

I wasn't wrong. The night plodded on and on, just like my dance partners. I began to wish a vampire would show up just so I'd have something interesting to do. If I hadn't promised Mina I'd dance with Mr. VanderBleeth and keep him away from Lurelia, I would have sneaked out after three dances.

However, the first of my waltzes with Mr. Dancy was a definite bright spot.

"Miss Stoker, at last. I have been waiting all evening to take you into my arms"—I gave him a look of pretend shock, but a little smile twitched free—"and spin you around on the treads," he continued. His smile made him even more handsome, and flashed a dimple I didn't realize he had.

"Your Highness . . . if I may," said a flat American voice behind me. "Gee, I've never danced with a princess before."

I rolled my eyes as my partner led me toward the sea of dancing and swirling couples. As Mr. Dancy settled me into position, I saw Lurelia had taken Mr. VanderBleeth's arm and was looking up at him as if already infatuated. I couldn't blame her. Even with the mustache, he was the most handsome of her partners thus far this evening.

But then again, she hadn't had a turn with Mr. Dancy yet.

I smiled up at him as we eased smoothly into the flow of circling couples. "Why, Mr. Dancy, I do believe you are quite aptly named."

"Well, yes, of course, because Richard is such an appropriate name for the son of an earl who—" His eyes crinkled at the corners as my laughter drowned out his words.

"No, that is not what I meant, and I am certain you are fully aware. I meant to compliment you on your skill at the waltz, Mr. *Dance-y*."

"Ah, that. Well, yes, then of course. One cannot have a surname like Dancy without intending to live up to it." To emphasize his words, he slipped into a particularly sweeping and complicated step, which, to my surprise and delight, I was able to follow. Our toes did not even brush, and somehow we were on the opposite side of the dance floor without ever having come close to another couple. That was the mark of an excellent dance partner: he should be able to direct his counterpart easily and efficiently without misstep or verbal direction.

"Miss Holmes," I heard a voice say over my shoulder. "If you would allow me to lead . . ."

I giggled when I saw Inspector Grayling struggling to keep Mina from directing him all over the floor. I was surprised to see him present at the ball, but not terribly surprised to see him dancing with my friend. She liked to spar with him just as much as she did with me. From the looks of the red at the tips of his ears, she was doing an excellent job interrogating him about the murder.

"I'm glad you're enjoying yourself," said my own partner. "I've been trying to find an opportunity to spend time with you since you put me off by spilling lemonade on yourself."

"I . . . what?" I looked up at him. Shock washed over my face just as the lemonade had done to my gown.

His dimple appeared again but his voice was wry. "At the Rose Ball, last May. You bumped into Miss What-Was-Her-Name on purpose, did you not? I don't know why you chose to put me off that evening, but I can only hope it wasn't me you were avoiding, but that some other task or responsibility took precedence. Otherwise, I would be utterly dejected."

"Mr. Dancy," I said, looking up at him from under my lashes, "you know a woman never tells her secrets."

"And I suspect you might have quite a few of them, don't you, Miss Stoker?"

"Don't we all?" I replied sweetly, then was surprisingly sad. Mr. Dancy was so very nice—and charming and handsome, of course, and somewhat wealthy. And if my sister-in-law, Florence, was here watching, she would have us engaged in a trice. But he was getting a bit too familiar, and a little too close to the truth. The problem was, he could never understand a person like me. Vampire hunters didn't marry.

And for a moment, I regretted that reality. I regretted the fact that I had no chance of ever being a normal woman with a normal life. I realized at that moment I could never let a man truly get to know me.

I would always be alone.

And along with the loneliness I'd surely feel, I'd also have to bear the disdain of Society. A woman who didn't marry was looked down upon, called a spinster or described as "being on the shelf"—like something that's been put aside or no longer useful.

But little would the rest of Society know that I was much more than useless—married or not. I'd be the one saving their innocent lives from dangers and death at the hands of red-eyed demons. I'd be the one free to patrol the streets at night, watching over my charges and keeping the city safe.

The waltz ended, pulling me from my thoughts, and before Mr. Dancy could question me further. I took the opportunity to excuse myself to the ladies' lounge. On the way, I grabbed Lurelia as she and Mr. VanderBleeth were leaving the dance floor. "Let's go freshen up," I said, slipping my arm through hers. "I shall see you soon for our dance, then, Mr. VanderBleeth."

"I'm looking forward to it," he replied with a deep bow. "Thank you, Princess Lurelia. I reckon I'll have lots to tell everyone back home about dancing with a princess." He hardly rose before giving her an even deeper bow.

I had to practically tow Lurelia off with me to the lounge. Once inside, I did a quick look around. No, no one was putting on vanilla face powder with gold dust in it.

There, I'd done my duty, and Mina Holmes could stew on that for a while.

"He is a divine dancer," the princess said. "That Mr. VanderBleeth. And rather amusing too. I don't think I've laughed so hard in ages. Americans say such funny things, yes?"

She'd laughed? That was a bad sign, because she sure hadn't even twitched a lip since I'd met her. "Tell me about your fiancé," I suggested. "When is the wedding? Did you have a long courtship?"

What little bit of light that had been in her expression faded. "We had no courtship. I've only met him twice, and he's ten years older than me."

She sounded miserable. "Is he nice? Is he handsome? He must be rich . . ." I tried to think of something positive to say. But Lurelia was rich in her own right. She was a princess.

And princesses had arranged marriages. That was how it worked. It even worked that way for non-princesses here in London. If a young woman was wealthy and from a good family, she was more often than not married to a "perfect match," whether he was of her choosing or not.

"He's the Duke of Sparling. He owns a large estate and is very rich. He's the elder son of one of my father's trusted advisors. He's barely as tall as I am. He has bad breath. And he likes *cats*. I hate cats."

Blast. That didn't sound promising at all. No wonder Princess Alix was concerned about Lurelia's time here in London. "You don't sound happy about the engagement." Maybe it wasn't as bad as she made it sound.

"Happiness has nothing to do with it. But of course, I must marry to carry on the family line. And do what my father, the king, commands." She sounded brave and resigned at the same time.

Now I understood why she wasn't very lively. She was a princess and had no choice in her future. So it was up to Mina and me to make sure she had fun while in London . . . while directing her away from the likes of Mr. VanderBleeth.

And Mr. Dancy, for that matter.

I kept Lurelia occupied in the ladies' lounge for as long as I dared. It would be nice if Mina would come along and play nursemaid too, but she didn't. So, trying to buy time, I encouraged Lurelia to show me the steps for the *kelva*, and pretended she had a row of lace on the back of her gown that took me some time to fix.

Just as we were practicing the *kelva* for the second time (I pretended to be a slow learner), the lounge door opened. Three women, all of whom were older than Lurelia and I, swept in.

"Why, Princess Lurelia! I haven't had the opportunity to tell you how lovely you look tonight." Lady Isabella

Cosgrove-Pitt said with a graceful, generous curtsy. "I hope you are enjoying our little celebration," she said on the upswing.

"I am, thank you."

"The princess was just demonstrating the steps to the national Betrovian dance," I said, for they were all looking at us curiously.

"Ah, the *kelva*, is it? I remember it . . . a four-step beat. One-two-*three*-and-fourrrr," murmured Lady Cosgrove-Pitt, perfectly executing the steps Lurelia had just taught me. She spun on the last beat with a smooth dip, then stepped back into the rhythm without a hitch.

"Excellent!" Lurelia clapped, and Lady Cosgrove-Pitt bowed again. "How did you know it?"

"From my youth," the older woman replied. "I visited your country more than once. And excuse me, Your Highness— I have been rude. Allow me to introduce my friends. I dragged the two of them from the ball, for my gown is in need of some little repair." She showed us the tiny blue and green butterfly that had come loose from a row along the edge of her gown's bodice.

The other two women—Lady Merceforth and Mrs. Rathbottom, both married to wealthy and powerful men as well—seemed pleased to meet Lurelia. They curtsied and engaged her in conversation as I looked on. I was tempted to slip away. However, I decided better of it. It wasn't so much Mina's temper I wanted to avoid, but the disappointment from Miss Adler or, worse, Princess Alix, if something went awry with Lurelia.

After sewing on Lady Cosgrove-Pitt's butterfly, the ladies fixed their hair, pinched their cheeks, adjusted their gloves, and even brushed a subtle bit of color onto their lips. It wasn't until Lurelia and I were leaving the lounge that I remembered I was supposed to be trying to get samples of face powder. But by then, they had departed in a flock of chatter, and I was out of excuses for delay.

When we left the lounge, Lurelia and I went to check our dance albums. To my disappointment, one of the dances I'd missed was my second, and last, waltz with Mr. Dancy. Blast it all! And I was startled to realize my dance with Mr. VanderBleeth was next. We had been in the lounge for longer than I'd expected.

"Mr. Southerby," Lurelia said, peering at her album. "I hope he is a good dancer."

I knew for a fact the young man was fairly light on his toes. But he was also deadly boring (I had a feeling he couldn't make conversation because he was counting steps the entire time) and very shy, and therefore no threat to the princess's reputation. I watched with relief as Mr. Southerby led her away.

"Avoiding me again, Miss Stoker?"

I turned to find Mr. Dancy at my elbow. "I beg your pardon?"

"You missed our second waltz." He frowned mockingly. "But at least I have reserved my place for a third one—and the final waltz of the evening." He extended his arm with a warm smile.

"Er . . . but I believe there must be a mistake." I turned to retrieve my dance album, but it had already been taken away to be erased. Not that I wouldn't rather take a turn with him than Mr. VanderBleeth, but duty called.

"A mistake?" Mr. Dancy frowned. "I don't see how . . ."

"But you've only signed up for two dances. And—"

"Well, hello there, Miss Stoker. I reckon it's time for our waltz now, isn't it?"

I turned in time to find Mr. VanderBleeth in mid-bow. When he came up, he captured my hand and looked at me with laughing, dark eyes.

Familiar laughing, dark eyes.

Miss Stoker

The Third Waltz

"Well, that explains the confusion," I said to Pix once I'd recovered from my shock. I gripped his arm firmly as he led me to the dance floor. "You crossed off Mr. Dancy's name in my album and added your own. That's why I could hardly read it."

"It was to be the bloke's third waltz with you, luv," he said. His voice was somewhere between his usual Cockney and the American accent he'd been using all evening. "'E was bein' greedy."

Pix's hand was steady and solid at the back of my waist as he shifted me into position for the waltz. Lurelia claimed he was a divine dancer, and I was curious to find out whether that was truly the case.

But I was more curious about other things. "Should I even ask what the blazes you're doing here? And how on earth did you manage . . . *this*?" I removed my hand from his shoulder to encompass his whole character, and the fact that he'd gained entrance to a very exclusive ball. "Unless . . . good gad, you aren't really named Martin VanderBleeth, are you?"

"Bloody hell, of course not!"

"Well, you'd think you'd pick a less ridiculous name than VanderBleeth if you were choosing one."

He laughed, but I could hardly see his mouth because of the absurd mustache. "That was the point, luv."

His fingers, gloved in proper coverings for once, curled around my left hand and we stepped into the fray on the dance floor. Smoothly, but more leisurely than with Mr. Dancy. In fact, Pix held me tighter than was strictly proper for a waltz. Our legs brushed against each other as we stepped *one* two-three, *one* two-three, swirling almost lazily around the room.

He smelled delicious: of cinnamon and clove and other things. His movements were graceful and confident, his hands firm and yet gentle. His dark eyes—the only recognizable part of him—looked steadily down at me. I could see only a hint of his full lower lip below the luxurious blond mustache. I wondered what it would be like to kiss a man with a mustache like that . . . even if it was fake.

Blast it! What on earth was I thinking? He was a thief and a sneak. And I couldn't believe half the words that came from his mouth. Less than half. I didn't even really know what he looked like . . . although there had been one time he'd removed all of his disguise so I could see his face. But it had been shadowy and dark in my bedchamber . . . and who knows if he *truly* had removed it all.

"Right then. Why are you here? And why are you masquerading as a rich American? And how in the world did you manage to get an invitation? Is Martin VanderBleeth a real person?"

"In fact, he is," Pix said, executing a pass between two other couples. We came so close I felt the air move, but we didn't touch either of them. "Aye, and to the best o' me knowledge, the bloke remains in New York City, completely oblivious to the borrowing of his name."

"And you chose to borrow his name, as you put it, for what reason?"

"Perhaps it's jus' so I can see 'ow the other 'alf lives. See wot it's like t'dance at Mister Oligary's bloody Midnight Palace . . . and maybe even take a gander at ye and yer Mr. Dancy. Ye make a fine lookin' couple, the two o' ye, even though the fop thinks he ought t'be worthy of three dances." The smile curved his mustache but did not extend to his eyes. Instead, they glittered darkly. And his Cockney accent had become even thicker than usual.

"I believe your motives are that innocent about as much as I believe you're an American heir," I returned.

The mustache curved even more, and now his eyes danced. "Ver' well, then, luv, ye've caught me out. Me motives are never innocent."

"So why *are* you here?"

The humor faded from his gaze. "I thought me new customer—the one wot's causin' me some consternation—would be likely t'be 'ere tonight. The most exclusive gatherin' o' the wealthy an' powerful. I was hopin' I might identify 'im. Or 'er."

"You think it's the Ankh."

He didn't respond, but his fingers tightened over mine a trifle.

"How did you think you'd identify him or her by coming here? You only have the paper, the note, you gave me . . . how would you know? Have you ever seen him? Or her? Or spoken to him?" Once more, he remained silent, but I wasn't going to let it go. "Tell me what else you know about this new customer, Pix, and why you're so blasted worried about him. Or her."

"Bloody 'ell, Evaline, yer gonna be th' death o' me—or at leas', the death o' me peace."

"I hardly think you have any peace to speak of, Pix. Sneaking around in the stews, wearing disguises all the time, dealing with whatever illegal trade it is you do. That doesn't seem like a very peaceful life at all. It doesn't seem like a *life* at all."

I was one to talk, being a vampire hunter and all, but he was making me angry. Always half-truths. Always hiding. And blast it all, even though I didn't trust him, I couldn't stop thinking about him either. That was what infuriated me the most.

His expression turned blank and I felt his body become rigid as steel. "Do ye think I'd choose such a life if I 'ad the choice?"

"Pix . . ." I didn't know what to say. There was something raw, something real about his words. Bleakness darkened his eyes. "What do you—"

"Leave it, Evaline. Just leave it *be*." He'd never spoken to me in that tone before. Cold, hard, cutting.

I scrambled for something to say, but no words came to mind. Instead, we paced through several more steps until the waltz ended. At least he hadn't abandoned me on the dance floor.

"There's yer Mr. Dancy," Pix said as he escorted me off the dance floor. "Waitin' for ye like a pantin' hound dog."

"Thank you for the dance, Mr. VanderBleeth." My voice matched his chilly one. "I do hope you enjoy the rest of your evening."

I spun smartly and took myself off to locate Lurelia, managing to avoid Mr. Dancy at the same time. The princess should have just been finishing the same waltz with Mr. Southerby. I nearly bumped into Mina, who grasped me by the arm and towed me off.

"Well? Have you learned anything? Did you see anyone using vanilla face powder?" she demanded.

"No. I—"

"And where's Lurelia?"

"She was dancing with Mr. Southerby—"

"*There* is Mr. Southerby. And Lurelia is not in his vicinity."

Mina and I both spun in different directions to scan the room. "It's impossible to find anyone here," she muttered over her shoulder. "With all those ridiculous flowing draperies and so many alcoves, and the lights are always moving about. And now that the dancing is finished, everyone is in the way. Drat it! Where could she have gone?"

"Surely she can't be far. The waltz just ended."

But Mina didn't reply. I turned back to see her pushing through the crush of people, heading toward Mr. Southerby. By the time I joined them, she'd already begun questioning the poor man.

"You mean to say you didn't even dance with her at all?" Mina's voice rose alarmingly.

"I intended to, of course, but we were nearly to the edge of the dance floor when she stopped and asked me to fetch her a glass of apple-tea, with a caramel cinnamon swirly-stick. When I came back, she was gone."

"Double-drat!" Mina whirled on me. "How could this happen?"

"Calm down," I said, even though I felt a little disconcerted. "Perhaps she merely wanted to freshen up. There's no reason to panic. Surely she's not gone far."

But we couldn't find her anywhere. We checked the ladies' retiring room, then Mina and I split up. We went in different directions, meeting up at pre-arranged locations. I didn't see Lurelia or Mr. VanderBleeth, although I did have another near encounter with Mr. Dancy. But I managed to avoid him at the last minute, for I had a feeling he would become difficult to dislodge if we met up.

Suddenly, my arm was grabbed in a deathly grip. I spun around, ready to lose my temper, when I saw Mina's face. It was strained and white, and for once, she wasn't telling me what to do.

She was looking up . . . up . . .

There, on the highest balcony overlooking the room, was Lurelia, teetering near the edge. Even from here, I could see she was disheveled and wore a terrified expression.

Oh my gad. She is going to fall!

Miss Holmes

Wherein Our Heroines Make an Exceptional Blunder

L urelia didn't fall.

I never believed it was an imminent possibility; for she merely stood at the balcony, which had a waist-high railing, looking as if she were in shock, but Miss Stoker certainly did. She dashed off like a madwoman, pushing through the crowd and bolting up the moving stairs.

I followed at a slightly more sedate pace, though still very quickly. Unfortunately, our hasty actions garnered the attention of some of the other party-goers, and I heard the low rumble of concerned murmurs.

My insides churned and my palms were sweaty beneath my gloves. I wasn't eager for Miss Adler or Princess Alix to realize we'd lost custody of our charge on the very first night of duty. And from the looks of the younger princess, something unpleasant had befallen her. I just hoped it wasn't anything too awful.

By the time I reached the balcony, I was breathing heavily due to my blasted corset. Evaline had moved Lurelia away from the edge, out of sight of the curious in the ballroom below. It was a lovely space, for the other side of the chamber opened onto a large terrace that overlooked the city. The fresh night air would have been welcome if this weren't such a desperate moment.

The princess sat on an upholstered bench, looking more forlorn and timid than ever. Half of her hair sagged in loose hanks, and she was missing a glove and one of her pearl earbobs. There was even a tear on her overskirt.

"It was awful," she said over and over again. "So terrible!"

"It's all right. You're safe now," said my partner. I wasn't at all surprised she didn't have a handkerchief to offer the tearful princess, so I extricated one from my small drawstring bag and thrust it at Lurelia. Honestly, how did Evaline think she would be a successful vampire hunter if she was never prepared for emergencies? She hardly even remembered to bring money for the street-lifts.

"I was so frightened!" Lurelia made good use of my handkerchief with decidedly unprincesslike sounds. "And he . . . he . . . Oh, it was terrible!"

"He who?" I demanded, for clearly Miss Stoker had no concept how to conduct a thorough and efficient interrogation. She merely stood there looking disgusted. Someone had to take control and guide Lurelia into coherence. "What happened? Did someone attack you?"

"Y-yes. Yes. I—I went to wash my face . . . I was feeling rather warm. I didn't really want to dance the last waltz, and so I sent my partner off to find something to drink. But I wanted some air, so I . . ." She buried her face in the handkerchief.

"Yes? What did you do?"

"I went up to . . . up here. Someone . . . Lady Cosgrove-Pitt? Or one of her companions . . . had mentioned to me there was an open terrace on one of the lower roofs, and I thought if I could just breathe some of the night air I would be . . ." She dissolved into tears, hiding her face in trembling hands.

"Your Highness . . ." It was a struggle for me to keep my tone respectful, for this was precisely the sort of emotional breakdown that frayed my nerves. "If you would attempt to focus your thoughts and tell us what happened, Evaline and I will see what's to be done."

Lurelia lifted her damp face from the scrap of white linen. "It was awful. He was so . . . he was so frightening. He . . . he . . . at least, I *think* it was a he."

I went cold. "What?"

"I thought it was a man at first. He was dressed in black, and he wore a hat. And gloves. And it was dark and shadowy." My sharp words seemed to have forced Lurelia to collect her thoughts. "But then, the way he spoke . . . and moved. It couldn't have been a woman, could it? A woman dressed in men's clothing?"

"What did he—or she—look like?" I demanded, feeling as if I'd been plunged into a pool of water. Everything was slow and murky. I had seen Lady Cosgrove-Pitt just before the final waltz. She had been standing in a corner, conversing with Mr. Oligary and Lady Bentley-Hughes. And she had been the one to tell Lurelia that the terrace was here. Could she have had the time to change her clothing and come up here to accost the princess?

"Forget what he looked like! What did he say? What *happened*?" Evaline's voice was as tense as I felt.

"He . . . she . . . w-wanted me to tell h-him . . . h-her . . . where it was. 'Where is it? Where is it?' He kept saying it over and over. 'Where is it?' He had his hands around my throat . . . f-first he shook me by the shoulders, then he put his hands around my neck . . . and he wasn't so very tall. Perhaps he was a woman."

"What did he want? What was he looking for?"

"He—he wants the chess queen. The Byzantine chess queen." Lurelia's voice quavered. "He said if I don't give it to him, he'll . . . he'll . . ."

"Do you mean the Theophanine Chess Queen?" I was confused. "How would you know where it is?"

"I don't know!" Lurelia burst into tears. "I told him the letter is missing, and he s-said the letter didn't matter. That he knew I could find it. That that was why I c-came to L-London . . ."

I had to blink several times before I could determine where to begin to untangle this tale. "So a man—who might have been a woman—accosted you here on the terrace and wanted you to tell him where the Theophanine Chess Queen is. And even though you don't know where it is, not only does he believe you do, he believes you came to London for the express purpose of retrieving it? Is that correct?"

The princess had stilled during my speech, and now she looked up at me with confused gray eyes. "Y-yes. I believe so."

"Why on earth would he—or she," I added grimly, "believe you know where it is? The chess queen has been missing for three centuries."

"Be-c-cause I . . . I . . ." Lurelia swallowed hard. "Because I was the one who r-realized the l-letter was a-about the chess queen. I found it in a trunk of old papers and r-realized what it w-was—a letter from Queen Elizabeth to my ancestor the Duchess of Fedeway. But I d-don't know what it means!"

"So the man threatened you. If you don't tell him where the chess queen is, he'll . . . what did he say he'd do?"

Lurelia bowed her head. "Nothing," she whispered.

I exchanged an impatient glance with Miss Stoker, and she took the opportunity to speak. "Your Highness . . . Lurelia. We're here to help you. If you're in danger—of anything— tell us so we can help. You must trust us."

But she just shook her head silently. Before I could press her further, Inspector Grayling burst through the entrance. Hardly sparing either Miss Stoker or me a glance, he rushed to the distraught princess.

"Your Highness, are you hurt?" Because of his excessive height, he found it necessary to crouch next to her in order not to tower over the diminutive girl—something he never had the consideration to do when speaking with me. The toe of his shiny boot squeaked softly on the marble floor. "What has befallen you?"

"She isn't hurt," I told him, deciding an interruption with a clear and simple response was better than the halting, timid answer Lurelia would no doubt provide.

Grayling flashed me an exasperated look just as Mr. Oligary, Miss Adler, and Lord Regent Terrence swept into view. Oh *drat*.

"Princess Lurelia! Are you injured? What has happened?" exclaimed Mr. Oligary. He hardly leaned on his walking stick as he limped to the princess's side. "Your Highness, I am terribly sorry for whatever occurred to upset you at my social hall. I shall make certain the captain assigns the very capable Inspector Grayling here to handle the investigation, and he will make any arrests as quickly as possible. Please, allow me to see you to a more comfortable location so you may be . . . er . . . put to rights."

Miss Adler gave me a cool glance, and I knew at least in her mind, Evaline and I were being held responsible for this event. Double drat!

"Miss Holmes, perhaps you can shed some illumination on the events?" Inspector Grayling sidled up to me. He looked down his long nose as if *I* were the one who'd attacked the princess, clearly taking his assignment seriously.

Before I could formulate a polite response, Miss Adler ushered Lurelia from the terrace, plying her with platitudes and assurances that she would be just fine. They were followed by the Lord Regent, who appeared to be quite inebriated, if his unsteady footsteps and the stench of spirits wafting from him was any indication.

This left Mr. Oligary, Grayling, Evaline, and myself on the terrace. I had never met the famous businessman, inventor, and philanthropist, and wasn't pleased about making his acquaintance under these circumstances. Aside from that, I felt as if I should assist Miss Adler with Lurelia.

But as it turned out, I didn't have much choice in the matter.

"You're the Holmes girl, then?" Mr. Oligary fixed me with a pair of piercing blue eyes. One of them was magnified slightly by a single-lens spectacle, held in place by a curious brass fitting that curved around his temple and ear. It was very cognog, and I decided if I was ever required to wear spectacles, I would want something of similar design.

I knew Mr. Oligary's age—at least as reported in the papers—was forty, and meeting him in person gave all indication this was true. His attire was the height of fashion, with exquisite tailoring and excellent fabric. His coarse brown hair was just beginning to thread with gray at the temples, and while his face wasn't perfectly handsome, the man had an air about him that my mother would call charisma.

As I took in the details of his person, I observed several nuances that had never been reported in the press: he smoked Joseph & Gargantan cigars, preferred Imported Empress Earl

Grey tea to spirits, had recently changed the blade on his mechanized shaver, and owned a white dog who desperately needed its nails clipped.

"Yes," I said. "My name is Mina Holmes. It's very nice to meet you, Mr. Oligary. I had the pleasure of attending the Grand Opening of the New Vauxhall Gardens several weeks ago, and look forward to visiting again, for I was unable to find the time to ride on your Observation Cogwheel." I carefully avoided looking at Grayling, who'd fished me out of the river in a most mortifying episode that evening.

"Indeed. And what a shame. The Observation Wheel is my favorite part of the pleasure park," he said. "Please. Be my guest any time at the Gardens. These will allow you to ride as many attractions and as often as you like." He reached into his pocket and withdrew a handful of triangular brass tokens, which he offered to me and my companions.

We thanked him profusely—especially Grayling, which caused me to wonder just whom he might be planning to take to the Gardens. Then I introduced Miss Stoker.

"Isn't your brother Bram Stoker?" Mr. Oligary said. "The manager of the Lyceum Theater? I've been speaking with him about replacing the current steam engine that powers the lighting system. We have a new model that runs much more quietly. Although I prefer the soft, sibilant hiss of steam—it's so relaxing and comforting, isn't it?—but when one is at the theater, one does wish to hear what is being said onstage, I suppose." He smiled benignly at us. "And steam power is much safer and more efficient than electricity. We are very fortunate here in England not to be exposed to the dangers of that terrible invention." His voice, which until now had been casual and friendly, tightened a trifle.

I dared not look at Grayling, for I was fairly certain his terrifying steamcycle did not, in fact, run on steam, but on something illegal. Such as electrical power.

"The Moseley-Haft Act has made certain of that," said Grayling in a well-modulated tone. "Keeping Mother England safe from the evils of electricity also enables you to keep your steam and cogwheel factories in business, and therefore a good number of our countrymen and women employed."

"Precisely." Mr. Oligary smiled. "I shudder to think what would happen if we legalized that abominable, invisible white-hot power they use in the States." He gestured absently to his leg using the walking stick. "You may not know this, but I actually considered supporting its widespread induction to England until the event which caused this very injury." He shook his head. "Perhaps you heard about the incident, which resulted in the death of my business partner, Edgar Bartholomew."

"It was no mere accident," Grayling said, glancing at me.

Mr. Oligary shook his head gravely. "Tragic. If only I had arrived in time, perhaps I could have prevented the tragedy." He looked at Evaline and me, chagrin in his expression. "Pardon me, ladies. Ambrose and I have discussed this case numerous times, and I apologize for bringing up such a tedious topic in front of you. It's one of the few unsolved crimes on my young friend's docket, and I'm certain he shares the same frustration I do."

Grayling nodded. "Very well, then. Miss Holmes, shall I find your wrap? It's well past two o'clock and the orchestra and food have long quit. Most of the guests have gone as well."

I avoided Miss Stoker's sudden look of interest and inclined my head in acquiescence, ignoring the rise of heat in my cheeks. I knew Grayling also wanted to quiz me about the attack on Lurelia. I would be most forthcoming with him, of course . . . as long as *he* apprised *me* of the details regarding the not-so-accidental death of Mr. Oligary's business partner. "Certainly, Inspector Grayling. I have one thing I must do, and then I shall meet you by the door through which we entered. Miss Stoker, may I have a word?"

Evaline grinned broadly as we left Mr. Oligary and Grayling on the terrace. "You didn't tell me the inspector was your escort this evening. He certainly looks well put-out in his tailcoat and gloves."

"Oh, Evaline, do hush about that." My cheeks were flaming. "I want to visit the ladies' retiring room one last time to see if there is any trace of that face powder. If the Ankh was here this evening, there is always the chance she made use of the chamber."

I *think* my companion rolled her eyes, but I was walking too quickly—just ahead of her—to know for certain. I stepped onto one of the elevators and yanked Evaline on board before the gate closed. "Did you dance with that Mr. VanderBleeth? Do you think there is any chance at all he was the one who accosted Lurelia?"

To my great annoyance Evaline began to laugh. "There is no chance he accosted the princess. I'm certain of it. Did you not recognize him, oh Mistress of Observation? Surely the great Miss Alvermina Holmes wasn't taken in by a mere disguise!"

I turned to glare at my partner. What on earth was wrong with her? I had no idea what she was taking about, but I ground my teeth and chose not to reply.

"Oh, don't sniff at me," Evaline finally said as the elevator gate opened. We were on the ground floor and the ladies' retiring room was across a small alcove. "You always do that when you don't know what to say. Mr. VanderBleeth is actually very well-known to both of us." She lifted one eyebrow at me in a manner I find very irritating.

Mr. VanderBleeth had been in the trolley car ahead of Grayling and me when we entered the ball, and I had thought he seemed familiar. All of a sudden I understood. "That disreputable Mr. Pix! How on earth . . . ?" Well, at least we didn't have to worry about Mr. VanderBleeth luring Princess Lurelia into eloping with him.

At least, I didn't think so.

Evaline was still laughing as we slipped into the ladies' lounge. The space was empty, and still illuminated with a great number of soft gaslit sconces, which made it much easier for me to spy any traces of face powder. I had, of course, come prepared with a number of small paper envelopes with which to collect samples.

I carefully scooped up several dustings from the counter-top in front of the long row of mirrors where ladies generally put themselves to right. I'd have to examine and test them at home, but I did catch the faintest scent of vanilla from one of them.

"Oh, dear. Lady Cosgrove-Pitt lost another of her butterflies."

I turned sharply. Evaline was rising from the floor, something in her hand.

"Let me see that," I said. For some reason, my heart was pounding.

With an odd expression, she offered me the small embroidered butterfly. It was no larger than my thumbnail, very delicate and trimmed with green and blue stitching. I remembered seeing them all along the neckline of Lady Isabella's gown; they were quite a lovely accessory.

I lifted the butterfly, looking at it carefully in the light. Did I see the faint glitter of gold there? The faint dusting of white powder? Indeed I did.

My hand shook a trifle as I brought the decoration to my nose.

I sniffed.

Vanilla.

Miss Holmes

Cause for Termination

Inspector Grayling sat stiffly across from me in the carriage. "For the last time, I am not going to discuss the Bartholomew case, Miss Holmes."

I lifted my chin. "No one is fond of discussing one's failures, Inspector Grayling, but perhaps I could be—"

"*No.*"

"There is no need to raise your voice."

"Apparently there is, for you seem to have become hard of hearing. And I don't have failures. In fact, I have the greatest number of closed cases on the homicide team. There are only two unsolved—" He clamped his lips shut and glowered at me. "Since you've spent so much time badgering me about the Bartholomew case, our ride is almost over. We'll be at your house shortly, so perhaps you would do as Mr. Oligary suggested and apprise me of what Princess Lurelia told you, and your observations about tonight's incident."

I gave him a withering look but complied with his request. I did *not* mention my suspicions that the princess's assailant was the Ankh. He could come to his own conclusions.

"As for my observations, Inspector Grayling, I confess there were few relevant clues. The assailant left no trace of his presence, either on the terrace or on Her Highness's person. My suggestion for conducting this investigation is to determine which guests or servants at the ball match the physical description of the villain, and then attempt to determine who had the opportunity to slip away and—"

"*Thank you*, Miss Holmes."

I sniffed and peered out the window. We had turned past Cavendish-square. In two more streets, I would see the bell-shaped gas lamp that hung from the porch at my house.

"Perhaps you could at least enlighten me about the homicide you are investigating related to the robbery of the Queen Elizabeth letter," I suggested stiffly. "After all, you were the one who raised the topic."

"Indeed I did." He sounded as if he regretted it. Nevertheless, he did go on to answer my question. "The connection to the robbery is fairly evident, even to a non-Holmesian investigator such as myself, although I must clarify that it is a *possible* homicide. The body of one of the museum guards was found near the lighting controls for the North Wing of the museum—where the Arched Room is located—"

"I'm aware that the Arched Room is in the Northwest Quadrant of the museum, Inspector Grayling."

"Pardon me, Miss Holmes. Of course you are."

"Presumably the location of the body is relevant to the fact that the lights were extinguished so the thief could carry out his plan?"

"Indeed. There are indications the museum guard was actually the one to cause the blackout. His hands showed traces of burns, and there was black around the control box as well as on his person. There was one more curious thing, Miss Holmes, and I'll leave it to you to consider," he said as we turned onto my street. "There were two tiny marks on the back of the guard's shoulder. Perhaps six inches apart, hardly larger than pinpricks."

"Fascinating," I murmured, mulling over this tidbit. "I do appreciate the information, Inspector."

As the royal carriage glided to a smooth halt, Grayling cleared his throat. "Er . . . Miss Holmes . . . that is, I wish to say . . . it was an honor to be your escort this evening—"

"Why, thank you, Inspector Grayling." I replied in surprise.

"—in spite of your tendency to take the lead during every dance."

I gave him a dark look, but my lips had begun to quiver. "That is a gross exaggeration. I did not attempt to lead during the quadrille."

His mouth twitched as he helped me out of the carriage. "That's because, as you very well know, Miss Holmes, the quadrille is a country square dance. Even *you* wouldn't be able to manage a group of eight couples."

I couldn't keep a straight face any longer and began to giggle in a horribly girlish fashion as I looked up at him. For some reason, his ridiculous height no longer bothered me. "If only they would all listen to my suggestions to follow the tiles on the floor, the dance squares would remain uniform and no one would cut the corners short and tread on the ladies' hems!"

His eyes crinkled charmingly when he laughed, which he did now. "Miss Holmes, you are quite—" He froze and his arm lashed out, halting me from taking any steps up my walkway. "Get back in the carriage."

Before I could speak, he reached beneath his formal coat. Something metallic gleamed in his hand and he gestured for me to heed his command. Of course, I was to have none of that.

"What is it?" I brushed against him from behind.

"Miss Holmes, I told you to—*You!* There! Show yourself! I'm with Scotland Yard!" He stalked up the walkway, pointing a magnificent-looking hand-weapon toward the shadows. "I said *show yourself!*"

But by now I'd seen him. "Dylan! What on earth are you doing here?" Heedless of Grayling's weapon, I charged past him toward my friend, who had emerged from the side of the house.

"Mina! Where have you been?"

"I had an engagement this evening. What are you doing here?"

"It appears to me this gentleman was attempting to break into your residence," said Grayling. "Perhaps he didn't learn his lesson previously."

The inspector was referring to the first time I'd met Dylan, for the newcomer had broken into the British Museum and been jailed shortly afterward. Since then, Grayling seemed certain Dylan was some sort of criminal.

"You had an engagement?" Dylan's voice was none-too-polite.

"Why, yes. Miss Adler requested my attendance at—oh, never mind. What are you doing here?" I hadn't seen him for more than a few minutes since the incident with the vampire pickpocket gang, for Dylan had been spending all of his time working at the hospital with Dr. Lister and Dr. Gray.

"There are some things—I—well." He stopped and glanced at Grayling. "Can we can go inside, Mina? I don't really want to talk about it out here."

I had the feeling he meant he didn't want to talk about it in front of the inspector. "Very well. I shall . . . I will . . . just one moment, Dylan." I dug in my handbag and produced the house key, which I handed to him. Unlike at Miss Stoker's home, there was no butler or footman to greet us at the door.

As Dylan started toward the entrance, I turned back to take my leave of Grayling. He had a most peculiar expression on his face—as if he violently wished to say something, but dared not open his mouth. He was still holding that hand-weapon, with its fascinating array of bronze cogs and gears. It had a slender barrel like a firearm, and a small orange light glowed on one end. I had half a mind to ask him if I could examine it, but decided to wait until I had better illumination.

"Thank you again, Inspector—"

"Are you quite certain you mean to allow that character into your home? In the dead of night? What on earth are you thinking, Miss Holmes?" Apparently he had given up on restraint.

"I've nothing to worry about with Dylan—"

"And so it's *Dylan*, is it? And not Mr. Eckhert? Miss Holmes, do you recall that gentleman has been jailed for breaking and entering? And that no one seems to know who he is and from where he's come? Do you not have a care for your reputation?"

The fact that Grayling knew Dylan's full name, and quite a bit more about him than I realized, came as a surprise to me. Still, I didn't care for the tone of his voice. "I don't give a whit about my reputation. And I'm perfectly capable of taking care of myself, Inspector Grayling."

"Except when you are falling out of a bloody *window*. Or *drowning* in a creek because your corset is too tight." He drew in a breath. When he spoke again, his voice was marginally quieter. "Very well, Miss Holmes. Good evening. And never say I didn't warn you about consorting with criminals." He gave a smart, sharp bow, then turned and strode back to the carriage.

I watched him go, then turned back to the house. Dylan stood on the porch, waiting for me.

"What are you doing here? Tell me at once, Dylan, for I am exhausted. It's been a very eventful day."

"I need you to come to the hospital. There's something I need you to see. It's important."

"*Tonight?*"

"Yes. Please, Mina?"

"What is it?" I asked wearily. The only thing I wanted to do was get out of my corset and pinprick-heel shoes and climb into bed.

"I think . . . I'm pretty sure we have some patients who've been bitten. By vampires."

⊰•⊱

I don't remember what time I finally fell into bed, but dawn was imminent and I could hardly form a coherent thought.

As I slipped into slumber, my mind was filled with grotesque images of twin bite-marks and the deep, bloody weals on three of Dylan's patients at Charing Cross Hospital.

I had no doubt the damage had been caused by one or more UnDead.

I dreamt in those early hours of dawn . . . of the red-eyed, sharp-fanged vampires, with their blood-tinged teeth and foul, claw-like hands . . . of my mother, trapped with Evaline while they fought off hordes of the UnDead from attacking Miss Adler as I watched helplessly from behind a solid glass window . . . of my mother and Evaline laughing and sipping tea in the parlor as Lady Cosgrove-Pitt served them biscuits while a dead vampire lay slumped and bloody in the corner.

But then I dreamt of the Ankh. Of her calm gray eyes and her small, strong hands as she faced me across a massive chessboard. With a flick of her wrist, she set a large fire around us. I was somehow chained to my chair, and she forced me to play chess . . . and then she reached out, smiling, and petted me on the head as the flames roared and licked at the backs of our chairs . . . and the black tendrils of smoke snaked around us like an evil vine, as if binding us together . . . *Checkmate*, she whispered. *Checkmate . . . checkmate . . . checkmate . . .*

"Mina!"

I bolted awake, chest heaving, hair plastered to my face and throat. Mrs. Raskill stood over me. She was holding the top of her Phinney's Instant Butter Mill in one hand, and the fingers of the other were wrapped around my arm.

Though my heart still thudded beneath the twisted blankets, I forced away the remnants of the dream. "Yes?"

"You all right, there, missy? I've been knocking for ten minutes, and then I heard you carrying on like a caterwauling cat!"

"I must have been dreaming," I said, avoiding her eyes. Sitting up, I pushed the tangles of hair from my face.

"A message has come for you," said my housekeeper, looking at me with concern.

"From whom?"

She shook her head and firmed her lips. "I'm not about to give it to you until you eat some breakfast. This is the second time in three days I've had to wake you from whatever it is you're dreaming about."

Since I had no other option, and I *was* hungry, I freshened up and dressed quickly. Moments later, I sat at the kitchen table eating the results of Mrs. Raskill's latest household gadget, the Flippers-Fryer & Toaster. The double-layer pan was quite a time-saver, she boasted, and it never broke a yolk.

Though the bacon and eggs tasted heavenly, I had only a few bites before I held out my hand. "The message, if you please, Mrs. Raskill."

She eyed me balefully, but dug the note from her apron pocket. I immediately recognized Miss Adler's penmanship—unslanted, purposeful, and very neat—and my stomach dipped a little. I broke the seal and read:

Please present yourself in my office promptly at 10 o'clock.

I squeaked when I realized it was beyond half-past nine, and bolted from my chair. My teacup went tumbling, followed by a rasher of perfectly crisp bacon (a terrible waste!), and Mrs. Raskill began to bellow.

I dodged the dripping tea, stepped on the bacon (unfortunately crushing it into the floor), then slipped past the housekeeper as she descended upon the mess, griping loudly as she mopped it up with vigorous sweeping motions.

I would have helped her clean up, but I'd learned from experience that not only did I not do it to her satisfaction, I got in her way while *she* was doing it. Instead, I swooped up my reticule, jammed on a hat, and snatched a pair of gloves from the front table.

I would never be able to find a cab in time to get to the museum for our appointment, but I dashed out the door anyway. Not for the first time, I wondered why someone as important to the Crown and National Security as Sir Mycroft Holmes didn't have a telephone or ready access to transportation from his residence. But I already knew the answer: because he was never at home.

I pounded down the steps and had just reached the walkway when a familiar horse-drawn carriage pulled up in front of my house. Evaline!

"Apparently you received the summons as well." I pulled the door open without waiting for Middy to step down to assist. "To the museum," I told him.

Evaline watched with undisguised amusement as I fairly tumbled into my seat—crinolines, bustle, reticule, and all. "Yes. I knew you would need a ride as well."

"I can only imagine there is a new development in the Princess Lurelia incident. Or perhaps the princess wishes to visit Bond-street. I was telling her about the lace shop, and she seemed interested in patronizing it," I said calmly.

Miss Stoker eyed me, but didn't speak. I lapsed into silence as well, for I was unable to dismiss a growing sense of trepidation. Perhaps something had happened to Lurelia. Or, on a more optimistic side, perhaps the stolen letter had been found.

The ride to the museum seemed longer than ever, but Evaline and I arrived just as Big Ben struck ten. Moments later, the door opened to Miss Adler's office, and we bustled in.

Our mentor sat at her desk. Her favorite wrist-clock rested on the surface next to a steaming cup of Darjeeling and a plate of paper-thin slices of lemon. A cunning pair of scissors with double circular blades rested atop a small wooden box. Miss Adler had a stack of papers aligned neatly at her elbow, and her dark hair was pulled back into a particularly severe hairstyle.

"Please sit."

Her expression did nothing to ease my trepidation, and I glanced at Evaline. She didn't appear to be the least bit concerned.

"I trust Lurelia has recovered, if not fully, then at least somewhat, from last night's incident?" I asked.

Miss Adler nodded briefly. "Yes. She seems to have come through it with little ill effect."

"I'm very relieved. She seemed quite frightened—"

"Mina." Miss Adler spoke quietly, but it was enough. "I've called the two of you here today because it's quite clear you have given little interest or attention in fulfilling the request Princess Alix has set before you. Not only have I noticed a decided lack of enthusiasm for this task, but this disinterest and inattention have already resulted in two unpleasant and embarrassing incidents. I thought you were aware how vital it is that this Betrovian visit be free of scandal and upset, but apparently . . . well, suffice to say, Miss Holmes and Miss Stoker, that, due to the circumstances, you are hereby relieved of your duty. Your services are no longer needed."

MISS STOKER

Miss Stoker Interrogates

For a moment, I thought Mina was going to faint. Her face went deadly white and then a dark flush swept her cheeks. And for once, she didn't have a thing to say.

On the other hand, I was ecstatic we no longer had to watch over the colorless princess. Now I could set my attention to Pix's mysterious customer and forget about balls and shopping and holding royal hands.

However, I did hate for Miss Adler and Princess Alix to think poorly of Mina and me. I wished there had been a better way for us to give up the task.

Now that Miss Adler's news had been delivered, I saw no reason to remain in her office. I rose and thanked her, then excused myself.

Mina—still more subdued than I'd ever seen her—pulled to her feet as well. "Thank you, Miss Adler. I'm sorry to have disappointed you and Her Royal Highness."

She didn't speak again until we were in the carriage and Middy closed the door. "Well," was all she said. "*Well*."

That was when I realized the tip of her nose was red and she was blinking rapidly. Blooming fish! Was Mina Holmes *crying*?

"Uh . . ." I didn't know what to say.

"You needn't look so *pleased* about it all," she snapped. "You look as if you were just—just given an entire ballroom of vampires to stake! Doesn't it matter to you that we have been terminated from the princess's special service league? And that we've disappointed Miss Adler? Did you see the way she looked at us? Whatever am I going to do *now*? A Holmes, *fired* from a case! A failure!" She snapped her jaws closed and stared out the window, still blinking.

"Well . . . er . . . maybe you'll have more time to try and catch the Ankh, now that we don't have to watch over Princess Lurelia."

"I shall be relegated to my laboratory working on a treatise over—over *coffee grounds*. Or—or embroidery threads. Or something equally useless."

"Well, you never know, Mina. If there were ever coffee stains at a crime scene, your—um—treatise might come in handy."

She whipped her head around. There were two spots of pink on her cheeks. "I suppose I should tell you . . . there are indications that UnDead are present in London. So at least *you* will have something to do."

I sat upright. "There are? How do you know? What makes you think—"

"I don't *think*, Miss Stoker. I *know*. I saw the evidence myself in the pre-dawn hours this morning. At Charing Cross Hospital. Three victims, and none are expected to live."

※

I wasn't nervous. Not really.

Why should I be?

"You killed my brother! Murderer!"

I pushed away the memory of that horrible shrieking accusation, and blocked the image of the wide eyes and furious mouth.

I was a vampire hunter. I was descended from one of the most famous Venators of them all, and I had already slain a dozen of the UnDead.

But I was a little queasy as I felt for the stake in the hidden pocket of my trousers. Pepper, my maid—the only other person in my household besides Bram who knew about my secret calling—had helped me dress in men's clothing tonight.

Loose trousers held in place by dark suspenders, a plain, undyed shirt that buttoned down the front, and a hat had turned me into a slender young man. The mass of my pinned-up hair made the flat-topped newsboy cap bulge on top. Pepper had sneaked a pair of her nephew's shoes for me, because my feet were so small.

Mina and I had visited the hospital after leaving the museum and I tried without success to speak to one of the victims. Although in the past, Dylan had been able to save others whose blood had been drained by UnDead, this time each of these patients were so badly wounded there was little hope for survival.

Since none of the victims were coherent enough to give me any information about where they'd been attacked, I didn't know where to start looking. All I could do was listen, watch, and wait for that telltale, eerie chill over the back of my neck that told me a vampire was near.

So I walked and wandered in the darkest part of night, and then I walked some more. Aimless and yet with purpose . . . for somehow, I found myself in Whitechapel: the darkest, dingiest, dirtiest, and most dangerous area of London.

It was also the place Pix called home, and where he reigned supreme over an underworld of pickpockets and other thieves, as well as a seedy pub called Fenman's End.

Actually, I didn't know if he truly reigned supreme. But I did know an awful lot of violent criminal-types in the stews showed Pix nothing but respect and obedience. Including a large, grabby-handed facemark known as Big Marv.

I wondered, not for the first time, how such a young man— for he couldn't be older than twenty-three or twenty-four— could command that amount of power in such a violent world. Surely he hadn't been around for that long. And I was fairly certain he hadn't been *raised* in the dark, dangerous rookery.

I just didn't know where he'd come from.

Or, as Mina would no doubt say, from where he'd come.

The fact that my route took me to Fenman's End did make some sense. The last time I was here, I'd staked a vampire—much to Pix's fury. I was saving his life, but he wasn't the least bit appreciative.

That was also the first time I'd seen the small palm-sized device I was so curious about. The intriguing machine that was apparently Pix's "business."

I strode into the pub, glad I'd decided to dress as a boy tonight. I wasn't in the mood to attract the attention I would have done if I was wearing a skirt.

As usual, Bilbo was tending bar. I took a stool at one end of the counter so I could watch for trouble—as well as Pix—and glanced at the older man. His sparse tufts of hair looked as if they grew thinner by the hour. And he had a very large, ripe pimple on his chin. I found it hard to look any-where else.

He remembered me. "Wotcher pleasure, miss? Lemonade or ale?"

"Neither. I'm looking for Pix."

"'E ain't 'ere." He scratched the dark stubble that grew on his chin, narrowly avoiding the ready-to-burst pimple. "I ain't seen 'im."

It was on the tip of my tongue to ask if he'd seen any vampires, but I held back. "How's Big Marv?"

Bilbo might have cracked a smile. Or he might have grimaced. "'Is finger's mostly 'ealed up, fin'lly."

"Maybe that'll teach him to keep his hands to himself."

"Don' know 'bout that. 'E ain't too smart, Big Marv."

"That's the truth." I sat there for a minute, then realized what a golden opportunity I had. "So . . . how long have you known Pix?"

Bilbo gave me a sidewise look as he turned to fill a tankard with foaming ale. He shoved it at a customer and demanded payment, then turned back to me. "Long enough."

"Right, then. So did you know him when he was a little boy? Or more recently?"

"'E warn't no boy first time he come in 'ere. But I can't as right tell ye 'ow olden 'e was. I ain't 'is blooming pappy!"

"Of course not."

"But it warn't that long ago," he added a little less loudly.

"Right. So was he . . . well, why did he come in here? What I mean to say is, was it an accident or did he come here purposely? To Fenman's End. To Whitechapel."

This time, there was definitely a smile, and even the hard bark of a laugh. "*No one* comes purposely to Whitechapel, Molly-Sue. Thought ye 'ad more brains'n that."

I decided to try another tactic. "Does he own Fenman's End? Is that why everyone—er—fears him so much?"

"Fear? That ain't the way I'd call it. Respect, maybe. An' ye'd 'ave to ask 'im about that."

I gritted my teeth. I'd hoped the old man would be an easy solution to the problem of who was Pix. Bilbo turned away to serve another patron, giving me the opportunity to think about my next question.

He didn't have to make his way back to my end of the bar counter, but he did. Which told me Bilbo was either just as curious about me as I was about Pix, or he'd been told to keep an eye on me if I came into the pub.

"If I wanted to place an order with Pix, how would I go about doing that?" I asked casually.

The bartender lifted one bushy eyebrow and wiped his nose with the back of a hand . . . then with the front, for good measure. When I saw the shiny streak left on his skin, I decided never again to allow him to serve me anything to eat or drink. "An order? An' wot would ye be orderin' then, girl?"

"Er . . . one of those little gadgets." I smiled innocently. "I don't know what they're called, but they're just this big"— I showed him with my hands—"and have some wires curling out from them. I could use one."

"An' wot would the likes o' ye be doin' wi' something that could land yer pretty self in th' clapper?"

I kept my smile in place. "I'm willing to take the risk. After all, you've seen me in action. You know I'm no easy mark."

He nodded in acknowledgment, his eye lighting with appreciation at my use of slang. "Well, now, oy can't argue wi' that, Molly-Sue. Anyone 'oo can take Big Marv ain' gonna go easy."

"So, if I wanted to place an order, then, how would I do it? In order to keep my identity secret." I leaned closer, caught a whiff of the pungent tobacco and sweat scents that clung to him, and eased back a little. "Pix refuses to sell to me, so I don't want him to know it's me who wants it."

Bilbo considered me for a moment as he toyed with the ripe pimple on his chin. I braced myself, ready to dodge if it should burst. "Pix don' wanna sell t'ye? Woy not? I ain' never knowed the boy t'pass up a bit o' flimp."

I shrugged. "He won't say. So tell me . . . how do I get one?"

He narrowed his eyes. "I could get in th' black wi' him if'n 'e finds out."

"How will he find out? I'm not going to tell him. No one else in here is paying any attention to me. All they want is ale from you." I made my smile as innocent as a baby's.

"Awright. There's a place. Bridge & Stokes is wot it's callt. On St. Albans, way over t'Pall Mall where all them dandies be. An' inside summere, there be a book in a case. Ye ask t'see th' book an' when ye put th' book back, ye've got yer order slipped inside. Ye granny all 'at, Molly-Sue?"

"Right. Bridge & Stokes on St. Albans-street. Ask to see the book in the case, put the order inside."

"Aye. In the back o' the book, it's hollered out wi' a spot fer the paper where it's writ."

"And then . . . what? How do I pay? How do I get it?"

"Questions. Allus questions." He paused and shouted at a customer near the other end of the counter. "Shut yer trap. Oy'll be wi' ye when I'm wi' ye! I gots busy-ness 'ere." He was shaking his head when he leaned on his elbows, bringing his aromatic self a little too close for my taste. "Ye tell in th' order where ye wan' the communi—communicay—th' messages t'go. And ye get d'rections fer the rest then."

I nodded. That seemed reasonable. I eased back on my stool as Bilbo left me to tend to the cluster of patrons that had gathered while we talked.

Pix wouldn't tell me what the little device was. He also wouldn't give me any information about his mysterious customer. So I would become a customer myself.

There was more than one way to cut a cogwheel.

I was ready to make my way home. No vampires tonight, but at least I'd made some progress in another direction. I'd better leave before Pix arrived and saw me talking to Bilbo. It would be best if he didn't know I had been there.

I gave the bartender what I hoped was a masculine farewell wave—in case anyone was watching. I'd taken three steps toward the exit when I caught a movement from the corner of my eye.

Turning, I saw that the door leading to the tunnel for Pix's underground hideaway was sliding open. Blast! He'd see me in an instant, and I had no doubt he'd recognize me. My only hope was to blend in.

I ducked toward a crowded table in the corner and slid onto an empty seat that angled away from the secret door.

"Ay! Wot ye think ye're doin'?" one of my tablemates exclaimed.

I had barely enough time to register the five faces goggling at me—one of them vaguely familiar—before I looked over at Pix's door.

"If'n yer gonna sit 'ere, yer gonna entertain us blokes." Someone's hand slammed on the table hard enough to make it lurch.

"Patience, gentlemen." I made a sharp gesture at them. "And I use that term loosely. I'll be gone in a moment. I just needed to rest my feet."

I was glad I'd moved quickly, for it was Pix who stepped through the opening door.

And he wasn't alone.

"Ye ain' gonna sit 'ere! 'At's *Pete's* seat! 'E don' like it when no blokes sit in 'is *seat!*" The table jerked, punctuating each sentence.

"Hey! That ain' no bloke! 'At's the slavey wot broke Big Marv's fingers!"

"I don' care if'n it's the Queen o' England—har, har—no one's gonna set in Pete's seat wif'out his say!"

"I ain' mollyin' wi' *her*, ye fool. I was th'ere. I saw it. She can sit 'ere if'n she wonts."

I hardly heard the exchange, for my attention was completely focused on the pretty blond woman with Pix. In her clean and fashionable clothing, she stood out in the rough and dingy bar like the sun breaking through a cloudy day.

He had offered her his arm and he guided her through the pub—fortunately, without glancing in my direction. Pix appeared to be enjoying himself, smiling and chatting with her in that charming way of his . . . and she was responding in kind.

And then, with an unpleasant jolt, I recognized the woman.

Her name was Olympia Babbage, and she was the grand-daughter of some famous inventor. Mina had dragged me to the Oligary building to look at a display of the grandfather's work a few weeks ago.

That also happened to be the day I'd staked my first vampire—a vampire who'd been trying to feed on Olympia. So I'd saved her life—although the air-brained woman hardly seemed to notice. She was more interested in writing down mathematical calculations than thanking me.

But more importantly, and more unsettling to me, at least, was the fact that this young woman seemed to have inherited her grandfather's talent for inventions—a talent someone like Pix would appreciate.

This wasn't the first time I'd seen Pix and Olympia together. When everything came to a head during the spirit-glass case, they both happened to be there—and it was obvi-ous they were already acquainted.

There was a strange curdling in my belly. Suddenly, I felt a great jolt at the back of my neck, and something tightened around my throat. The next thing I knew, I was airborne.

"I tol' ye 'at was *Pete's* seat!"

The words rang in my ears as I crashed into the wall and landed in a heap on the floor.

I remembered to clap a hand over my cap, which had gone askew, and gingerly opened my eyes.

No one seemed to be looking at me, except the man who was presumably Pete—for he was sitting in my chair. He gave me a dark look, and I pretended to cower.

I could best him in a fight, of course, but not tonight.

When I looked around the pub, Pix and Miss Babbage were gone. I scrambled to my feet and dashed to the door, faking a limp as part of my disguise.

But when I got outside in the fog-shrouded night air, the couple was nowhere to be found.

Miss Holmes

Wherein Mr. Holmes Is Pressed into Service

After Miss Stoker brought me home from our meeting with Miss Adler, I spent the rest of the day, and well into the night, closeted in my laboratory.

It was either that or sulk in my bedchamber, and a Holmes doesn't sulk.

Even when she gets terminated from a case.

Even when she shames herself in front of a member of the Royal Family.

Even when she realizes both of her parents prefer to be anywhere but in her vicinity.

But I wasn't the only one with failures.

So when I woke up the next morning slumped over my desk in the laboratory, surrounded by samples of coffee grounds, it was with new resolve.

I might no longer be wanted or needed by the Crown, but there were other puzzles and unsolved crimes to which

I could turn my attention—such as the case of Mr. Oligary's partner's death. And in the meantime, no one could keep me from building a case against Lady Cosgrove-Pitt as the Ankh.

I dashed off a note to Uncle Sherlock asking for his assistance, as well as a copy to Dr. Watson, in the event my relative was otherwise occupied.

Though I hadn't slept well or long enough for the last two nights, I managed to put myself to rights, dark circles under my eyes notwithstanding. My attire was not as uniquely fashionable as the ensemble I wore to the Midnight Palace, but it was nevertheless neat and smart, and befitted a young female detective. My spring green day dress attempted to lift my spirits with its bright hue, and though it was trimmed with a subdued navy bric-a-brac and grosgrain ribbons that gathered at the bustle, I donned robin's egg gloves and pinned a matching saucer-hat over the thick coils of my hair. I surveyed myself in the mirror and thought the dancing yellow, blue, and green feathers quite enchanting.

My large reticule in hand, I accepted a piece of toast from Mrs. Raskill and swept from the house. I had three destinations on my agenda: Charing Cross Hospital, 221-B Baker-street, and, finally, the Met—better known as Scotland Yard.

As expected, I found Dylan doing what he called "making rounds." Apparently that was a futuristic term that meant he was checking in on all the patients he had been treating.

His weary face lit with pleasure the moment he saw me, and a good portion of my own megrims faded. Dylan never failed to make me feel worthy and interesting—and even, occasionally and surprisingly, attractive.

"Mina!" He strode down the hospital ward, the white coat he insisted on wearing flapping with alacrity. Since a white jacket was utterly unfashionable in London—or anywhere else as far as I knew—he'd had to have it made specially for him.

Affixed to the lapel of his coat winked Prince Albert's pin, which had been given to Dylan by the Queen herself. She was so appreciative of his service to her that she'd bestowed upon him one of her precious husband's diamond and onyx cufflinks. Just beneath it he wore a small sign that read "Dr. Eckhert."

"Good morning, Dylan. I hope I'm not interrupting anything." I examined his countenance. He was one of the most handsome young men I'd ever met, and now that he'd gotten his thick blond hair cut so that it no longer fell into his eyes, he looked even more appealing.

However, he appeared peaked, and he was due for a shave. I narrowed my eyes and looked more closely to assure myself he wasn't as worn down as he'd been during the spirit-glass debacle.

Shoes stained with dried clumps of mud—*he hadn't left the hospital, nor changed his shoes since Friday, when it had last rained; it had poured early this morning, but fresh mud would still be damp.*

Shirt collar pressed straight and upright, and smelling faintly of cedar—*a fresh shirt, taken from its closet within the last several hours.*

Deep diamond-shaped creases on the side of his face—*he'd recently awakened from a nap in the upholstered chair in his office.*

Crumbs nestled in a fold in his collar, accompanied by a pale brown stain, and a faint vinegary scent wafted from his person—*he'd recently eaten a sandwich—likely ham—with mustard and pickles.*

Dylan moved toward me in such a way that I thought he was about to embrace me, but seemed to collect himself at the last minute. "I'm so glad to see you! I know I haven't been around much lately, but there's so much work to be done here."

He was correct. I'd hardly seen him in the last three weeks, and even when he brought me here two nights ago to look at the vampire victims, I was too tired to stay for long.

In fact, I'd hardly spent any time with Dylan since the night he'd kissed me in a carriage. The very thought made my cheeks bloom hot and my attention slip to his mouth.

And then I couldn't help but wonder if that was *why* I hadn't seen very much of him . . . because the kiss had been unskilled? After all, it had been the first (and only) time I've ever been kissed. Perhaps I'd done something wrong. Perhaps he hadn't liked it . . . as much as I had.

Had that been yet another failure on my part? A sudden lump formed in my throat and I sharply redirected my thoughts. "Have there been any more vampire victims?"

Dylan's gaze lost some of its pleasure at seeing me and turned grave. "Two more. Just came in last night—well, early this morning." He gritted his teeth; I saw his jaw move. "I can stem the loss of blood, Mina, and even replace it, but it's the infected wounds that are killing them."

I rested my hand on his arm—something I would never have done to any other gentleman, certainly not Inspector Grayling. "I know you're doing everything you can do."

A familiar expression of frustration washed over his face. "But I should be able to do *more*. In my time, in 2016, it would be a piece of cake to save them! We just need antibiotics— and then I could save a whole *lot* of people from a whole lot of things. Not just vampire bites."

There was little I could say. I'd heard this speech— and variations on it—before, and I thought I understood his helplessness. But at the same time, I knew the prospective dangers of time travel, and suspected changing history wouldn't bode well for the future. I wasn't altogether certain it would be a good thing if Dylan had access to more futuristic medical treatments—even if it meant saving more lives.

If we ever found a way to send him back to his time, what if things were different for him? What if he altered things so that he was never born?

"Could you take leave for a bit? I'm going to visit Uncle Sherlock. Perhaps you'd like to come with me." The first time he'd met my famous relative, Dylan had been dumbstruck. I knew he'd enjoy speaking with him again, and it would get him away from the hospital and his frustrations for a while.

His brilliant blue eyes—fringed with abnormally thick, sandy-brown lashes—lit for a moment. Then the interest faded, and he shook his head. "I can't, Mina. I can't leave here. There's just too much to do."

I squelched a rush of disappointment. "Very well, then," I said briskly. "I hope you shall endeavor to get more sleep than you apparently have been getting, and perhaps empty the pockets of your coat occasionally. And you might eat something other than a moldy crust of bread." He looked at me and I lifted an eyebrow. "There is one sticking out of your pocket."

He jammed a hand into his pocket, then sheepishly removed said crust of bread. "There's no mold on this," he said, grinning. "You were wrong, for once!" It was ridiculous how much I appreciated the way his eyes sparkled when he was happy.

"Quite. At least for today. But if you'd left it any longer in your pocket, it's sure to grow mold. One wouldn't want those tiny green spores growing all over the inside of your coat!"

"No, that's for su—" His eyes widened. His mouth opened. He goggled at me for a moment. "Mina! That's it! Oh, Mina, you are *brilliant*. You are so brilliant, I could—I could kiss you!"

My cheeks flooded with warmth. "Er . . . right, then."

"Really! You just gave me the absolute best idea ever! I don't know why I didn't think of it!"

"Erm . . . quite. I'm very pleased to be of assistance. What idea precisely did I . . . er . . . ?"

"This! This is it!" He was shaking the crust of bread at me. "Moldy bread! That's how he started it! Dr. Flemming! I wonder how long it will take to grow? And then how will I administer it?"

He descended into a soliloquy of muttering and mumbling to himself as if I were no longer present—rather like that female inventor Olympia Babbage tended to do when she got caught up in the plans for one of her inventions. I confess, I found it only mildly less annoying when Dylan fell into the habit than Miss Babbage.

I realized he no longer remembered I was present, and reluctantly, I decided to take my leave. I had other things to attend to, and despite my disappointment that he wouldn't join me, at least I was feeling slightly less morbid than I had earlier.

I could kiss you!

Despite his words, I wondered if he would ever do so again.

***

"I am very grateful for your assistance, Uncle Sherlock."

We had left 221-B Baker-street, where he kept his apartments, and were traveling in his carriage to Scotland Yard. Not incurring the expense of another cab was an additional benefit to having visited him in person rather than merely sending a message.

Aside from that, Mrs. Hudson, Uncle Sherlock's landlady and sometime housekeeper, made a delicious, filling snack she called Stuff'n Muffins. They were, she informed me, like a stuffed turkey but in the form of small, bite-sized muffins made of seasoned bread chunks—stuffing with chopped cranberries, and pieces of turkey. She always pressed several of them upon me when I visited.

"As it happens," said my uncle, "I intended to make an appearance at the Met today anyway. Inspector Lestrade has been bumbling through another investigation, and I decided it would be best to offer my assistance before he travels too far down an incorrect deductive path—and note that I use the term 'deductive' liberally. I don't believe Lestrade could deduce in which direction a horse crossed the street even if he came upon a pile of its dung!"

"What sort of investigation?" I was genuinely interested, for listening to my uncle describe not only a case, but also the errors and detours made by other less-skilled investigators, had been my earliest form of education. I had long since graduated from listening to Uncle Sherlock lecture on such topics as explosive detritus and its makeup, the science of bloodspatters, and, most recently, how to determine the height and weight of an individual by measuring the depth and surface displacement of his footprint.

"I haven't been apprised of the details yet. My attention was absorbed in another puzzle involving a mathematician named Dr. Moriarty. He is a worthy challenger, and I look forward to exercising my powers of observation and deductive reasoning in competition with his robust intellect. I am given to understand, however, that Lestrade's latest debacle of a case involves the location of an abandoned underground Carmelite abbey off Fleet-street. There seems to have been an unusual number of deaths in the vicinity—mostly the toshermen who scavenge in the sewers, and some of the less fortunate who live in the area as well. It's an unpleasant fact of life that those who subsist at the lowest levels of society will, in fact, meet their demise more quickly and at a younger age than those of us who do not . . . but still, it is a tragedy. Death—regardless of whom it touches—is *always* a tragedy, Alvermina. Never forget that."

"Of course not, Uncle Sherlock."

"Apparently the number of deaths is sufficiently noticeable even in that poverty-stricken area to have caught the attention of the Met. And so Lestrade is attempting to put an end to it. And here we are." He gestured with his walking stick as the carriage rolled to a halt.

As we alighted—my uncle forgetting, as usual, that it was a generally accepted societal nicety to assist a skirt-attired person down from a vehicle—he nevertheless turned to me and said, "You are quite clear where to go? I shall do my part, of course, but you shall have to move quickly in order to accomplish your task."

"Yes, Uncle. And thank you once more," I replied as I carefully navigated onto the ground.

"I am always willing to be of assistance when it comes to the pursuit of justice. It is imperative we Holmeses do our part by contributing our skills and abilities to the authorities—even when they do not realize they require them."

And with that, we walked into the offices of the Metropolitan Police, better known as Scotland Yard.

As usually happened, the moment Sherlock Holmes made an appearance at the station, everyone in the vicinity became interested. Policemen, detective inspectors, clerks, and every manner of employee gathered in the corridor to speak to him—or, more accurately, to hear him speak.

This was the opportunity I needed, and the one I'd created by asking him to accompany me today. I trusted my uncle would have no difficulty finding topics on which to discourse while I sneaked off to search the files of unsolved cases.

If Inspector Grayling wouldn't tell me about the Bartholomew case, I would find out on my own. The unsolved case—especially since it was one of Grayling's, and tied to the most famous businessman in England—was a temptation I could not resist, particularly in light of my most recent failure.

I hurried down the corridor, following the instructions Uncle Sherlock had given me about where to find the files. I'd had to listen to him complain about the disorganization of the administrative process at the Met—secretaries had to laboriously hand-copy each paper report, and they were arranged haphazardly in boxes by date rather than alphabetically by name—but it had been worth it to learn where to go.

As it happened, the route took me past the office Inspector Grayling shared with his partner, Inspector Luckworth. The two were as unalike as Holmes and Watson, and, truth be told, Holmes and Stoker. Grayling was a devout cognoggin, possessing gadgets and devices that stirred my envy and fascination, while Luckworth was more dedicated to plodding about on his large feet and blustering at—er, I mean interviewing—people.

I couldn't help but peek in as I approached. I told myself it was because I didn't want Grayling to take me by surprise, or to see me rushing down the corridor. But I was also desirous to take another look at what the ginger-haired detective called his "case board."

To my relief, the office was devoid of homicide investigators and any other two-legged beings. There was evidence of Luckworth's recent departure—a trail of crumbs currently being devoured by a flop-eared beagle with a mechanical leg—and no sign of Grayling. No coat, no hat . . . good. That meant he wasn't lurking about.

Angus, Grayling's beagle, gave me a baleful glance, but he was more interested in his midday snack than greeting me. I had no complaints about this, for the last few times the black, brown, and white canine had attempted to converse with me, I ended up with pawprints on my skirt and vigorous licking on the part of my wrist bared by my glove.

"Hush," I told him when he looked as if he might vocally interact with me. The crumbs were gone, and apparently there was nothing edible in the waste can beneath Luckworth's desk. There was nothing *in* the waste can, as far as I could tell, but instead crumpled papers were piled around it. "There's no need for you to bark, Angus. I'm just going to look at your master's board over here."

The last time I was in this office, I'd noticed the pinboard on the wall above Grayling's desk. It held photographs, drawings, maps, notes, and other items pertaining to the cases he was investigating. I intended to create a board of my own, dedicated to my investigation of the Ankh, and I wanted to examine his more closely.

I'd been looking at it for only a moment when it occurred to me Grayling's files would be in the very desk on which my palms were placed. Surely he would have a copy of the Bartholomew case in one of the drawers . . .

With a glance at the door, then a stern order to Angus to keep quiet, I pulled open the drawers. The first one held writing implements and small notebooks. The second one contained personal grooming accoutrements—such as a comb, hair pomade, tooth polish, and a fascinating device I realized was a nail clipper. I found this surprising; not that Grayling wasn't well-groomed—he certainly was—but that he would think to have such accessories on hand. There was even something I'd never seen before called "chewing gum." I sniffed it. Ah. That explained why he often smelled of peppermint.

The third drawer was locked with a dual-gear, brass-plated device that appeared to require two keys. I struggled with it for a moment, then moved on to the fourth and final drawer.

It was here that I found success. My sound of delight caused Angus to lumber to his feet on short, stubby legs—one of which clicked dully. He appeared to be waiting for me to reward him for my success, for he looked up at me with big brown eyes and barked.

"Hush!" I hissed, looking about for something with which to bribe him. Grayling's desk was utterly devoid of anything except gadgetry, pencils, and neat papers. Not a single photograph or tidbit of food.

Angus barked again, this time more forcefully, and I considered fleeing the office and going about my original plan. But I had seen the words "Oligary" and "Bartholomew" on a collection of loosely bound papers, and I didn't wish to lose the opportunity to investigate further.

Angus barked and whined, and he put his brown paws on my pretty spring green dress, batting at me as if to elicit a response. Then, with a jolt of delight, I remembered the Stuff'n Muffins. Mrs. Hudson had insisted I take several for later, and I had two of them tucked inside my bag.

"Here you go, doggie," I said, breaking off half of one muffin. I let him smell it, then tossed it over toward Luckworth's desk—he'd never notice another crumb or stain—and turned back to my perusal of the documents. One thing I had to admit: Grayling's reports were impeccably organized. Bound together with sturdy wire rings, his notes consisted of handwritten information, photographs, and envelopes with more tactile items slipped inside.

I skimmed the details of the Bartholomew case as quickly as possible. Hmm. There was a suspect in the not-so-accidental death of Hiram Bartholomew, but the individual had yet to be apprehended for questioning. I regretted I couldn't take the file with me as I'd intended to do. Surely Grayling would notice it missing.

Angus barked again, and clattered back over. Goodness, the beast had eaten quickly. He panted up at me hopefully, and I tossed the other half of the muffin. I was just about to put the report back into the drawer when something caught my eye on a second collection of papers below it.

The Individual Known as the Ankh.

Well, now, wasn't that interesting. Perhaps Grayling wasn't as certain as he pretended that the Ankh was gone for good.

I picked up the stack, intending to read through it as well (surely he hadn't pinpointed his own distant cousin Lady Cosgrove-Pitt as the culprit) . . . but then I saw the report below it.

Possible Evidence of Vampires in London.

I snatched that packet up just as Angus barked again. The short yip was so loud and unexpected, right at my elbow, that I jumped and lost my hold on the papers. The packet tumbled onto the desk.

"Really, sir! You must cease to be so annoying. Now, this is nearly your last one, so please take your time and savor it." I gave Angus a sharp look, and to my surprise, his rump dropped to the ground and he closed his mouth, waiting silently and expectantly.

Quite interesting.

And ridiculously adorable.

I tossed him half of the last muffin and returned to the files. I was stunned, to say the least, to realize Grayling was not oblivious to the fact that UnDead existed.

However, I didn't even begin to read that report, for I automatically glanced down into the drawer once more. The bottom file was the most aged, the most thumbed-through and annotated one of them all. It was not written in Grayling's hand.

When I read the name on it, I slowly reached down to pull it out. My heart thudded, and my insides felt as if a collection of butterflies had been released.

Melissa Grayling.

I had to read only a half-page to comprehend: Melissa Grayling was Ambrose Grayling's mother. She had been stabbed by an unknown person when he was nine.

And he had been the one to find her body.

I must have gasped or otherwise made a noise that recalled Angus, for there he was again, bothering at my skirt. But before I could foist the last bit of muffiny-bribe upon him, he suddenly stilled and looked toward the door. If his ears hadn't been so long and heavy, I am certain they would have pricked up with interest.

My palms went wet and my insides turned to ice. Angus, on the other hand, was ecstatic, and began to yap excitedly. He ran in circles around the office, tripping over his soft brown ears every third or fourth step.

I shoved the files back into the drawer in their proper order, knowing this canine excitement portended only one thing. My pulse was racing and I dove to the floor just a moment before Grayling appeared in the doorway. He wore a hat and coat, and looked as if he were in a rush.

"Miss Holmes?" I didn't believe I'd ever heard him sound so utterly bewildered.

I did my best to look innocent and as if it were completely natural for me to sit on the floor (how was I ever going to get up again with this corset binding me?) playing with Angus.

"Why, Inspector Grayling. I hope you don't mind—I just came to visit Angus." I wheezed a little, for the unexpected dive to the floor made my corset compress my torso at an awkward angle. Then I smiled down at the little beast and offered him the last bit of muffin. "I accompanied my uncle here, and while he was busy discussing a case, I decided to see if Angus was in residence."

The white-faced, brown-spotted beagle looked up at me with a jaundiced expression, clearly shocked at my bald-faced lie. Nevertheless, he took the muffin and seemed to have no problem wolfing it down.

"Ah. Mrs. Hudson's Stuff'n Muffins are a great favorite of Angus. How did you know?" Grayling asked. He looked only mildly less confused.

"It was a happy serendipity." I was more than a little bewildered myself to learn that he knew Mrs. Hudson. Additionally, the excessiveness of his height was even more pronounced now that I was at ground-level and he loomed over me.

"Right then. Er . . . since you are sitting here utterly unagitated and at ease, I can only assume you haven't heard the news."

"News?" I wanted more than anything to bolt to my feet, but that was impossible given my position on the floor and the vise-like corset around my waist. I would definitely either look ridiculous trying, or land on my rump in the process. Or both.

Grayling offered me a hand, which I had no choice but to accept. He pulled me smoothly to my feet before responding. "Princess Lurelia is missing."

Miss Holmes

Miss Holmes Investigates

"Missing?" I echoed.

"More precisely...it is believed she's been abducted." Grayling glanced at his desk, then back at me. Was there a light of suspicion in his gray-green eyes?

I did my best to look innocent, and to direct his attention to more pressing matters. "Are you investigating, then, Inspector?"

He sighed. "I suppose you'll want to go with me."

"Naturally." I started toward the door, then hesitated.

Grayling seemed to know what I was thinking. "I will arrange for a conveyance other than the steamcycle if you prefer, Miss Holmes. Although that vehicle will get us to the scene more quickly than any other mode of transportation."

I struggled with indecision for a moment, then capitulated. It was imperative I arrived at the location before the hordes of bumbling inspectors, well-meaning servants, and other curious-minded folk trampled through any clues that might be there. "Very well. The steamcycle it is. *If* you would be so kind as to not drive it so very speedily."

He smiled—a full-on, delighted grin—and I nearly jolted at the spectacular change in his countenance. "Whatever you wish, Miss Holmes."

Somehow . . . I didn't believe him.

⁂

I was correct in my assumption that Grayling was not to be trusted—at least in regards to the speed of his steamcycle.

The last time I'd been required to utilize the vehicle, I rode on the back, clutching my driver around the waist from behind.

This time, however, in deference to the fact that I wasn't wearing split skirts and had many more layers of crinoline and petticoat, Grayling insisted I sit in front of him.

In an utterly mortifying discussion, he indicated I should hook my left knee around a small knob on the front of the seat so I could sit side-saddle, as I did the rare times I rode a horse, with both my lower appendages on the right side of the beastly machine. I spared only a moment of thought regarding why he had such a contrivance on the steamcycle— how often *did* he take females for a ride?—before he handed me a leather aviator cap with ear flaps, and a pair of goggles. Then he climbed on behind me.

Moments later, Grayling's arms blocked me in on either side as he reached for the steering bars, and, most disconcerting of all, his right leg slid firmly beneath mine.

I was incredibly thankful I had donned the over-large cap (and gad knew what my saucy feathered hat would look like when I took it off) and that I was facing away from him, for I can only imagine how red my face must have been due to this immodest proximity.

I was about to tell him I'd changed my mind when the cycle roared to life. I caught my breath, half-turning to speak to him over the rumble of the engine, and suddenly the vehicle leapt forward.

I stifled a shriek and gripped the small handles he'd pointed out earlier. The vehicle roared out of the small garage in which he'd parked, took a sharp turn, and then began to weave between carriages, cabs, and vendor carts.

I closed my eyes and concentrated on *not* noticing the strength in the arms that embraced me, and solid torso nearly touching my spine. But every time we went around a corner, I was forced to lean into one or the other of Grayling's protective arms.

Yet, for all the speed and swerving and jolting, I confess I felt relatively safe, and was even beginning to enjoy the race, peeking through slitted eyes . . . until he took an unexpected turn and the next thing I knew, we were barreling below-ground along the track of the underground trains.

It was dark, and close, and the only light was from a small headlamp at the front of the cycle, and something glowing beneath it. I don't like dark, close, or underground places, and my fingers turned cold and stiff as I gripped the vehicle's handles as tightly as I could.

I squeezed my eyes shut, praying a train wouldn't come along behind us . . . or in *front* of us.

I was definitely going to give Inspector Grayling a decisive talking-to when we arrived at our destination.

But when we finally did roar up the drive of the Domanik Hotel, and I saw the carriage with Her Royal Highness Princess Alix's seal on it, I forgot about my exasperation with Grayling. As I slid off the cycle—my posterior still vibrating from the roaring vehicle, my arms still warm from the proximity of his—I felt a combination of determination and apprehension.

What if Princess Alix ordered me to leave? What if she did so in front of *everyone*?

"Is everything quite all right, Miss Holmes?" Grayling said as I handed him the aviator hat and goggles. His expression was one of barely concealed amusement, but when I made no comment, his attention strayed to a location above my head. I could only suppose what condition my jaunty feathers were now in.

"Yes, indeed," I told him briskly. "Whatever could be amiss? After all, I've just barreled through the underground of London at breakneck speed on a vehicle that is surely in violation of Moseley-Haft."

"Are you suggesting that I, a member of the Metropolitan Police, am in possession of an illegal vehicle?" He looked down his long, narrow nose at me. I couldn't tell whether he was amused or insulted.

I sniffed and started into the hotel without an escort. Trepidation regarding the uncertainty of my reception by Princess Alix returned as I made my way inside, but I hurried along in an attempt to leave it behind.

Although I didn't know precisely where the Betrovians had been staying in the hotel, it was a simple matter of logic and observation for me to navigate to the largest and most comfortable apartments—the rooms where, presumably, Lurelia had last been seen.

Grayling was on my heels as I entered the chamber, and uncertainty knotted my belly. If Princess Alix, or Miss Adler, or anyone else demanded to know what I was doing there . . . or, worse, ordered me away, I suspected I might never be able to show my face in Society again.

Princess Alix was present, and so was Miss Adler. The Lord Regent was there, along with a prune-faced man who was presumably the hotel manager, a terrified-looking maid, and a variety of other individuals . . . including my father.

I felt a rush of heat followed by nausea. It would be bad enough if I were turned away in front of everyone, but if my father were to witness such a humiliating event . . .

Everyone looked toward the doorway as Grayling and I entered. For one absurd moment, I considered the option of escape.

Instead, I did what any proper English miss would do, regardless of the awkwardness of her situation. I stiffened my upper lip and I curtsied.

"Miss Holmes," said Princess Alix. "I cannot imagine how you arrived so quickly. Thank you for making all haste. Is Miss Stoker soon behind you, then?" Her eyes were warm and filled with gratitude.

I successfully hid my surprise. "Yes. Of—of course, Your Highness." I cast a cautious glance at Miss Adler, whose expression was inscrutable. She gave me an imperceptible nod. "Erm . . . I'm not certain of Miss Stoker's whereabouts. I'm sure she will respond as soon as she learns her presence is required, Your Highness."

Then I looked at my father. It took me a moment to remember when I'd last seen him—other than at the Welcome Event at the museum, and from a distance. My quick calculations told me it had been more than a month.

"Sir," I said, by way of greeting.

"Do come in, Alvermina," he ordered. "There's work to be done, and apparently you're to be the one to do it."

Still confused, but doing my best to mask the bewilderment, I did as I was bid. Fortunately, Miss Adler took charge and began to apprise me of the situation.

"Princess Lurelia has gone missing. All indications are that she's been abducted. She was last seen in the chamber adjoining this one"—Miss Adler gestured to a door—"last evening at ten o'clock by her maid. This morning when the maid went to awaken her, she was gone. Her bed had been disturbed as if slept in, and we found this piece of paper in the waste can. There was no sign of a struggle."

"This is a highly sensitive incident," said Sir Mycroft, fixing his piercing blue eyes on me. "The Lord Regent has agreed to keep this information from the public for the time being, but if word should leak out that Princess Lurelia has disappeared, we could have a significant international conundrum."

"Of course." My head wanted to spin with all the information—and lack thereof—and implications of the situation, but I stopped it firmly. Now was the chance to prove myself again to the princess and Miss Adler . . . and my father. I must be more observant and careful than I'd ever been.

"Here is the note." The hotel manager, whose face was generously wrinkled, handed me a piece of paper that was in the same condition as his countenance.

I had no way of immediately knowing whether the hand was that of Princess Lurelia, but all indications were that it was. The letters were precisely formed, definitely in the penmanship of a female who was right-handed (which I'd already observed, of course, that she was), and the script held extra flourishes that befit a royal personage. I could tell the words had been scribed slowly and with care. In addition, curiously enough, none were scratched out or corrected, and there was a surprising lack of ink-spots.

Dear Mina and Evaline:

> *I told you there was nothing, but there is something.*
> *You will know how to find it and if you don't help me,*
the worst will happen.

If anything should happen to me before we next speak, you will know what to do.

—*L.*

"Interesting," I said as a myriad of thoughts rushed through my mind. I glanced at Grayling, who until now, had neither moved nor spoken, and I offered him the letter. I was curious as to whether he would draw the same conclusions I had.

"I presume you comprehend what it is Her Highness is attempting to communicate," said my father.

"I have my suspicions. And no, I have not as yet received any messages from her." I gestured to the door. "May I see Lurelia's chamber?"

The maid managed to keep her emotions in check as she brought us into the adjoining rooms—a bedchamber, a walk-in wardrobe, and a private bathing chamber. Nevertheless, her voice quivered when she described the activity of the night before. I directed her to give me every detail of the evening, regardless of how insignificant it seemed.

"I brushed my lady's hair one hundred thirty times as usual. And then I braided it in one large plait and tied it with lace and helped her into her night rail."

"What did the night rail look like?"

"It was blue. With lace, here." The maid indicated where the flounces would go.

"Go on."

"And then she got herself into the bed and when I left the chamber—for she dismissed me"—the maid cast a worried look at the Lord Regent—"she was reading that book. I never saw her again."

"What time did you leave the chamber, and what time did you come in this morning?"

"It was five minutes after ten o'clock according to that clock, and this morning I finally knocked on her door at noon, when she hadn't rung for me, miss." The maid gave a brief curtsy as if to indicate the end of her speech.

But I wasn't yet finished with her. "Did the princess ask you to post any letters for her? Or to have any messages delivered to anyone?"

"No, miss."

"Did you notice whether the paper was in the waste can before she got into bed last night? Were the writing implements on the desk? Are those her writing tools? Can you confirm this is her writing?"

"No, miss, the paper wasn't in the waste can. I noticed for certain because I tidied up the entire chamber, and emptied it myself. Yes, miss, that is her pen, and yes, that is her writing, as far as I can tell. When I tidied up, I put her pens away in their writing box, and left the box on the desk where she liked it. The paper is from the hotel, miss. You can ask the gentleman." She glanced at the hotel manager.

"Very well. Thank you. You've been extremely helpful . . . miss?"

The maid bobbed a curtsy, clearly ready to make her escape. "Derrica, miss."

After the maid fled, I commenced with interrogating the hotel manager, whose name was Mr. Bentford, about the security of the building as well as these apartments.

He took exception to my implication the security was lacking, and informed me that every entrance was either locked or guarded by robust doormen. "And this suite of apartments we reserve for our most important guests because it is the most luxurious and the most private and inaccessible. Of course it is on the fifth floor, and not reachable but through the main stairway—and of course the servants' hall. We have never had any complaints from our guests, and we have had *many* important visitors." He glanced at my father as if to confirm his statement and Sir Mycroft made a sound of agreement. I trusted my father's opinion about this, at least.

I examined the chamber and made several curious observations. All the while, I sent covert glances toward Grayling to see if he noticed the same.

"*The Guidebook to London*," he mused as he picked up the book Lurelia had been reading. "Fascinating."

"I agree. And note the last page she has read."

"I have."

"And the strand of hair . . . here." I withdrew a pair of small forceps, lifting a long dark hair from the floor near the door."

"Quite right, Miss Holmes. And of course, the impressions left on this notebook of paper."

"Indeed."

We eyed each other speculatively, then I went to examine the doorknob and the entrance to the chamber. Just as I finished, I heard the arrival of Miss Stoker in the adjoining room.

It was difficult not to.

She swept into the chamber like a small windstorm. "So the princess has gone missing? She's been abducted, then? Is there a ransom?" Evaline's eyes sparkled with enthusiasm, surely anticipating a dangerous adventure.

I hated to disappoint her.

"I'm afraid not," I said. "Princess Lurelia is indeed missing, but she has not been abducted." I glanced at Grayling, giving him an arch look.

To my disappointment, he didn't look the least bit nonplussed. "Not only has she not been abducted," he said with a nod in my direction, "but she left the chamber early this morning, and under her own steam—so to speak."

"Quite correct, Inspector," I interjected, ignoring his little jest. "And I know precisely where to find her. She has gone to see—"

"Westminster Abbey," Grayling and I announced together.

"Oh," said Evaline. "Drat."

Miss Stoker

Wherein the Mechanics of Vampire Slaying
Are Considered

While I was disappointed there wasn't to be an exciting rescue of Princess Lurelia from the clutches of her abductors, Mina was puffed up with satisfaction that she'd so easily solved the case. However, I was delighted my evening would be free.

Tonight I was going to Bridge & Stokes.

I'd had Middy drive me down St. Albans-street today so I could see what type of business Bridge & Stokes was. Bilbo could have been a little more specific with his information. But now I knew Bridge & Stokes was a gentlemen's club.

I could hardly contain a smile. Visiting a gentlemen's club would be a welcome distraction—and an exciting challenge.

I glanced at Mina. If she came with me, I'd have to save her if things went awry, *and* listen to her lecture all the way there and back. She would tell me things I needed to know, and a lot more things I *didn't* need to know. My head hurt at the thought.

However, if she accompanied me, she would no doubt know what to expect at Bridge & Stokes—that is, how to play all of the card games—and she would probably notice things I didn't. She looked more like a man than I did, too, being taller and less curvy. Aside from that, it would be helpful to have a second person watching out for Pix . . . and the Ankh.

It turned out the Lord Regent wanted to personally retrieve Princess Lurelia from Westminster Abbey. "We will make a public event uff it," he said, glancing at the formidable Sir Mycroft. "In an attempt to qvash any rumors about zhe princess's reputation. We shall make it appear as if we planned zhe entire visit." He stroked his mustache, then worried its dark ends into tight pincurls.

When she heard this news, Mina's face fell. "Of course. I—and Miss Stoker—were happy to be of service."

"But how did you come to this conclusion?" asked the hotel manager, whose name I did not recall. He appeared quite relieved that his security was no longer in question.

"It was quite simple. There are no traces of any individual other than Derrica entering the princess's chambers—with the exception of this single dark hair." Mina glanced at Grayling. "Recall the heavy rain overnight and into the early hours of the morning, and note the absence of any streaks of mud or dirt inside her apartments. Thus one can only conclude that individuals have *left*, but have not *arrived*. Therefore, no one has taken her from this location against her will."

I still didn't follow. "But the dark hair? Her Highness is blond, and so is her maid, and—er—the Lord Regent." Mostly, anyway.

"If one looks closely, one will easily note that the single strand of dark hair is not human, but from a horsetail. One will also note, if one examines it even more studiously, the tiny blob of adhesive that had attached it to a wig. Therefore, my Lord Regent, when you arrive at Westminster Abbey, if you do not immediately see Princess Lurelia, I would recommend searching for a young woman dressed in a blue walking gown—the only dress missing from her closet, according to her maid—with dark hair."

"But . . . how did you know she was traveling to Westminster Abbey? Oh, wait . . . it was the last page she looked at in the travel guide, wasn't it?" I was supremely proud of myself for *deducing* such a thing on my own.

"In fact, it was not, Miss Stoker." Mina's voice was smooth. "An amateur's error, but I won't hold it against you. You're rather new at this—"

"Right," I interrupted. "So how did *you* know she was at Westminster Abbey?"

"Inspector Grayling noticed it as well—the impressions on this page in the princess's notebook. If one looks closely, one can see it is a list of times, and also one can make out the words 'St. James's.' Clearly, the princess was noting down the Underground schedule, and the name of the station on which she would disembark—St. James's Park."

"In fact, Miss Stoker, the last page Her Highness appears to have looked at in the *Guidebook* described the fees for the Underground trains, as well as a description of how to utilize the system for transportation. Being a member of the Royal Family, one wouldn't expect her to be familiar with such plebeian modes of transportation," said Inspector Grayling without a trace of the condescension I heard in Mina's voice.

"I see. But how did you know she meant to visit Westminster Abbey? St. James is near so many other possible attractions. She could have been going to see Parliament or Jewel Tower. Or was that a lucky guess?"

"Evaline, you should know by now that *guessing* is not a valid part of detecting. I—and Inspector Grayling as well—deduced that Princess Lurelia was going to visit Westminster Abbey because of the very faint check marks she'd made in the table of contents of this guidebook—presumably attractions she meant to visit whilst here in London. It was the only check-marked item near St. James's station. It was, really, quite an elementary deduction, if one is paying attention."

"Right."

"Ferry well done, Miss Holmes," said the Lord Regent, who had followed our conversation with interest. "I zhank you ferry much vor helping us."

"Indeed," replied Mina. She appeared to want to say something more, but instead she turned to me. "May I share your carriage, then, Miss Stoker?"

"Of course."

"Thank you again, Inspector Grayling, for . . . er . . . providing me transportation here. I'm not certain my hat will ever be the same again, but it was . . . appreciated."

He bowed and excused himself, and Mina and I took our leave as well. I didn't have the chance to tell her about my plan for the evening, for as soon as we settled into the carriage, my companion began to talk. Big surprise.

"Well, that was quite an interesting turn of events, don't you think, Evaline?"

"Um . . . yes. I think so." I hadn't the foggiest idea what she was talking about.

"Lurelia may not be as simple and timid as we supposed. But why did she sneak out of her chamber to go to Westminster Abbey, of all places? I have several theories, Miss Stoker. But feel free to share yours first."

"Your feathers are drooping," I told her, a little meanly. Of course I didn't have any blasted theories!

She reached up and patted vaguely at the decorations on her hat. "Drat. Next time I—never mind. There will never be a next time. I will never set my—my posterior on that dratted vehicle again!"

I snickered, for I had seen Grayling's steamcycle parked in front of the hotel. Then I became serious. "I'm going to Bridge & Stokes tonight. Do you want to come with me?"

"To a gentlemen's club? And why? Are you mad? Do you have any idea how to play poker? And you do realize, this would *not* be a night to forget your money. And one cannot simply walk into a gentlemen's club—even if he is a gentleman. One must be a member—or have a member who is a sponsor. Honestly, Evaline, do you *ever* plan ahead?"

I grinned. I could see the light of interest in her eyes. "Hardly ever."

"I presume you have a good reason for this foolishness."

"Of course. It's where Pix's customers place their orders for his devices. You'll want to go with me, then?"

"Someone must, to keep you from getting into trouble."

⤝—⤞

Creating a foolproof disguise meant a visit to the Lyceum Theater. Fortunately, Bram never minded when I raided the costume and makeup rooms under his roof, as long as I returned them.

My brother was typing madly in his office, working on the book he called *Count Dracula*, when Mina and I knocked on the open door. He looked up and I nearly laughed, for his hair was standing up in wild waves every which way.

"How do you kill a vampire?" he asked as we walked in.

"You stab him in the heart with a wooden stake," I replied. "Preferably one made of ash wood. And then he poofs into dust. Which smells disgusting, by the by."

He frowned and glared at me. "That doesn't work."

I shrugged. "I'm sorry. I didn't make the rules. We're going to borrow some things from the men's wardrobe, all right, Bram?"

"I'm going to have to change that," he muttered, still frowning and glaring. "It's not *interesting* enough. It can't be that simple. Stab an UnDead in the heart, and suddenly he's gone. It doesn't even work that way for mortals! We at least have a body afterward. And blood. What about the vampire's clothing?"

"You could always behead the UnDead. One stroke with a sword works just as well as a wooden stake, and it's a little more exciting."

He looked interested. "And what happens afterward? Does the head roll away and the body slump to the ground? Is there blood splattering everywhere?"

"My word, you're blood-thirsty," I told him affectionately. "I do hope that doesn't put off your readers."

"No, indeed. People love to hear about gruesome and horrific things—as long as they aren't happening to them. To whit—think of all the terrible things that happen in Shakespeare!"

"Well, I'm sorry to disappoint you, but the same thing happens when you behead an UnDead as when you stake him: he explodes into ash. Which is messy, you know. It gets everywhere, and it smells like a dead body."

"Perhaps a more complicated, more—er—ceremonial approach?" Mina asked. I could tell she was only half serious. "Sneaking up on the creature when he is unaware, and . . . oh, perhaps, binding him down? Shoving a head of garlic into his mouth—they don't particularly care for garlic, do they?

Maybe a pike that affixes the creature to whatever he is sitting or lying on? It would be rather gruesome to imagine, but it would certainly be more *interesting* than the simple thrust of a stake to the heart. Why, anyone could do that." She cast me a look.

I rolled my eyes. I hadn't seen her stake a dozen wild-eyed, sharp-fanged, out-for-blood UnDead when the opportunity presented itself. In fact, I hadn't seen her stake one. "Right." I turned back to Bram. "Do you mind if we dig through the wardrobes?"

"No." He was looking at Mina consideringly. "A pike that holds the creature down. And what if it went through each arm? No, no . . . too Christ-like. Ah. His *head*. Perhaps through his head?"

Mina shuddered. "I shall leave that to you, Mr. Stoker. Incidentally, we met Mr. Oligary recently. Apparently you know him quite well."

"Aye, yes, one could say that. He's a great lover of the theater, and a patron as well."

"Are you going to get a new steam-machine for the lighting? He indicated the one you have is too loud and a bit outdated."

"Frank—Mr. Oligary—has been trying to convince me to trade up to a better machine for a year. I wanted to install electric lights four years ago, but then Moseley-Haft came along and now that's impossible." Bram glanced longingly at his typing machine.

"So you aren't afraid of the evils or danger of electric lighting?" Mina asked.

"No, indeed. Not at all. Why, they have begun to install electric lighting at the Broadway Theater in New York, and there hasn't been one hint of problem. And they certainly don't have to account for the constant smell from the coal burner . . . or that incessant *hiss*. In our last performance of *The Merchant of Venice*, it nearly drowned out Shylock's best speech!"

"Fascinating. And did you know Mr. Oligary's business partner, Edgar Bartholomew?"

"Yes, yes, of course. He was a fine gentleman. Tragic." Bram's sentences were getting briefer, which meant he was becoming distracted. "Wasn't fond of Moseley, though."

"No? Are you saying Mr. Bartholomew wasn't a supporter of the Moseley-Haft Act? That he would have wanted electrical power to remain legal?"

"What? Oh no, I don't know about that." Bram's fingers strayed to the keys of his typer. "He didn't care for Lord Moseley himself. There was rumor the man wanted to buy out Bartholomew and partner with Mr. Oligary."

I had no idea why Mina was wasting our time with this, but I was bored, and Bram clearly wanted to return to his work before the actors and actresses arrived for the evening performance. "Let's leave my brother to his make-believe vampire killing," I said, pulling her out of the office.

"Well, that was enlightening," she said, yanking her arm out of my grip. "I wonder if Grayling knows about that."

"How so? And what's this nonsense about *anyone* could stake a vampire?" I glared at her as we pushed into the dimly lit men's wardrobe chamber.

It smelled faintly like tobacco and mothballs. In the drassy light, the ten rows of clothing looked like an eerie lineup of gentlemen.

"I was simply speaking theoretically," Mina replied. "And it is possible—anyone could stake an UnDead. If they knew what to do. It's not as if one needs special skills or knowledge."

"Right. Especially since vampires are stronger than the strongest of mortal men, not to mention much faster, and they can't be killed or injured any other way—unless you could get them to walk into the sunlight and stay there until they burned. No, it would be as simple as a walk in the park, staking a vampire."

And there would be no regrets about taking a life that had once been that of a normal person. No "*You killed my brother!*" accusations living in one's nightmares.

No. It would be as unnerving as swatting a fly.

Mina sniffed and turned to a mechanical box on the wall. She pushed a button, and lights—gas lamps, of course—popped on one by one with their familiar yellow glow. Then she turned a dial and one of the costumes began to rise toward the high ceiling, revealing another one behind it. Then it too lifted, showing another, then another, in one tall circuit. The rotating mechanism creaked and hissed and rattled.

"What I meant to say was it was fascinating to hear about Mr. Bartholomew, Mr. Oligary, and Lord Moseley," Mina said as she turned the dial back. The circling costumes came to a halt and she made a sound of satisfaction as she reached for the simple black suit hanging in front of us. I thought it looked like something a funeral director would wear.

"Excellent. This looks as if it will do nicely." She turned to me with a cool smile. "I shall be masquerading as the Ankh this evening, Evaline. What about you?"

Miss Stoker
An Overdue Discussion Occurs

Unlike in the past, when Mina insisted we don our disguises separately and meet up later, this time we prepared for our visit to Bridge & Stokes at the Holmes house. My home, the spacious Grantworth House, would have been closer and more convenient. My bedchamber was larger, and there was the benefit of my maid, Pepper. But there was the problem of leaving the house unnoticed by my sister-in-law, Florence, or the rest of the staff while dressed as men.

We were in Mina's bedchamber again—which felt surprisingly familiar to me. Of course, I'd been here only a few days earlier preparing for the Midnight Palace.

"Why are you dressing as the Ankh?" I asked as my partner smoothed a thick, shiny substance over her hair to keep it from kinking up.

"Because I suspect she has been to Bridge & Stokes—if indeed she is the one who is Mr. Pix's mysterious customer.

And if she has been there, then others might remember her. And if they believe I am she, who knows what we might learn about her."

"And . . . what if she is there tonight too?" I confess, I had a spike of thrill when I thought about that possibility.

"Then it will be very interesting," Mina replied with a small smile.

I helped brush her hair back in a smooth, sleek cap and then pinned it in several large flat pin curls to her head. Not as perfectly as Pepper would have done, but well enough that they would stay.

"I'm not certain you look that much like her," I said.

"As you recall, Miss Stoker, the Ankh has never looked the same every time we encountered her. Yes, she favors male attire—a simple, stark, black suit with a white shirtwaist. And she alters her height, color of her hair, facial hair—and lack thereof—and even the shape of her nose and brows. But there are two things that do not change. First, her eyes. They cannot be altered in any way other than by makeup or obstruction. When one looks into the eyes of another, one sees the unchanging iris—and the essence, the very *life*, of that person—regardless of how dark the lashes or liner is, how much hair is falling into them, or how slightly elongated the shape of the eye has become due to the application of a bit of spirit-gum at the corners."

"Well, since you don't have her eyes . . ."

Mina gave me an exasperated look. "Of course not. And hers are a chameleon-like gray hue that appear to change color according to what she is wearing. But the other thing—and really, Evaline, I cannot believe with all of the encounters we've had with that villainess—including the time you were in close proximity to her—"

"Do you mean the time she tried to electrofy me? Oh, yes, right, of course. I was observing her very closely as I dragged her to the floor while a massive statue tumbled on top of us."

Mina gave one of those sniffs of hers. "The Ankh always wears gloves, Miss Stoker—for the simple reason, as I know I've previously informed you—that one's hands cannot be disguised. Additionally, one cannot often remember to suppress one's natural habits, like the movements of a hand or the way one nods one's head . . . In the game of poker—with which you must become familiar before tonight—those personal quirks are called 'tells.' But, as I was saying, not only does the Ankh always wear gloves, she also always sports a small but noticeable—if one is looking, of course—diamond stud on her right ear. I believe it must be held in place with a minuscule magnet placed at the back of the earlobe."

I blinked. "So you will wear gloves and a tiny diamond earbob and dress like a man, and the people at Bridge & Stokes will believe you're the Ankh."

Mina smiled. "That is my intent and my belief. Now, shall we attend to your disguise, Mr. Kevin Newman, distant cousin of Sir Mycroft Holmes—who shall, incidentally, be our sponsor this evening? Yes, of course my father is a member of Bridge & Stokes. He is a member of most of the clubs in London, regardless of whether he visits them."

I took her place in the chair in front of the mirror. As she battled my thick, curling hair into a smooth braid that could be tucked under the blond wig we'd selected, my attention strayed to the photograph of Desirée Holmes.

While Mina was definitely a Holmes—she had the prominent nose and tall, slender figure—I did see a resemblance between her and her mother. She had Desirée's—Siri's—green-brown eyes and chestnut hair. The shape of her mouth was similar as well. But while Mina was passably attractive, her mother was quite lovely.

And she was an excellent fighting mentor. She'd demonstrated spins and kicks and moves I could only hope to copy some day.

"What was she like?" I asked suddenly.

Mina's hands stilled on my scalp, then began to move again. Perhaps a trifle more firmly. She didn't respond, and I avoided her gaze in the mirror. We both knew who I was talking about.

It felt odd, knowing that a person I had known in such a familiar—yet unusual—way was also the mother of one of my friends. And that neither of us had known of the other's existence because of Desirée's secret life.

"She was nothing like me, or my father," Mina said finally. She too refrained from looking at me. "She liked to go to parties and balls. She liked to dress and shop and be around people. She was often quite amusing. She found my work in the laboratory . . . tedious. Claimed she had no patience for that sort of thing."

Mina was speaking of Siri as if she were dead. And for all we knew, she was. But we'd never talked about it. I didn't know what Mina knew . . . and she didn't know what I knew.

I'd never told her about my experiences as a vampire hunter, but, I realized, now was the time. "The first night I attempted to stake a vampire, I . . . I must have fainted. I remember Siri being there with me, and I remember pulling my stake out, and getting ready to use it. But there was *so much blood.* Everywhere. It wasn't like the two bites you had on your neck. The UnDead had torn open the belly of Mr. O'Galleghy and his . . . insides . . . were spilling out." I swallowed hard as my stomach lurched. I still dreamt about that night. "I don't remember what happened after that. I woke up in an alley. Alone. I haven't heard from her—from Siri—since."

I didn't know whether she had killed the vampire herself, or whether I had somehow done it . . . or whether something else much worse happened. Although she was an excellent trainer and advisor, Siri wasn't a Venator. She didn't have the superior strength and speed that had been bestowed upon me and the others of my family legacy. As Mina had pointed out, anyone could feasibly slay a vampire if one knew how to do it—but that didn't mean she had been able to get beyond the power of the UnDead.

Siri could be dead. Because of me. Because I had failed to kill the vampire. If that were the case, I wondered if I could ever look Mina in the eye again.

"What was the date of that event?" Mina asked.

"The tenth of February, last year. Or before dawn, in the early morning of the eleventh." I held my breath, because I knew her response would answer at least one of my questions.

"My mother left on the eleventh of February, last year. At least, that was the last time I saw her. That morning. I *did* see her, Evaline. She was alive. Had I known it would be the last time . . ." Her voice trailed off in an uncharacteristic fashion.

I felt a wave of relief, so tangible I trembled. Now I met her eyes in the mirror. I made sure she saw my gratitude, for I didn't trust myself to speak.

She nodded, then turned to dig in a box of hair pins. "What was . . . she like? As Siri?"

A rush of something like pity surprised me. Of course she would wonder, and be curious. And not just because she was a Holmes.

Being a mother and a lady of Society was commonplace and natural. But being a woman of physical action, of cunning and strategic hand-to-hand combat—things that only men did, and few as well as Siri—was so foreign to anything Mina or I would have known if things had been different.

"She was brilliant. She moved so quickly and gracefully."

"She was an excellent dancer," Mina said with a small laugh. "At least, so I've heard."

"She was a demanding taskmaster too. She made me work hard, and study history and facts about my family. I practiced for hours every day—most of the time without her. And I had to read a lot too, which I didn't like as much. But she came nearly every day to work with me. She could always tell when I hadn't spent enough time practicing or studying." I bit my lip. I realized then that the moments Siri spent with me were moments she could have been spending with Mina. "Did you do a lot of . . . things with her? Shop? Um . . . talk?" What would Mina do with her mother? "Go to parties?" That was a ridiculous question. I groaned inwardly. The last thing I wanted to do was make this awkward conversation even more awkward.

"No. Not very often. She did take me shopping on occasion; I believe I learned how to dress from her. That's how I came to know of that modiste off Fleet-street, in Chewston-alley. The one whose work is all the latest of Street-Fashion. I always thought it odd she liked that shop, for it wasn't particularly her style."

"You still haven't told me the name of it," I said, in an effort to lighten the mood.

"It's called Lady Thistle's. It's on the third street-level."

I wanted to ask more questions—about how her beautiful, social mother ended up married to someone like Sir

Mycroft—but someone knocked on the bedchamber door. Mrs. Raskill poked her head in.

"There is an individual here who wishes to speak with you."

Mina frowned. "I am not available. Please take their card and inform the person I shall be in touch tomorrow." When Mrs. Raskill left, grumbling, my friend said, "I am not about to receive anyone dressed in this fashion. And would it hurt Mrs. Raskill to use a pronoun when she announces a visitor?"

This time Mrs. Raskill didn't knock. She merely looked around the open door. "The individual is insistent and will not leave. I was given this." She offered a small ivory card with fancy red printing on it.

Sighing, Mina walked over to accept the card. When she looked down at it, her eyes widened in shock. "Good gad. Princess Lurelia is here!"

MISS STOKER

Wherein an Uninvited Guest Insists upon Poker

There was nothing for it; Mina had to receive Lurelia. One couldn't turn away a princess—especially one who traveled to one's door . . . in a *hired hackney*? I gaped as the vehicle rolled off down the street as soon as the princess stepped inside.

"Good evening, Your Highness," Mina said.

"Mina! Evaline! You are both here. I'm very pleased." Lurelia seemed slightly less awkward than usual. When she took note of how we were dressed, her expression changed even more. "Are you . . . you are wearing very odd clothing."

"Please, have a seat." My companion neatly ignored the implied question. "May I offer you some refreshments?"

"Oh, no, I'm not the least bit hungry." The princess chose not to sit down, but instead to walk through the front room toward the kitchen. "What a quaint home."

"Thank you." Mina gave me a look that, for her, was rather amusing. I'd never seen her look so discombobulated.

"What brings you to my . . . er . . . quaint home? Did you . . . er . . . travel without escort?"

"Oh, yes. Lord Regent Terrence is busy tonight—he is with your father, I believe, Mina, doing something boringly political. I sneaked out the back of the hotel and hired a—what do you call them? Taxi? Yes, a taxi. I'm here because I wish for you to entertain me this evening. Princess Alexandra assured me you would be available whenever I wished, and I wish to be entertained tonight."

"But . . . erm . . ." Mina looked helplessly at me. If I hadn't been in the midst of the same predicament, I would have found her expression hilarious.

"Where are you going dressed in that fashion? Are you pretending to be men? I shall do the same. It will be a grand adventure. I have always wanted to wear trousers!"

"But . . . erm . . . Your Highness, it's not quite—"

Lurelia lifted her chin and gave us an imperiously royal look. She was almost more frightening than my sister-in-law, Florence, when she got annoyed with me. "I wish it, Mina. I should not want to report to Princess Alexandra that you disappointed me—or her. *Again.*"

"But, Lurelia . . . where we are going is not quite . . . well, it isn't precisely the best location for a young, affianced *princess* to—"

Lurelia lifted her chin, and for the first time, I saw a real spark of emotion there. "If you do not take me with you—dressed as you are, on whatever adventure you are going—then I shall follow you. All on my own."

And that was how the three of us ended up in a carriage disguised as young men.

Mina still looked mildly nauseated, but I was beginning to appreciate the humor in the situation.

"Besides wanting entertainment tonight," Lurelia said as our carriage made its way from Grosvenor to Pall Mall, "I have another request of you."

I had a feeling her idea of a request was more like a command, but I kept that thought to myself.

"We are happy to serve you in any way, Your Highness." Mina's words were smooth, but I saw the trepidation in her eyes.

How ironic that what we'd—or at least I'd—anticipated being a dull, quiet assignment might yet turn out to be quite amusing.

"You must help me find the chess queen."

Mina relaxed a trifle. "The letter describing its probable location is missing, but presumably you have made a copy of it."

"Correct." Lurelia seemed pleased.

"Why do you want to find the chess queen?"

The princess's gaze darted away. "I'm to exchange it for some . . . letters. Letters that I . . . wrote."

"Ah." Mina and I exchanged glances. Blooming fish, this was going to be a mess!

Nevertheless, my companion nodded. "Of course I—we—will assist you to find the chess queen, provided it is still to be found. It has, after all, been missing for centuries. But I am afraid I cannot allow you to give it up to the perpetrator of this blackmail scheme."

"But—"

"Your Highness, you must trust me. I am a Holmes. We will find the chess queen and we will unmask your blackmailer and retrieve those letters for you." Mina didn't seem to realize—or care—that she'd interrupted a princess. I decided not to point this out. Mina interrupted everyone.

"Very well." The princess smiled behind her false mustache. Mina had made certain to hide as much of the girl's face as possible behind bushy sideburns, thick hair, and a mustache. "Now, will you teach us how to play the game you call poke?"

"Er . . . poker. Yes, but you must learn quickly, for we have nearly arrived at our destination."

Although the sign for Bridge & Stokes was at the third street-level above the ground, I discovered (I say *I* because Mina claimed she was already aware of this) that the actual establishment was at the sixth, and most elite, level. In fact, in most areas of London—at least the ones outside Whitechapel and Seven Dials, where reputable people frequented—there were only four, and on occasion, five street-levels.

Each level was accessed via a street-lift, which required coin as payment. The higher one wished to go, the more one had to spend.

The lower the level, the darker and dingier the walkways, shops, and vendors. The ground, or street-level, was traversed mostly by vehicles, for there were few shops or businesses at the lowest level. The streets were nothing more than a conduit and a place where refuse and other waste collected and puddled in the sewage canals. Even the Refuse-Agitators couldn't keep up with the amount of waste from our good city.

Lining each side of the street, along the shops, were walkways with waist-high railings. Vendor carts were moored to the edge of the walkways with massive clamps, floating out over the street below. Occasionally there were sky-bridges connecting both walkways that allowed pedestrians to cross the "street."

It was an ongoing gripe of Mina's that I often forgot to bring money for the lifts, but this evening I had stuffed a good number of coins and bills in my coat pocket. That was fortunate, for it cost two pounds to take the lift to the sixth-level.

"I could buy an entire meal for two pounds," I grumbled.

"Or an excellent brandy," Mina said in a deep voice, giving me a quelling look.

Unlike most street-lifts, which were public and merely needed payment to enter, the one that traveled to Bridge & Stokes was operated by a burly man wearing a uniform and a cap. He had no intention of allowing us on board. Mina jabbed my foot sharply with her walking stick and I remembered the card engraved with Sir Mycroft Holmes's seal. On the reverse was a note in which he confirmed the sponsorship of his cousin, Mr. Kevin Newman.

"This way, gentlemen." The burly man allowed us to enter after I showed him the card and paid the lift fee.

As we rose smoothly above the ground, I couldn't help but gawk at the sight. The ornate brassworks that created the sides of the lift allowed an excellent view of the buildings as we passed by. The higher we went, the fancier the storefronts became. When we reached the top and stepped out of the platform, we found ourselves on a terrace-like balcony overlooking the city. For a moment, the three of us simply stared at the ragged array of rooftops in row upon row upon row below us, as far as the eye could see. We were higher than any other building in the vicinity; the only structures taller than us were the distant white face of Big Ben and the jutting black spires of the Oligary Building.

Even the sky-anchors danced and buffeted below us, moored to the cornices of buildings built too tall and narrow to keep from swaying at the top. The sky-anchors were large balloons meant to keep the tall, spindly buildings from crashing into their nearby neighbor.

The sun had sunk beyond the rooftops in the west, and the sunset left a spectacular red-pink color in its wake. Even the ever-present fog clouding our city didn't seem to be present at this height. Behind me, to the east, the sky had turned dark and I could see the beginning of a glitter of stars, and in the distance . . .

Was that an airship? I felt the tiniest shiver. Was it the same one Pix and I had seen twice? The one that portended something bad? The eerie, shadowy thing that slid silently through the night like evil? Blooming fish, was I getting poetic!

Still . . . I couldn't drag my eyes away from the oblong shape that could very well be an airship. It was too far away to fully recognize, and the sky was too dark.

"Shall we?" Mina broke into my thoughts.

I saw the flicker of hesitation in her eyes. If we were recognized inside a gentlemen's club—especially with Princess Lurelia—not only would our reputations be ruined, but surely Princess Alix and Miss Adler would be beyond furious. I couldn't imagine how much trouble Mina and I would be in. It would be an international incident.

But I *had* to obtain one of Pix's devices. We needed to find out what exactly it was, and he'd taken back the one I had stolen from him. And this was also our chance to learn what we could about his mysterious customer—whether it was indeed the Ankh or not.

And besides . . . it would be an *adventure*. I couldn't imagine doing anything more exciting than mingling elbow to elbow with gentlemen in their private club. I could hardly wait to see what they got to do!

Females didn't have any place similar to these clubs. We were restricted to sitting politely at tea and making nice conversation, or being chaperoned to within an inch of our lives at highly regulated dances. We couldn't visit pubs or fighting clubs or music halls or even the pleasure gardens like

New Vauxhall without a proper chaperone. And our bodies were just as restricted—by corsets and stays and layers of petticoats.

Hmm. Perhaps that was the Ankh's point all those months ago, when she railed on about society and its restrictions against women.

And poor Lurelia . . . destined to marry an older man who was boring and had bad breath. She was owed a little bit of fun.

Without another thought, I breezed toward the door.

The words "Bridge & Stokes" glowed in soft yellow light, somehow fashioned out of a long slender lamp forming the script. The door opened as we approached. I remembered to speak in a deep voice, and to act imperiously, as if I and my companions had every right to be accepted inside.

And, miraculously, we were.

Sir Mycroft's card—which, I admit, had been Mina's brilliant idea to forge—seemed to be the magic key. Not only did we gain entrance, but the butler called a porter to give us a tour of the club so we would know where we wished to spend our time.

I glanced at Mina, giving her a smile of success. She didn't smile back. In fact, she appeared more than a little uncomfortable. Lurelia, on the other hand, seemed just as enthusiastic as I felt—at least, as far as I could see behind all the facial hair. My last bit of nervousness evaporated. No one would recognize the Betrovian princess; Mina had done an excellent job with her disguise. And aside from that, who would even believe it if they *thought* they saw her here?

As we were led down the corridor, I noticed the plush, royal blue carpeting beneath our feet. It felt as if I was walking on a goose-down mattress. The ceiling was high, and the walls were stained dark brown. Ornate brass and copper cogworks decorated the intersection of every corridor along with the upper framework of every doorway. Large brass fixtures spanned the ceiling from one wall to the other, and oblong gas lamps hung suspended from them at regular intervals. Massive pictures in thick gold and silver frames depicted things like *The Hunt at Dawn* or *Two Mechanized Engines*.

The porter pointed out "The Brandy Room," "The Poker Room," "The Whist Room," "The Library," and "The Smoking Terrace"—and advised us that we could, of course, order food, drink, or cigars in any of the chambers regardless of their name. As we trooped up a flight of stairs, it occurred to me to wonder how on earth Pix gained entrance to such an exclusive establishment.

Surely he must need to come here regularly to retrieve his orders. He didn't strike me as someone who would trust another person to collect and deliver them.

But how?

As we passed by on our tour, we encountered several gentlemen of the peerage along with some wealthy businessmen—

many of whom I'd met. No one seemed to take notice of us, for they were either deep in conversation, card-playing in their armchairs, or otherwise occupied. Several of the bachelors Lurelia and I had danced with at the Midnight Palace were present. I thought if anyone were to recognize us, it would surely be one of them. But no one did.

"And this chamber is known as the Founders' Room," said the porter as he stopped at the largest and most ornate door yet. He pushed a button, and the brass and copper cogworks along the top of the entrance clicked to life. The double doors swung gracefully inward. I looked inside to see a comfortable, luxurious chamber decorated in rich blues and browns.

A large fireplace graced one wall. Overstuffed leather chairs studded with metal pins were arranged around low tables. Soft wall lighting gave the place a pleasant glow. The place was just as I would have imagined a gentlemen's club to look.

"The portraits of our three founders can be found on the wall adjoining the cigar table. And there in the cabinet beneath them is an original copy of the Domesday Book. Feel free to page through it, gentlemen. The Keeper will be pleased to open the case for you."

My pulse spiked. There it was—a book in a case. It had to be the place I was to submit my order. I'd already written it out, with Mina's help, and I tried not to appear too eager as the three of us entered the chamber.

As we made our way to an empty table and group of chairs, I looked over at the glass-front cabinet. Wasn't the Domesday Book an important artifact? It had all the history of England written in it, or something like that, from medieval times. Had someone really cut out some of the pages in order to accept orders? Miss Adler would be devastated. Mina would be compelled to lecture. Then I nearly stumbled over my walking stick. I'd looked up from the book's case and recognized the portrait directly over the cabinet.

It was of the one and only Mr. Martin VanderBleeth. His name was emblazoned in large type on a plaque below it.

Blooming fish.

"I suppose the founders visit the club on occasion?" I asked the porter innocently. This explained a lot of things . . . but also raised many more questions. "Such as Mr. Vander-Bleeth there?" I nudged Mina, and she looked over. Her eyes widened in comprehension, then narrowed with irritation. I could almost read her thoughts: *that dratted, disreputable Mr. Pix!*

"Oh, no," said the very proper porter, rearing back as if I'd insulted him. "Mr. VanderBleeth has long been deceased. I believe he passed on in 1875, only two years after the opening of Bridge & Stokes in this location. He did, however, provide all of the original glass for the windows."

"Oh." I frowned. Then, I figured it out, for the portrait wasn't of Pix arrayed in mustaches, but of a man who resembled the way he'd been disguised. "His son, then? Surely he visits the club on occasion."

"Indeed not, unless he were to fly across the Atlantic every month or so—which is, of course, impossible." The man looked as if I'd suggested he himself sprout wings and do the same. "The grandson, however, makes an appearance now and again. Apparently he has been touring the Continent."

The so-called grandson, also known as Pix. How very convenient.

"Is the junior Mr. VanderBleeth expected tonight?" I ventured.

The porter lifted his nose. "I don't presume to know the gentleman's schedule, nor his intentions. Might I remind you, this is a private club, and the gentlemen who are members expect the utmost in discretion and privacy. Perhaps you and your guests would like to select a cigar? Or choose from the food menu? The prime rib of beef is excellent."

I do believe that was the first time I'd ever been set down by a servant. However, I *was* hungry. "That sounds quite excellent. I shall have the prime rib of beef."

Mina gave me a "What are you doing ordering food/ Are you never not hungry/We can't just sit here forever" look, but I ignored it. And, thankfully, Lurelia did as well— or perhaps it was just that Mina didn't dare glower at the princess. Regardless, Lurelia ordered the roasted chicken, which came with whipped potatoes. I immediately began to second-guess my choice of beef with turnips.

However, I rose and sauntered over to the cabinet, which held the Domesday Book. As I approached, a small, wizened man who could only be the book's Keeper, appeared. He was hardly tall enough to look over the top of the cabinet.

"I should like to peruse the book," I said in my fake male voice. I hoped Bilbo hadn't forgotten to tell me anything—like a password or some other signal.

"Of course, my lord." The tiny man, who was no larger than an eleven-year-old boy, produced a delicate metal implement. He slipped it inside the back of the case, and then, with a soft, continual whir, the glass doors atop the cabinet rose and then slowly split open. The book lifted inside the cabinet on its own platform as I watched with interest.

"I suppose Mr. VanderBleeth finds this book quite fascinating." I felt as if I were fishing around in a murky, muddy puddle with my bare hand, hoping to come across something other than slime.

"Oh, yes. Of course."

That was helpful. But not really. "As well as many others." *Perhaps a woman dressed as a man, wearing a single diamond earbob?* But of course even I knew I couldn't ask such a question. When the Keeper remained silent, I indicated the massive volume. "May I?"

"Please."

The moment I lifted the book from its display, I realized it wasn't really a copy of the Domesday Book. It was actually a small box, made to look like a book. I felt much better about flipping it open to the back, and yes indeed, where the last fifty or sixty pages would have been, there had been a hole cut into the papers. A small box—currently empty—fit into the space. I glanced at the Keeper (who had turned away to adjust the wall lamp), then placed my folded-up order into the box.

I felt as if I'd accomplished something significant when I handed the book back to its Keeper—much less carefully than I had retrieved it, now that I knew it wasn't a priceless artifact.

"May I interest you in a cigar, my lord?"

I turned to what the porter had called the cigar table, and looked down at the long, glass-covered expanse. Inside the display table were rows of cigars, arranged alphabetically by whatever it is cigars are categorized. The type of tobacco? The geographic location of origin? I had no idea.

I didn't even like the smell of cigars. And of course, I'd never tried one.

A little bubble of daring rumbled up through me.

Tonight I was a gentleman for all intents and purposes. Why *shouldn't* I see what a cigar was like? I didn't have to actually *smoke* it . . .

"What do you recommend?" I asked in a deep voice that sounded ridiculously fake to me.

"Do you prefer a more floral, herbal taste, or a spicy, chocolatey one? Or perhaps one with the flavor of citrus?"

"Er . . . floral sounds about right."

"Very good, my lord. Perhaps you might take your pick from one of these." The cigar-keeper began to push some buttons on a small panel at the back of the case.

The glass top lifted up and back toward him. Then, seven different cigars located randomly throughout the case ascended from their slots. I realized each was on a curved brass holder that cradled the cigar.

I wasn't certain what to do next. "Er . . . that one looks excellent." I laughed gruffly as I pointed to one of them.

"Would you care to smell it first? Or shall I clip it for you?"

I had no idea what he was talking about. Bram didn't smoke cigars, and the only time I was ever exposed to them—which was never, for gentlemen didn't smoke in polite company—was if I caught a peek of the men in the study after dinner. "Of course."

Fortunately, the cigar-keeper asked no further questions. Using tongs, he took the cigar I'd identified and placed it on a small machine flanking one side of the cabinet. There was a sharp little *snip* and one pointy end fell away. Then he put it on a small silver tray and offered it to me.

"Very good. Thank you," I said, picking it up. The outside was leathery and papery at the same time. I lifted it to my nose and sniffed. The smell was musty and faintly like dried roses, but not particularly pleasant—at least to me. I turned to rejoin Mina and Lurelia.

"Shall I light it for you, my lord?"

Argh. I turned back. "Er . . . not at this time. Perhaps after my dinner."

"Very good, my lord." The cigar-keeper bowed, and I fled to my seat.

"What on earth do you think you're doing, Evaline?" Mina said from between gritted teeth. "You aren't actually going to *light* that thing, are you?"

"I might." But I slipped it into an inner pocket of my coat.

We glared at each other, then looked away. I decided Mina's bad mood was due to worry that we'd be discovered.

"Do many men wear ear-studs like yours, Mina?" Lurelia said suddenly.

My head—and Mina's—spun to look at her so quickly I feared I might have left some of my brain behind.

"Pardon me?" Mina said.

"I just noticed the diamond ear-stud you're wearing; it must have been too shadowy in the carriage and you were wearing a hat. I've never seen earbobs on a man before, and since I arrived, I've seen it twice. Is it an English fashion?"

"No." Mina's voice sounded strangled. "Where else have you seen a gentleman wearing earbobs?"

"I don't recall where it was. Perhaps when I was shopping yesterday? Or at Westminster Abbey? The gentleman did have a tiny diamond in his ear; I noticed him because I thought it was unusual."

"That is excellent information, Lurelia. Thank you for mentioning it." She looked meaningfully at me—as if I hadn't realized the importance of the princess's comment.

I considered taking out my cigar just to needle Mina. I didn't know why she was so tightly wound. No one had even looked twice at us—even with her being dressed in the style of the Ankh. That likely was a disappointment to her.

And I supposed most of the reason she was nervous was because Lurelia was with us. Perhaps she'd be less irritable if the princess wasn't tagging along.

No. Probably not.

Regardless, I was beginning to feel bored. Somehow, I thought being in a gentlemen's club would be more interesting. But we were just sitting there, waiting for our dinners to arrive. I'd done what I had to do, and now there was nothing to keep my interest.

I considered ordering a brandy. Just to see what it tasted like. Not that I couldn't sneak a sample from Bram's liquor cabinet. But there was the added danger here of getting noticed. Maybe I'd go join the table of young bachelors playing whist in the next chamber. Some of them had seen me in a gown only three days ago, and one had even waxed rhapsodic over my—what had he called them? Oh, yes—"lips like crushed, velvety rose petals." I shuddered at the memory. I wondered if any of them would recognize me. It was a good thing Mr. Dancy wasn't here. He of all of them would be the one to see through my disguise.

I rose from my chair.

"Where are you going?" Mina demanded.

"Just need to—er—freshen up," I lied.

"*Freshen up?*" Her eyes goggled. "Where on earth are you going to freshen up? There are no ladies' lounges here!" She spit the words from between gritted teeth.

"Then I shall be required to use the *gentlemen's* retiring room, won't I? After all, I am in trousers!" Goodness, didn't the woman have a sense of humor? I glanced at Lurelia, but she had risen and walked over to the cigar-keeper's cabinet. I wondered if Mina would berate *her* if she chose to light a cigar.

My partner might have said something else, but just then I felt the subtle rush of chill over the back of my neck and shoulders. Had someone opened a door? Perhaps onto the Smoking Terrace? My hair was pinned up so high and tight that any change in the air was immediately noticeable on my exposed skin.

I sank back into my seat, heart pounding. Would the draft dissipate? Or did it mean UnDead were present? I'd been uncertain in the past . . .

"What is it?" Mina's voice was less demanding than before. Maybe she noticed my expression.

The eerie chill remained like little prickles of ice above the collar of my shirt. The nape of my neck felt as if a cold hand rested there, curling around me.

There was no mistaking it. And—oh, *blast it*! I hadn't thought to bring a stake with me tonight. Blasted, blooming, *pickled* fish! How could I be so stupid? I'd been so concerned about looking like a man, and getting dressed at Mina's house, that it hadn't occurred to me to include one in my disguise.

I looked at Mina. "Take Lurelia and leave now."

"They're here? Vampires?" Her expression was grave and her gaze darted about as if she had the ability to identify an UnDead.

"Yes. I don't know how many. I'm not sure where they are. Take Lurelia and go. I need to find something to use for a stake."

Mina shook her head in exasperation. "Your walking stick. It's wooden, Evaline. I thought that was why you selected that one."

Right. Maybe it was. Feeling more in control, I rose from my chair, walking stick firmly in hand. "Are you leaving now?"

"Are you certain you wish me to?"

I gave her a look that made even Mina decide not to argue. "The less people I have to worry about saving, the better. You'll just be in my way."

"The *fewer* people," she muttered under her breath, but she scooted—rather quickly, due to the freedom of her trousers— off to retrieve Lurelia.

I would leave it to Mina to make the proper excuses. I had a vampire to track.

MISS HOLMES

Quick-Wit

L urelia was understandably startled when I informed her we must leave.

"But so quickly? And my roasted chicken hasn't arrived. I want to know what are whipped potatoes. And where is Evaline?" she asked.

I hesitated to put my hands on a member of the Betrovian Royal Family—or any royal, for that matter—but if she didn't come with me, I was going to have to put that concern aside and drag her out. The vampires could show themselves at any moment, and I knew from personal experience how quickly they moved and how frighteningly strong they were.

"Miss Stoker felt ill and left to go home." It wasn't one of my better fabrications, but I couldn't worry about that.

"But I don't wish to leave until I've eaten. The chicken sounds delicious. We don't eat much chicken in Betrovia."

I held up my hands in a genteel effort to remind her to keep her voice low. No one needed to hear the word "Betrovia."

"I'm feeling rather nauseated myself . . . perhaps it's being so high up in the air. I really must leave before I . . . well, it may not be pleasant if I don't find a carriage soon." I put my hand over my midriff and attempted to appear as if I were ready to retch at any moment.

Though Lurelia continued to gawk at me as if she couldn't quite comprehend the situation—perhaps she was afraid I actually *would* vomit—she allowed me to escort her from the Founders' Room.

Naturally, I had paid strict attention to the layout of the club, so I knew precisely where we were and which route we must travel to find the main entrance. Because the porter had taken us on a very thorough tour, we had several turns to make, and one set of stairs to descend. As we made our way down the corridor, I did my best to keep the princess moving quickly without appearing to rush.

We passed a number of gentlemen in groups or walking along independently. Fortunately, none of them took any notice of us and I made certain not to meet the eyes of anyone we encountered. And, also fortunately—and to my disappointment—no one seemed to recognize me as the Ankh. I wasn't certain what that meant, but I didn't have time to mull over that now.

Instead, as we hurried along, I listened carefully for the sounds of altercation or distress, but heard nothing besides the same chatter and occasional bursts of laughter or exclamation from behind the closed doors.

Down the stairs, then two more short hallways, pass by the Brandy Room, and Lurelia and I would be one turn from the main entrance.

One might wonder about the ease with which I allowed Miss Stoker to convince me to take Lurelia, while leaving my partner to fend for herself, but it was the best and only option. Not only was Miss Stoker equipped and prepared (at least, once I reminded her of the wooden walking stick) to combat any UnDead, it was imperative the princess be removed from the vicinity of any sort of threat.

In fact, the nausea I had so easily manufactured was now becoming a reality the more I thought about what would happen should the princess not only be discovered here in Bridge & Stokes, but also, more seriously, if she became a victim of the UnDead.

Thus, I quickened our pace down the short flight of stairs. I paid little attention when we brushed past one of the butlers, who seemed to be in a state of agitated hurry as he flung open a door marked "Porters." As we approached the second-to-last turn before we would reach the main entrance, I learned why he was in such a tizzy.

"Sir Mycroft Holmes . . . and the Lord Regent Mikalo Terrence of Betrovia have arrived!" announced the butler into the room of his colleagues. "Everyone must attend immediately."

I stopped so quickly Lurelia nearly bowled me over. When I grabbed for her arm to steady both of us, she looked at me with the same appalled expression I presumably wore.

"No!" she mouthed, her eyes wide.

"This way," I hissed, yanking her through the closest doorway.

She stumbled after me and we found ourselves inside a chamber decorated in a similar fashion to the others we'd seen. However, in this particular room, the only acceptable activity seemed to be some sort of game. Seven chairs surrounded an oval table, and in the center was a contraption made of metal and glass tubes.

The occupants of the chamber turned to look as we effectively burst into the place, and I fixed a bemused smile upon my countenance. Though I was certain at any moment my stomach was about to heave, I managed to say, "Oh, here we are, old chap. Just the place we were in search of."

I didn't trust myself to look at Lurelia; I had no idea what to expect from her. She certainly didn't seem to be as intelligent and quick-witted as even Evaline was, and so I had no illusions the princess would be helpful in extricating us from this very sticky situation. I didn't mind doing all the talking and thinking for both of us; I just hoped she wouldn't say anything that would give us away.

"Very good," said one of the gentlemen. He had thinning carrot-red hair. "We've been short a player since Pample-Bridge left. Who's going to play?"

"Er . . . I'll play first, all right, then, old boy?" I said to Lurelia. Since I had no idea what sort of game they were playing, it was only reasonable that the more quick-witted and observant one of us should participate.

"Of—of course, if you like." She remembered to keep her voice deep.

"Right, then. Will you sit your arse down, won't you, so we can get started?" said a different gentleman with a thick black mustache.

My cheeks flamed at his rudeness, but I heard voices in the hallway behind us and recognized the calm, even tone of my father. This prompted me to dive into the one vacant chair at the game table—thankfully with its back half facing the door. I was more relieved than I cared to admit when Lurelia did the same, choosing a seat near mine but not at the table.

To my dismay, the voices stopped right outside the door-way. I could hear the conversation as it reverberated through the walls. Though I couldn't discern what they were saying, surely they would move on shortly. Then Lurelia and I could make our exit.

I turned my attention to the table and the setup in front of me. There seemed to be a glass tube-like track that circled the table. It had dips, hills, and sharp turns. In the center was a tall, slender chute that spiraled down and ended above the tiny canal. In front of each player's seat was a small box attached to the track. On one side of the box was a button; on the other, a light, and on top of each box was a small drinking glass. The glasses were empty.

No sooner had Lurelia and I taken our seats than a footman appeared from an obscure corner and poured some amber-hued liquid into each of the seven glasses.

When I smelled the scent of whiskey, I realized what a tenuous predicament I was in. And when I realized the familiar voice still rumbled outside the door, I could only grit my teeth.

Drat it! How long must you stand there talking?

And what if someone remembers admitting two gentlemen to the club with your "cousin" tonight?

I felt the blood drain from my face.

No. I couldn't think about that. I would deal with that problem if it happened.

"Very well, then. Shall we begin? Gentlemen, place your bets for Quick-Wit, round the first," announced the carrot-haired man.

The game was called Quick-Wit? Well, that sounded promising. Surely I could hold my own in a competition of that name. Feeling more confident, I waited to see what the others did before digging in my pocket and producing a pound note, which, after observing my companions, I fed into a small opening on the side of the box in front of me. It didn't go all the way in; a short piece protruded.

"Ready, gentlemen? Remember, you have only one chance per round to open your gate. You have to be the most quick-witted! Whoever stops the ball drinks!" crowed the vociferous leader.

"Aye! Around and around, the ball she goes, and wherever she stops, he pukes on his toes!" shouted the mustached man. From the sound of it, that particular gentleman had stopped the ball a number of times already.

The footman pushed the button on a mechanical device at the far end of the table. There was a *click-snap*, and a small gate popped out of my box, blocking the canal.

The spiral chute above the table began to spin, and I heard a metallic rattling. It became louder and faster, and I put my hand on the button of my box just as the other players had done. Suddenly a small brass ball shot out of the chute into a small funnel that fed it sharply into the tube. The ball began to ricochet through the tube, up and down the hills and dips, rattling along at top speed.

It took me only a moment to realize I had to push the button at precisely the right time to allow the ball to pass by my "gate."

I hit it too early.

The gate clicked back out of the way, then shot forward again almost immediately. The brass ball thunked into it and the light on my box blinked on.

My competitors shouted and cheered, and the pound note I'd fed partway into the machine disappeared completely. I had no idea what would happen to it now, but one thing was obvious: it was no longer mine.

"Ahh, beginner's luck!" cried someone. "And down the hatch it goes!"

"Drink up, sirrah!" shouted the red-haired man in a much-too-ebullient voice.

I eyed the glass of whiskey with trepidation. Clearly I had to drink it—all of it. While they watched.

"Drink! Come on, now! Time's a-wasting."

I took a deep breath, picked up the glass, and sipped. *Fire.* Gad, it was like fire burned my lips.

I couldn't drink this!

"What's wrong with you? You came to play—now drink up, won't you, old chap!" This was from the man with the black mustache—obviously happy to have someone else taking on the role of loser.

I didn't think I could sip it . . . it would take forever, and it tasted *awful.* But I sensed if I gulped it too quickly, the whiskey would burn and score the inside of my mouth. The last thing I needed was to be coughing and choking—then they'd know something was wrong. I'd be exposed, my disguise for naught, and Lurelia would be discovered. I tightened my fingers around the glass, steeling my resolve.

"Drink it all in one gulp," came a soft voice near my ear. "And don't breathe in while you're doing it!"

The princess knew how to drink whiskey? Maybe she should be playing the dratted game instead of me! Despite my frustration, I did as she suggested, fairly tossing the contents of the glass down my throat. It worked rather well. Yes, the liquor burned my mouth and down into my chest . . . but I managed to swallow it with little more than a tiny cough, though a few tears welled in my eyes.

"Ante up, there, good fellow!" cried the red-haired man

(whose name was Mr. Stanley), which I took to mean I should put another pound note into the machine.

Another one? At this rate, I was going to be many pounds poorer by the end of the night.

I hadn't heard any more conversation rumbling on the other side of the door. Hoping Sir Mycroft and the Lord Regent had left, I strained to listen. After this round, surely Lurelia and I could leave.

The whiskey had spread from my throat to chest, and now my appendages, down to my fingers and toes, felt pleasantly warm. The scratchiness was gone from my throat.

"Ready gentlemen? *Go!*"

The footman dropped the ball into the top of the spiral chute, and it clattered and clanged down as the chute whirled around at top speed. This time I knew what to expect. It was a combination of the speed of the ball, plus the uncertainty of where it would shoot into the canal that required the skill of perfect timing to open one's gate.

And clearly, the more one lost, the more one drank—and the more impaired the player became. And then the less likely one would have perfect timing. I could already feel the effects—small as they were—from the single gulp I'd taken.

The ball shot around and around, everyone pushing the button on their gate at the appropriate moment. The gates clicked away, then snapped back in a sort of rhythm that grew faster and more furious as the round went on. The men shouted and called out insults to each other as the ball picked up speed, ricocheting in its glass-covered tube.

Click . . . snap. Click . . . snap!

The door to the chamber opened.

"Sir Mycroft Holmes and the Lord Regent of Betrovia!" announced a footman. My hand jerked.

Click . . . snap!

Clunk.

The ball slammed into my gate. My light went on.

A great cheer went up from my competitors.

"Drink up, old boy!" cried Mr. Stanley. Who made him the game manager, anyway?

Everyone was looking at me, chanting, "Drink! Drink!"

My father and the Lord Regent walked over to the table . . . and came to stand *right behind my chair.* The whiskey churned in my stomach and I held my breath.

"Regent Terrence would like to sit in on a few rounds of Quick-Wit," rumbled Sir Mycroft. "Is there anyone who cares to give up a seat?"

I swore I felt his words sift down over the top of my head and settle there like a vise. Perspiration began to pool in a variety of areas on my person. The whiskey swished more violently inside my belly.

"Drink up, now, there, old chap! The Lord Regent wants to play and the time's wasting!"

If my father hadn't been standing behind me, I would have bolted from my seat and given it up for the mustachioed regent in a trice. As it was, I had no choice but to sit as utterly still as possible . . . and to slowly bring the glass of whiskey to my lips.

"Drink! Drink!"

I was just about to take a sip when the chamber door burst open so hard it thudded against the wall and bounced back.

"Murder!" cried the man who stood in the doorway. "Sir Wexfeld has been murdered!"

Miss Stoker

In Which Miss Stoker Is Subjected to Some Courting

Confident that Mina would get Lurelia out of Bridge & Stokes with her normal single-mindedness, I knew I could completely focus on the matter at hand.

As I hurried through the club, the cold, eerie sensation at the back of my neck remained strong. This made me sure there was more than one UnDead nearby.

Still, my inexperience left me with little else to go on. Were there two of them, or twenty? Or some number in between?

Clutching my walking stick, I hurried through the club, following the chilly sensation as well as I could. It ebbed and flowed, and I realized I needed to go up the stairs to the next floor.

I met few people on the upper floor, but just as I was rounding a corner, I heard a shout in the distance. It sounded shocked and fearful, and I heard "Murder!"

No! Oh, no! The UnDead had already created a victim. Horror, regret, and a little fear shot through me. It suddenly became very real: someone here tonight had died.

It could be someone I knew. Someone I had danced with, spoken to . . . *brought here.* No, surely Mina and Lurelia were long gone by now.

And if I didn't find the red-eyed demons, there would be more victims before the night was over.

It was up to me—only me—to stop it.

I spun around, the chill growing colder and more potent at the back of my neck as my insides bubbled nervously. Yet I was filled with purpose and determination. I heard noises above me, thuds and thumps, like a struggle, and realized I needed to find another set of stairs.

I sprinted around a corner and slammed full-force into someone. We ended up tangled on the floor, and when I opened my eyes I was looking up into the familiar face of Mr. Richard Dancy.

"What are you doing here?" I cried without thinking. "You have to leave immediately!"

It was only after I saw the confusion in his eyes, and then the sudden dawning of shock and recognition that I realized my mistake.

"*Miss Stoker?*" His eyes were wide, but, ever the gentleman, he assisted me to my feet. "What on *earth—*"

"There's no time for that now! You must leave!"

"I heard them crying murder. I don't know what's happened, but if anyone must leave, it would be you! Think of your reputation were you to be found here, not to mention the danger of having a murderer roaming about!"

He'd taken my arm as if we were at a ball and ready to enter the dance floor. I realized how surprising it might appear if someone came upon us and saw the way one man was looking down at another with something very much like affection. Nevertheless, a little wriggle of warmth shivered through me. Pix never looked at me that way . . .

And why on *earth* was I thinking about Pix at a time like this?

"Yes, yes, of course," I said. "I got lost. Will you please show me the way out?"

What else could I do but that? Now that he'd recognized me, Mr. Dancy's chivalrous character would never allow me to go off on my own. He was just as determined to see me out of the club as I was to make certain he got to safety.

Oh, gad, if I hadn't run into him—literally—*he* could have been the next victim!

But the chill at the back of my neck was just as intense as ever, and I knew I didn't have much time. At this very moment, a horde of vampires could be mauling a table of poker players in the chamber above.

"This way, Miss Stoker," said Mr. Dancy as he hurried me along. In fact, he didn't have to hurry me at all; I was moving as quickly as possible. The sooner I could divest myself of him safely, the better.

The hallway we turned down didn't look familiar, but that didn't matter. I was more concerned we'd encounter an UnDead before we got outside to safety, and certainly Mr. Dancy knew his way around Bridge & Stokes better than I did.

In fact, he must have, for all of a sudden, he opened a door and we were outside. A dark, starry sky arced over us, and the soft bubbles of yellow gas lamps studded the city below. There was no moon tonight, and a chilly breeze lifted the loosening hairs on the back of my head. I realized I'd lost my hat in our collision. Some of the pins had come free, and my hair was sagging in places.

We were on a small terrace filled with potted trees, climbing vines, and benches. Under any other circumstance, it would have been romantic to be here with the handsome Mr. Dancy—but I didn't have time to waste.

"What are we doing here? Is there a lift down?" I asked, looking about in vain.

"Yes, over there. But . . . Miss Stoker . . ." He turned me to face him. "If I may . . . just for a moment. We're safe here." He smiled down at me, never looking more handsome than he did at that moment.

Though I chafed and danced a little in his grip, I couldn't look away from his soft, warm eyes. "Yes, I know, but I must—"

"I cannot express how delighted I am to have encoun- tered you here tonight! I always believed you were unique and fascinating, but tonight my impression of you has become even more flattering. You are brave and bold and courageous. You must know I hold you in the highest of esteem, Miss Stoker . . . Evaline."

My heart was thudding and I felt soft and murky as he held me there under the stars. His face drew closer, and I knew he was going to kiss me.

I needed to go, to get back and save people—but just for a moment . . .

The walking stick fell from my hand as he bent closer. I lifted my face to meet his lips. And just as my eyes began to sink closed, I saw the red flare suddenly glowing in his.

My eyes bolted wide as he plunged his fangs into my throat.

Miss Holmes

Miss Holmes Makes a Prudent Exit

I had the presence of mind to fling the contents of my whiskey glass under the table while everyone was gawking and
bolting to their feet to the cries of "Murder?"

Due to the fact that my father still hovered behind me,
I was one of the few who did not rise. In fact, I remained res-
olutely facing away from him and the cacophony behind me.

Naturally, Sir Mycroft took control of the situation.
"Scotland Yard has been notified, I presume," he said as if he
were commenting on the weather. Though his voice wasn't
particularly loud, it held the sort of command that made it
heard without the need for volume. The general chaos in the
chamber settled into something more like quiet shock.

"Sir, if you will deliver me to the location of the tragedy,"
my father continued, presumably speaking to the footman
(my face was still averted). "And . . . it would not be remiss
if you were to notify my brother in addition to the Met."

The noise gave a brief uptick in volume, but Sir Mycroft's next words brought the chamber to a sudden hush. "No one is to leave the building. Everyone is to remain in their current location until the authorities have arrived and conducted their investigation. Everyone must be interviewed about anything they might have heard or seen."

My stomach dropped like a lead ball. This was it. Lurelia and I were in a complete and utter fix.

The only thing that would make it worse would be if someone remembered we had come in with Sir Mycroft's cousin.

No, the only thing that would make it worse would be if Inspector Grayling was part of the investigative team.

Now the lead ball in my belly broke up and began to churn like chunky butter. The liquid contents of my belly swished violently, threatening to surge back up. I swallowed hard, desperate not to allow that to happen.

I hadn't dared look at Lurelia since the unexpected appearance of Sir Mycroft and the Lord Regent, but as they made their way out of the chamber (apparently neither of them were required to remain in their current location—a fact which I, mostly, appreciated) I chanced a look over.

The princess's thick mustache and sideburns were still intact. She'd done nothing to draw attention to herself—not that that was a surprise, for that seemed to be her personality in general. I caught her eye and gave her a nod of encouragement. As soon as my father and the Lord Regent were gone, I rose and went to sit in the chair next to her.

"Where're you going?" exclaimed someone—and I realized he was speaking to me. "We have a game to finish here!" It was Mr. Stanley, the self-appointed manager of the betting game.

"Might as well keep playing since no one of us is going anywhere. Pass the time faster," added the man with the black mustache.

"Er . . . no thank you, old chap. I'm not feeling quite the thing at the moment," I said. "All this talk of murder makes my eye twitch."

They grumbled and tried to bully me into playing again, but I was firm in my refusal. Actually, it was desperation more than anything, for I had a feeling even the smell of whiskey would have me losing control of the swirling contents of my stomach.

Once they left me alone—after pressing the poor footman into making up the seventh person in the game (I had no idea who was fronting him the pound note)—I was finally able to give Lurelia my full attention.

"What are we going to do?" Her eyes were wide beneath the thick, too-long hair that kept getting caught in her bushy brows.

"Don't worry. I have a plan."

That wasn't strictly true . . . but one was forming in my mind.

I didn't like where my thoughts were leading, but at the moment it seemed the only possible way Lurelia and I might extricate ourselves without being discovered.

For the more I thought about it, the more I realized several things.

Under no circumstances could Sir Mycroft or the Lord Regent see us. That had to be the first priority.

(To be clear, it was the first priority *after* avoiding the UnDead and staying alive. But I had to trust Evaline had that element under control.)

Second, under no circumstances could I be seen by Uncle Sherlock. A master of disguise himself, he would immediately recognize me.

Third, if we were interviewed by Scotland Yard, we would need to provide our names and addresses, which we obviously could not do.

And finally, we would be asked to provide any information we could about the murder. Obviously, what I suspected about the crime—which was that it was the result of the vampire or vampires Evaline had sensed—was not going to be helpful to the police.

With the possible exception of one individual.

As much as it pained me to admit it, and as much as I dreaded the fact that it was the only solution, I corrected my thoughts to desperately hope that Inspector Grayling was going to be on the investigative force. Because if he were not, I suspected the threat of a vampire would be the least of my worries.

With this in mind, all I could do was wait until the investigators arrived, and hope whatever vampires might be present had either been exterminated by Evaline, or had fled the club. Never one to leave anything to chance, I spent my time examining the chamber in search of anything that might be used as a weapon against the UnDead, should we be confronted by them.

While there was no garlic to be found (I even lifted the lids on the used meal trays), there was a decorative cross hanging on the wall among several other items from the collection of the sixteenth Archbishop of Canterbury. I surreptitiously slid it from its mooring and tucked it into my pocket. Since it was made from iron, it weighed down my coat, but there was no help for it.

I was just searching for something that could be used as a wooden stake when I heard voices in the corridor. I spied an automated umbrella stand tucked in the corner and pushed the button, hoping to find at least one with a wooden handle. The machine was surprisingly old and slow for such a luxurious club, and I chafed at the delay as it rumbled ever so slowly around in its circuit. It offered me two different brollies I had to reject because they were too thick for me to break. The third one, fortunately, was more like a parasol and I snatched it out before the stand came to a halt.

I'd just managed—with greater difficulty than I care to admit—to break it in two over one of my knees when the chamber door opened. I jammed the shorter piece into the inside pocket of my coat, which was now beginning to sag unfashionably due to all of the accoutrements I'd stuffed inside. One of the benefits of being a female—one of the few— is the ability to carry a reticule within which one can hide numerous useful objects.

I hovered in the corner as several members of Scotland Yard, along with one of the butlers, and a gentleman who I deduced was the club manager, came into the chamber. Presumably none of them were UnDead, but none of them were Inspector Grayling either.

Drat!

The one time I wanted to encounter the infuriating man, and he didn't have the decency to make an appearance. I fumed and worried and tried to hide in the corner, in hopes no one would notice me and I could somehow slip away with Lurelia.

And then he strode in.

I felt almost faint with relief. I'd never been so happy to encounter the arrogantly tall, broad-shouldered, ginger-haired man. He was speaking in low, insistent tones to the club manager, who was gesticulating urgently as he responded.

Then without warning, Grayling nodded, then turned and left the chamber. I strained to hear his last words as he walked through the door, " . . . speak with Sir Mycroft."

Drat.

But the time of waiting and planning was past. I needed to take action, for the other inspectors were beginning to cull the gentlemen away for individual interviews.

I went to Lurelia and said, "Act sick. Now."

I don't know what I expected, but it wasn't for her to stand up and begin to cough violently, so hard she nearly doubled over.

I put my arm around her waist, and she staggered awkwardly against me. People were looking at us. "My friend needs to find a . . ." What did men call it? "He's going to be ill! Um . . . too much whiskey. Where is the nearest—er—"

One of the footmen sprang to action. Perhaps he was afraid Lurelia was going to stain the lush rugs on the floor, or be ill in some gentleman's lap. The result was precisely what I had hoped: he led us out of the chamber and down a hall. Lurelia was now making convincingly disgusting gagging sounds, and I began to worry she really was about to lose the contents of her stomach.

Apparently, the footman was too, for he simply pointed to a door, then fled back down the hall.

We didn't even bother to go inside the—whatever it was called. Although Uncle Sherlock claims every new experience is an invaluable part of detecting, I decided I could live without entering a men's retiring lounge.

"Now what shall we do?" asked the princess.

Leave.

We could just walk down the hall, navigate to the main entrance, and make our escape. But of course there must be men stationed at the exits to ensure no one left. If I were in charge of a murder investigation—not knowing the perpetrator was an UnDead—I would stake guards at every doorway in order to keep all suspects intact. (Knowing the perpetrator was, in all likelihood an UnDead, if I were in charge of the investigation, I would be *evacuating* everyone from the building.)

Regardless, the decision was made for me, for suddenly a policeman appeared in the corridor. Unfortunately, I recognized him from my visits to the Met. I certainly hoped Officer Thornbush didn't look too closely at me.

"What are you two doing out of the chambers? Everyone is to remain in the rooms until all of the statements have been taken."

"Yes, of course," I said in my deep voice. "We have pertinent information for Inspector Grayling. I was told he went to speak with Sir Mycroft at the scene of the crime, and that we should find him to give him our statements directly."

"Who told you—oh, never mind. The Inspector can deal with you. Come with me. I'm going there now."

As we walked with Officer Thornbush, I kept my face averted and conversation to a minimum except to ask, "How was the victim murdered?"

"Thought you knew something about the murder," Thornbush said suspiciously.

"I have information for Inspector Grayling. I didn't say it was about the murder precisely."

I heard my father's voice, and—oh *drat!*—Uncle Sherlock's too as we approached a chamber whose door stood open.

I gestured for Lurelia to wait and, drawing in a deep breath, I followed Thornbush into the chamber.

I scanned the space, my attention skipping quickly over my father, my uncle, and the Lord Regent—along with the two other gentlemen present—and toward the lumpy cloth on the floor. Presumably the body. Blood was already seeping through what had once been a curtain. I was rather relieved the mess had been concealed; my stomach was still queasy.

"Inspector, this bloke here's got something to tell you. Says it isn't *precisely* about Wexfeld here, but he claims it's about something important."

Now was my chance. I walked briskly toward Grayling, who, thankfully, had turned from the conversation at the sound of his name. As I strode past a small table to meet him, I flung out my hand and brushed an empty cigar-ash bowl off the table, directly into Grayling's path.

The metal bowl crashed onto the floor, bounced twice, then rolled to a halt right at his feet.

"Bloody hell," he muttered and crouched automatically to retrieve it.

I lunged to the floor at the same time and we both reached for the bowl. I'd removed my glove, so it was my bare hand he saw when our fingers closed over the dish.

As I'd hoped, he looked up at me in surprise, clearly noticing my hand was not that of a man. I met his gaze head-on, widening my eyes with entreaty.

Shock blossomed over his face, turning it a pleasantly ruddy shade under the freckles scattered over his high cheekbones. His eyes fairly bugged out for a moment and I thought he might be in danger of exploding right there. Then his expression turned to exasperation and, finally, unmistakable anger.

We rose in tandem, my heart thudding as I waited to learn whether he would divulge my identity or do as I'd mutely begged.

"I'll take your statement out here, er, sir," he said, even as his eyes bored furiously into mine. "Excuse me for a moment, Mr. Holmes. Sir Mycroft. My lord."

Nearly giddy with relief at his acquiescence, I preceded him out of the chamber and into the hall. He rounded on me the moment we were out of sight of the others.

He made little effort to keep his voice at a reasonable volume. "What in the bloody—"

"Inspector Grayling," I hissed, interrupting what was certain to be a diatribe by sending a pointed gesture toward Lurelia. "Please. If you would just attend to one thing for me, then you may lecture me and rail at me all you wish."

He ground his teeth, his face turning a dark red, but he snapped his mouth closed and turned to face my companion. It took him only a moment to discern the problem—a fact I had counted on—and when he spun back to me, his eyes were bugging out even more prominently and his face had colored almost purple.

"Are you *mad*?" He sounded as if he was being strangled.

As I had no logical response, I merely lifted my chin and glared back at him.

"Thornbush!" Grayling shouted in a much louder tone than was strictly necessary, considering the man was only half-way across a small room.

The other officer snapped to attention and approached.

"These two gentlemen have provided me with their statements, and they are free to go. Please escort them out of the building and *put them in a cab*, pay for the fare, and give the directions to the driver that he is to take them to their—homes—and *no where else*." He jammed a hand into his pocket and pulled out a collection of bills and coins, which he slapped into the hand of a bewildered Thornbush.

"Um . . . right, then, Inspector."

Lurelia made no hesitation, and began to walk with Thornbush down the corridor, but I wasn't quite ready to leave.

"*Miss Holmes*," Grayling said from between clenched teeth, after looking about to ensure that no one was within earshot, "if you don't leave this very minute, I will tear that bloody ridiculous hat and wig from your head and march you into—"

"Miss Stoker is here," I said in a low voice. "Somewhere."

To this day, I cannot describe the expression that covered his face. I almost felt sympathy for the man; the whole situation was like a rather horrific Shakespearean comedy, at least from his perspective.

"I will find her," he managed, although how he did so without moving any part of his jaw, I cannot say.

I realized Thornbush had paused and was now waiting for me, and I had only one more moment to give Grayling the information I'd promised. I reached into my pocket and pulled out the jagged wooden umbrella handle and, giving him a meaningful look, handed it to him. "You may find yourself in need of this."

I had no idea whether he would understand, but it was the best I could do given the circumstances. Thornbush was waiting, Lurelia was in danger of discovery, and my father and uncle's voices were drawing near.

So I did what any intelligent person would do: I took the opportunity to flee.

MISS STOKER

An Unexpected Farewell

It was more shock than pain that had me reeling from the thrust of Mr. Dancy's fangs.

Yet this wasn't the first time I'd been taken by surprise by an UnDead, and I also had my own advantage. He had no concept who I really was.

But as his mouth settled over my sensitive neck, I had to fight the sensations . . . the soft, sweet lull of my blood surging free . . . the smooth *kuh-kuh-kuh* of him gulping away my life in a breath-like rhythm.

It would be so easy to succumb . . . to just relax . . .

Remember who you are.

I marshaled my strength and gave Dancy a great shove.

As I pushed his face up and away, I slammed a heel down on his foot then twisted from his grip in one swift sequence of movements. He stumbled backward and nearly fell, his red eyes blazing with shock and excitement.

"Evaline Stoker," he panted as we circled each other warily. "You continue to fascinate me. You're the most attractive, surprising, delightful woman I've ever met." At least he didn't call my lips crushed rose petals.

He lunged before I was quite ready, almost catching me off guard. I dodged in the nick of time and came up beneath his arm. I caught him there, and with a quick twist, sent him stumbling off toward one of the potted trees.

I needed a weapon! My walking stick was somewhere on the floor, hard to see in the drassy light . . . Was that it?

I dove to the ground in a smooth somersault. My hand landed on something smooth and round—the stick!—but I rolled right over it and my face thudded into the stone tile. I grappled blindly for the stick. Miraculously, my fingers closed around it, and I slammed my foot down as I yanked up one end—*crack!* It splintered . . . just as a strong hand dragged me to my feet. He was there: all red eyes and sharp fangs, panting blood-scented breath in my face.

Then all at once, he was Mr. Dancy again. Handsome, smiling, coaxing. The red eyes and fangs were gone. "I so enjoyed waltzing with you, Miss Stoker. I do believe I could do so *forever*." He closed his hands tightly around me in the dance position—now, stronger than before, forcing me close to his body in an ugly rendition of the waltz. My free hand, which should have rested at the back of his waist, clutched what I hoped was enough of a jagged bit of wooden walking stick to do the job.

We stepped and swirled to a melody only he could hear. Mr. Dancy looked the same, sounded the same, even acted the same as the attractive young bachelor I'd flirted with many times. But there was no warmth emanating from his body, and at this close proximity, I could smell the faint aroma of death.

He smiled down at me, and I felt the soft tug of attraction. He was handsome. And charming. And funny. My limbs became heavier and I felt lighter on my feet. My fingers loosened and the piece of stick threatened to fall . . .

No.

I pulled my gaze away with effort and tightened my fingers around the weapon. I had to pick the right time . . .

He laughed quietly. "Tell me, now, Miss Stoker . . . why *did* you spill lemonade on yourself in order to keep from dancing with me all those months ago? Of course, back then, I was only a simple *mortal* boy. Now . . ."

"And now you're a simple, *immortal* boy. Too fresh as an UnDead—what, a day? Two at the most?—to know much about being one." With one sleek movement, I had the jagged walking stick pressed against his back. Right at heart-level.

One good thrust, and he was ash.

"What's this?" A flicker of concern marred his features, then smoothed away. "Sweet Evaline . . . you do know I am now impervious to firearm bullets or knife blades or any other weapon you might attempt to use."

"Then you won't mind if I shove this wooden stake in a little farther?" I asked.

His eyes widened, then blazed red. His fangs shot out, long and white and lethal. The sudden change startled me, and I inhaled a breath of UnDead. With a sharp movement, he twisted away, sending me spinning. I nearly stumbled to the floor, catching myself at the last minute.

Blast! Why hadn't I staked him?

I whirled back, makeshift weapon in hand, to find him bearing down on me. He was wild-eyed and furious, and his claw-like hands tore at me. I dodged and ducked, but he sliced at my face and arm with nails like blades.

"How dare you!" he cried. "I would have made you like me!"

"What? Foolish? I don't *want* to be immortal! Don't you know you smell like a grave?" I flung droplets of blood from my face and tried to ignore the pain lancing through my arm.

We circled around, facing each other like two boxers waiting to take the first jab.

"I liked you better when you were weak and mortal," I taunted. "At least then you didn't stink."

He made a sound of fury and lunged—just as I'd hoped. I grabbed him by the shirt to hold him off me as he dug his fingers into my arms and tried to pull me close. We twisted and struggled, locked together in an ugly dance. I tried to angle my arm up to stab him and he tried to tear into me with his fangs as we staggered around the terrace.

I saw the bench behind us and launched myself into him. The force of my movement sent him reeling back into the seat. He lost his balance, but brought me tumbling to the ground with him. As we fell, I raised my arm and plunged the stake.

"*Noooo!*" he cried . . . and the UnDeadness faded from his face. His eyes returned to normal, his fangs disappeared, and for one final moment, he was Richard Dancy . . . charmer, waltzer, suitor. Man.

Frozen in that moment, he looked up at me with such familiar eyes that I wondered if I'd somehow made a mistake . . .

And then *poof!*

He was gone.

And it was just me, and the wooden stake, and a cloud of foul dust wafting to the ground as I panted in the silence.

I staggered to my feet, trembling and chilled.

Bloody, perspiring, unsettled.

I'd just killed Richard Dancy.

I would never see him again. His *family*—his sister, whom I also knew, his mother—would never see him again. I swallowed hard, still gasping for breath, and felt the first pang of grief.

At the same time, I realized the back of my neck was still cold and prickly.

I closed my eyes tightly for a moment, then opened them. I couldn't think about all this right now. I had work to do.

I had just reached the door to the terrace when it burst open. Even in the murky light I recognized Inspector Grayling. He'd been running.

"Good gad," he panted when he saw me—and I realized how I must look, with my hair falling in thick hanks, bloody scratches on my arm and face, scrapes on my cheek. "Miss Stoker?" His attention went quickly from my face to the jagged stake in my hand, then back up to meet my eyes. "Are you—?"

I brandished my weapon. "There are more of them."

I would have charged past him, but he caught me by the arm. "Miss Stoker, I cannot let you—"

I pulled away. "Where's Mina? And—er—"

"They're gone. I sent them away myself." That was when he showed me his own wooden stake. "She gave me this."

Ah, Mina. Always thinking ahead. "How many victims?"

He followed me as I started back inside, seeming uncertain how to handle the situation. "One. That I know of."

I nodded, suddenly weary and yet determined. "There will be more soon—"

I heard voices, and with them, a definite increase of cold over the back of my neck. I threw up a hand to warn Grayling to be silent.

The conversation was coming closer. "Dancy? Where the bloody hell did he get off to? We were supposed to meet—"

They came around the corner, two of them, and along with them came the faint scent of blood.

I leapt forward, stake in hand, as Grayling shouted at me to stand back. But it was too late—I smashed into one of the UnDead and we tumbled to the floor. His eyes blazed red, and that was all I needed to be certain: I slammed my wooden weapon home.

Poof!

Behind me, I heard another shout, and the sounds of struggle. Someone had been thrown into a wall.

Ooh . . . now a second person thudded harshly.

Coughing from an inhalation of ash, I pulled to my feet just in time to see the remaining vampire rake his claws down Grayling's arm. He cried out in shock and pain, but in a sleek move grabbed the UnDead's arm and used the momentum to barrel him to the floor. They both tumbled down, grappling with each other as Grayling fought to free himself from the stronger creature.

I stumbled over to them. When the vampire came up on top, I thrust the stake into his back.

The UnDead exploded, covering Grayling with the disgusting dust. Coughing and brushing away the ash, he pulled to his feet. He was gaping in shock and curiosity.

I didn't speak; I was too busy paying attention to the back of my neck. It felt normal.

"That's all of them," I said when I was certain. Then, noticing the blood coursing down his arm, I added, "You need a doctor."

He was still staring at me. "I think you might need one more than I."

"I'll be fine." I reached up to touch the bite at my neck, which was still pumping blood due to my activity. "I just need to leave without being seen."

226

"Of course, Miss Stoker. I can arrange that."

I adjusted my coat and felt a slender item inside one of the pockets. A forgotten stake? No, it was the cigar. Suddenly, I no longer had the urge to try it out. I just wanted to go home.

"Congratulations, Inspector. You've met your first vampire." I handed him the cigar.

He took it, still giving me a look somewhere between admiration and wariness. "Let's hope it's my last, shall we?"

I shook my head, but didn't speak. *That* was not the least bit likely.

Miss Holmes

A Service of Tea and Prevarication

"I trust you've recovered from last night's adventures," I said to Princess Lurelia.

It was the morning after the events at Bridge & Stokes. We sat in a private parlor at the Domanik Hotel, where the three of us had just been served elevenses. Evaline had arrived a trifle late, wearing an unusually high-necked gown and long gloves. Her left cheek sported an ugly scrape, but I knew the wounds and bites on a vampire hunter healed more quickly than they would on an unexceptional person like me, so I had little concern for her physical health, at any rate.

But since my partner had come into the parlor without her usual energetic sweep, I sensed she wasn't feeling quite herself in other ways. I intended to make certain we had the opportunity to speak privately, for I suspected there were a number of things we needed to discuss.

"Indeed I have," replied the princess. "And I never saw Regent Terrence, so there was no chance of him discovering how I'd really spent the evening. I left word with the hotel doorman that I'd gone to a party with you and Miss Stoker." Lurelia looked at Evaline. "Some strawberry jam for your tea?" she said, passing her a small bowl filled with the jam. On the tray next to it was an array of dainty silver spoons—not even as long as my shortest finger, with the bowl of the spoon the size of my pinkie fingernail.

"In Betrovia, we take our tea like this." Lurelia spooned up some of the jam into her mouth, then lifted her teacup to drink. After she swallowed, she smiled at us. "Or, if you prefer, you may stir the jam into the tea itself, instead of using honey or sugar cubes as you English do."

"How delicious," I said. However, I wasn't interested in eating or drinking. "Now, to attend to the more pressing problem of your blackmailer, Your Highness." She opened her mouth to protest, but I shook my head. "I understand you wish to find the chess queen, but it is the blackmailer who is the greater concern. For if we do find the chess queen, and provide it to him—which we cannot allow to happen at any rate—what next will he demand from you in order to keep his silence?"

Lurelia wasn't able to muster a counter-argument to my position, but neither did she appear to want to be forthcoming. That wasn't unusual—Uncle Sherlock had pontificated many times about the crime of blackmail, and the individuals who tended to be subjected to such unpleasantness. If one has something worth being blackmailed about, it's generally a matter one would prefer not to divulge.

Therefore, it was incumbent upon me to question the princess in regards to not only the perpetrator himself, but also the subject of the blackmail—for that was also a valuable clue.

"The first question is the most important, Your Highness. Do you believe the individual who accosted you at the Midnight Palace is your blackmailer?"

Her eyes widened as if the thought hadn't occurred to her. It probably hadn't. Lurelia's playacting last night at Bridge & Stokes notwithstanding, she didn't seem to be the brightest of young women. "I'm—I'm not certain. I've never met the blackmailer before. Or spoken to him . . . or her."

This was a good beginning. I glanced over as Evaline filled her plate with tiny jelly pastries and thumb-sized salmon salad toasts. Right, then. If she was eating so robustly, whatever was bothering her couldn't be too serious.

"How has the blackmailer been in contact with you?"

"A—a letter. And then after the first letter, when I didn't respond, there were other signs. Signals. Things were left around for me to notice that were meant to remind me."

"Do you still have the letter? When was this?"

"It was before I came to London. Back home. And—and I burned the letter. I didn't want anyone to see it. The maids are so nosy."

I felt a sense of frustration. If the blackmailer was back in Betrovia, I would have a much more difficult time identifying and capturing the individual. "What did it say? Do you remember that? What did it look like?"

"It was very simple. The letter just said 'I have something you don't want to be seen. Payment will be required for the return of these items.'"

"But the type of payment wasn't identified? Was this before or after you found the letter about the chess queen?"

Lurelia screwed up her face in an unattractive manner. "Now that you bring it up, it *was* just after I found the letter. I was looking through an old Bible that belonged to one of my ancestors, the Duchess of Fedeway—she was a friend of your Queen Elizabeth. There were several letters tucked inside; they were very old. But one of them was wrapped in a thin cloth, and that was the letter from your queen. It was difficult to read, but I had heard the stories about the chess set and realized she was writing about it. I don't know if you were aware, but the board itself was in the possession of a Betrovian king for centuries after it was created—"

"Yes, of course. It was your King Thursted the Fourth who—er—forcibly intercepted the base of the chess set during an altercation in a Byzantine palace, if I recall correctly." My exasperation mounted. We were getting off topic, and there were several things I wanted to know about the blackmailer.

However, Evaline was actually showing some interest in something other than food or vampires. "So the board and the chess set were separated? They kept the game pieces in Byzantine, but—"

"*Byzantium.* Byzantine is the adjective, Miss Stoker. To whit, 'the Byzantine people retained the chess queen in Byzantium.' Byzantium is the ancient name of the Greek city that became known as Constantinople. Interestingly, when it was intact, the Byzantine culture embraced the monotheism of Christianity—like their Roman neighbors—rather than the Greek polytheistic religion. But there were influences from both cultures—"

"As I was *saying*," Evaline spoke loudly, "the chess set and the chessboard were separated. The board ended up in Betrovia, stolen by King Thursted the Fourth, and the game pieces . . . how did they get here to England?"

"Queen Eleanor of Aquitaine, who was married to King Louis of France and then to King Henry of England—and additionally, she was the mother of two English kings, King Richard the Lionheart and King John," I informed her. "Incidentally, if anyone should have had a chess queen modeled after her, it should have been Eleanor of Aquitaine. She was just as powerful and ruled as many lands as either of her two husbands. She was the regent for both her husband Henry and her son Richard. She was—" The other two seemed taken aback by my vociferousness. "At any rate, Queen Eleanor traveled on two different Crusades to the Holy Land—one with her first husband, Louis, and the second with her son Richard, after he was crowned king. Presumably, she obtained the chess pieces during one of those crusades, likely the latter—which is known as the Third Crusade. She would, I'm certain, being the powerful sort of woman she was, have been intrigued by and appreciative of possessing one of the first—if not the very first—known chess queen."

"And so this blackmailer wants the chess queen . . . why, exactly?" Evaline asked, reaching for another sandwich.

"If you'd been listening the first time I tried to apprise you of the details, you'd already know the answer to this, and we wouldn't be wasting time. The chess queen is the most important part of a key that unlocks the base of the chessboard. In order to use it, one has to have all of the original pieces of the set—for they are created specifically to act as weights and gears, as in a safe—and one must know the sequence of movements that will open the base. It's like a combination, if you will. Apparently the moves are scribed on the queen herself."

"So there's a treasure inside the base? What is it? And how did the base get here to London if the Betrovians owned it?"

I looked at Lurelia, who'd been following our conversation silently. "Perhaps you could explain to Evaline," I suggested. It wasn't as if I'd never tried before.

"Of course. But first, perhaps you'd like some tea, Mina? You've been doing a lot of talking . . . you must be parched."

I swore I heard Evaline choke back a laugh.

After pouring my tea, Lurelia took up the narrative. "Everything you've said is correct, to my knowledge. The chess table was gifted to Queen Elizabeth on the deathbed of her friend the Duchess of Fedeway, but the King of Betrovia at the time, Allfred—who was the duchess's father—did not approve of the gift, and he refused to send it to England. That is how the rift between Betrovia and England began, and it was only fifty years ago that there was an attempt to mend it. The chessboard was delivered by the Betrovians at that time, but you know what happened then . . ."

"Of course. That was the last State Visit between Betrovia and England, due to the embarrassing elopement of the prince with a commoner." I sincerely hoped history was not about to repeat itself with Princess Lurelia.

I suspected any letters she might have written, which the blackmailer claimed to possess, would cause just as big a scandal as the previous one, and were likely related to some *affaire de coeur* of her own. After all, over what other type of letter would it be worth blackmailing a young woman? Especially a young woman who was due to make a strategic marriage in the very near future, and who didn't love her betrothed.

"As far as what the treasure is inside the chess table . . . I've done a little more research on the specifics. Legend has it there are ancient writings—some from Atlantis, others from Babylon and Greece—that contain secrets to immortality and other unnatural powers, such as raising the dead. But there are other resources that claim the treasure is jewels—the missing Fire-Ruby of Ravenna or, even more far-fetched, the jewels of Helen of Troy."

"So why doesn't someone just smash open the chess-board? What is it made of, anyway? Stone, right?" asked Evaline with the blithe ignorance of one who has no concept of how ancient treasures should be hidden.

"Marble. It's made of marble, and apparently there is no way to break it open, as you suggest, without destroying the treasure inside. That was how it was protected for so long."

"And so this letter you found, Your Highness, suppos-edly tells where the chess queen is hidden?"

"Your Queen Elizabeth knew the importance of the chess queen, and since the chess set was separated from the chess-board, she wanted to ensure no one could unlock the secrets unless both the Betrovians and the English worked together. She and the Duchess of Fedeway agreed both countries should share the treasure, but that was not to be. So Elizabeth hid the chess queen . . . and I discovered the letter that explains where."

"The letter that was stolen during the Welcome Event," I said, giving Evaline a reproachful look. She was taking the last of the mint-orange muffins, and she'd already eaten three of them.

"You said you have a copy of the letter, Lurelia." Miss Stoker ignored me as she bit into one of the muffins. "I sup-pose Mina will need to see it if she's going to solve the puzzle where the chess queen is hidden."

"Yes, of course." Lurelia produced a piece of paper, which she handed to me.

I read aloud:

Dearest Bertina,

Many good thanks for Thy most recent message, and forsooth, thou knowest I would most Like to rest mine Eyes upon your face. But, marry, a visit to yon Betrovian city shall not come to pass, and 'tis my Dear Disappointment such that the pangs in my Heart pound strongly.

But knowest thou I have yet hiddest the Object of which we hast long spake, for 'twill remain in Safe-Keep until that time the two parts have thusly been Rejoined.

Knowest my Dear Friend all is well. Four Soldiers shall Guard Her Majesty, and below them shalt thou find the sailors Three. Our most Gracious Mistress shall rest in easy peace in the Bower of the Place which I haddest the Veriest Glorious of Triumphs and the most trying of Nightmares.

An' now, verily, 'tis the Time to send this Most Urgent missive to thou, my Belov'd Friend. God will, I shall meet Thou soonest anon. God save you, God keep you, until we shall yet again rest Eyes upon the Other.

Elizabeth Regis

"Was that some sort of code?" Evaline asked. "Or did they truly talk and write like that? I thought Shakespeare just . . . rather . . . made it up."

I shook my head, then returned to the paper. "It's actually quite a simple letter. The queen is sad that she is unable to visit her friend the duchess anytime soon. And clearly the 'Her Majesty' is the chess queen, for who else would a queen call Her Majesty but another queen? The puzzle now is to determine where the 'bower of the veriest glorious of triumphs' is located."

"A bower is generally a bedchamber, I believe," said Lurelia.

"Yes, but Queen Elizabeth would have had many bowers—bedchambers. For she had several residences and traveled among them regularly. Hmm. She speaks of soldiers and sailors . . . soldiers would be a common sight of course, for she commanded the English army at the time and even led them—and the navy too, let us not forget that—to war against Spain. Soldiers could also refer to the royal guards the queen would always have about her . . . but surely she wouldn't refer to actual people as guarding the chess queen. That would be too transient . . . No. 'Soldier' must refer to something permanent. Something that wouldn't be altered or changed for many years."

"A statue? A carving?" Evaline suggested.

"Something of that nature. Hmm. Our first order of business must be, then, to determine where the bower is. That will require some research—on my part, of course, Miss Stoker. Naturally, I would never suggest you should participate in such a . . . er . . . mundane task."

"Right, then. You can research possible 'bower' locations. I've got other things that must be done." She appeared entirely too pleased with this development, but I decided it was best if I did the research myself. After all, an assistant would likely miss something important.

"Now, back to the initial problem, Your Highness. I would like to get as much information about your villainous blackmailer as possible. Allowing such a scoundrel to remain free and unpunished goes against everything my uncle has taught me. The first thing we must determine is whether the person who sent you the letter in Betrovia was also the—er—individual who attacked you at the Midnight Palace. If it is so, then I have an excellent idea who that might be, and incidentally, that criminal is not unknown to me and Miss Stoker."

"Truly?" Lurelia's eyes widened.

"Indeed. The individual is a criminal mastermind who has managed thus far to evade the authorities. However, I am confident . . . he . . . or she . . . will be brought to justice due to my continued investigations."

"Do you think it's possible the blackmailer followed me here to London?" asked the princess. For the first time, she seemed actually frightened of the possibility—one which had naturally occurred to me from the beginning.

"If it is the same individual, there are three possibilities: First, the culprit is from your homeland and followed or accompanied you here. Which means he or she is likely in the Betrovian retinue. Second, the villain is English and was in Betrovia when he or she learned you had something worth blackmailing about. The criminal sent the letter to you while present in Betrovia. Or, the third and least likely option, in my opinion, is that the perpetrator has a partner that is either located here in England—less likely—or there in Betrovia."

Lurelia blinked, seemingly overwhelmed by the many scenarios I'd described. But there was more to consider. "It's unlikely there are two blackmailers, but we cannot completely discount the possibility. When did you discover that the—er—letters, did you say?—were missing?"

"Letters? Oh." Lurelia looked down bashfully. "I must confess, I haven't been completely forthcoming with you, Mina. I do hope you'll forgive me."

As I had been anticipating such a development, I said nothing. Miss Stoker, on the other hand, made a sound of surprise. Or perhaps it was just irritation that the crème-filled baked plums were gone. I was a little annoyed myself, for they looked delicious.

"Please go on," I said to the princess.

"I . . . er . . . was not attacked at the Midnight Palace."

"Of course you weren't."

She seemed surprised at my announcement. When I made no other comment, Lurelia continued. "I—mm—thought you wouldn't help me find the chess queen unless I gave you a specific reason. And . . . er . . . made the situation appear urgent."

"And so you pretended to be attacked at the Midnight Palace in order to gain my assistance. But then that plan went awry when Miss Stoker and I were relieved of our duty to be your companions. And so you had to find some way to have us brought back into Princess Alix's good graces, and so you wrote the note—which you didn't post and never meant to post—and 'disappeared' so we would be called in to consult. Correct?"

Lurelia resembled a fish with her bugged-out eyes and opening and closing mouth. It was not a particularly attractive look, but I refrained from pointing out that fact.

"Don't mind her, Lurelia," Evaline said jovially. "She does this sort of thing all the time. But I want to know how Mina knew you faked the attack at the ball. And how did you know the disappearance was just a ruse to get us back on the job?"

"There was simply no evidence of any other person on the terrace with you, Your Highness. Nor was there any evidence on your person that anyone had attacked you or that you'd fought them off. Your fingernails were unmarred, your face powder undisturbed, and I found nothing to indicate anyone else had been there. In addition, clearly the rent in your sleeve was deliberately cut and not torn—for that particular weave of silk would not be so straight and neat, but would tear on a diagonal along the grain of the fabric. However, since one cannot prove a negative, I couldn't be fully certain you had completely manufactured the attack. It wasn't until we were called to the Domanik Hotel after your disappearance that I began to suspect what was happening."

"But how?"

"There were several indications things were not what they seemed. First, the letter in the trash bin was clearly put there after your maid cleaned up. It was meant to be found. Also, there were no errors, ink blots, or corrections to the letter, which led me to believe there was no reason for it to be thrown away. Therefore, the information was meant to be read."

"But what if I'd simply changed my mind about sending it?" asked the princess.

"The letter was clearly written by someone with a purpose. There was no hesitation in the penmanship, no thoughtfulness. It was obvious whoever wrote it *meant* it. Therefore, the decision to send it had been made. In this case, it was never meant to be sent, but to be found and interpreted just as it was: that Evaline and I should be brought back to assist you."

"Incredible," Lurelia said.

"Now that we have that matter addressed," I said, folding my hands neatly in my lap, "perhaps you will be more forthcoming about why you are so intent upon finding the chess queen."

Now it was the princess's turn to look at me with remonstrance. "It's the Theophanine Chess Queen! Why wouldn't one want to find it? To discover the ancient treasure, and whatever secrets are hidden inside. After all, I was the one who discovered the letter."

"Perhaps." I shrugged. "But why do it in secret? Why not simply ask for my—our—help and set about doing so without all of the clandestine activity? Unless you are afraid the person who stole the letter during the Welcome Event might find it first."

Lurelia nodded vigorously. "How did you know? That is precisely why I . . . mm . . . why I didn't want to tell anyone."

"And there is no other reason?" I asked sternly. "Lurelia, if you want me to assist you, I must insist upon complete honesty. No more prevarication, no more half-truths."

Her eyes flickered away. "Very well. If you must know, I hoped to find it myself because . . . well, I hoped if I did discover the secrets of the chessboard, I could somehow use them to . . . mm . . . barter the end of my engagement. I don't want to marry Lord Avistali!"

That last statement was, I believe, the first time I'd seen not only real emotion in her eyes, but also unvarnished truth. There were still several things that didn't add up, and, I was certain, more half-truths, but this show of bald emotion was excellent progress.

I exchanged glances with Evaline and recognized the same pity and dismay in her expression I was feeling. But there was nothing to be done for it. Arranged marriages had long been an expectation of royal families, and also in the upper levels of society. There was nothing I could do to help extricate Princess Lurelia from her future. Nor did I attempt to soothe her with unrealistic platitudes. I simply responded briskly, "It's unfortunate you are to be subjected to an arrangement for which you have no affinity. And I will be more than willing to assist you in finding the chess queen—if she is still to be found, I am confident we will be the ones to locate her. But I would be remiss if I didn't express the opinion that finding the chess queen will be unlikely to lead to your broken engagement, Your Highness. Whatever is hidden in that chess table—if anything—is hardly going to change your father's mind."

I reached to touch Lurelia's hand bracingly. "If your father's mind is to be changed, I would suspect the only real way to make that happen is by speaking with him and appealing to his affection for you and presumed desire for your happiness."

Lurelia didn't meet my eyes, but I could tell she realized I was speaking the truth.

"Right, then," said Evaline after a moment. "Mina, perhaps we should leave Lurelia to her—well, you have research to attend to, and I have to go shopping with Florence. If you would like to share my carriage, now is the time to take our leave."

For once, I had no argument. And fortunately, Lurelia seemed to also agree.

Moments later, Evaline and I were settled in her carriage. "Now," I said as soon as Middy closed the door, "tell me what is *not* in the newspapers about the events at Bridge & Stokes. There was mention of only a single death at the club, with no details about how it occurred. Since you appear to be hiding a vampire bite, as well as some other wounds, I can only assume you were instrumental in keeping the victims to a minimum."

My companion gave me an acknowledging smile, then launched into a non-chronological, but still reasonably organized, description of what occurred after we separated. She finished up by saying, "And one of the vampires was Mr. Richard Dancy."

"Never say so!" I was rarely taken by surprise, but this was one such occasion. "But, how unfortunate." I remembered the gentleman as being one of the few of those in Society I could tolerate.

"I couldn't agree more." Evaline appeared to have much less bravado than she had in the past after describing her vampire-hunting exploits. "We were . . . well, I believe he wanted to court me. Not that I would have allowed it, for of course I will never marry, but . . . I did know him—and like him—better than any other eligible bachelor in London."

"But there is no body," I mused. "So no one will ever know what happened to him, will they? How terrible. Mr. Dancy just disappeared . . . forever."

"Not as terrible as his family learning he was turned into an immortal, blood-drinking demon, who has to take life from others in order to live. And he might have even been the cause of Lord Wexfeld's death." Her pretty mouth twisted with distaste. "He actually told me he wanted to make me like him—immortal and horrible."

I was silent for a moment, and apparently that caught Miss Stoker by surprise. "You aren't saying anything, Mina. Never tell me *you* would consider being immortal."

My attention flew to her, and my reaction was visceral anger and offense. "Of course not. Immortality is unnatural. Nothing lives forever. What a boring existence that would be . . . to live for infinity. And to be required to drink the blood of other humans for sustenance? Most certainly not. But . . ."

"But *what*? It's not like you to be so . . . quiet."

And it wasn't like Evaline to be so sensitive and insistent. Perhaps this vampire-hunting wasn't the simple, amusing activity she'd thought it would be.

"Whom do we know who *would* want to be immortal? To have that power? Whom do we know who has already tried to harness an ancient power so she could be omnipotent and in control? I'm certain I don't need to name the individual. It has just occurred to me to wonder if the Ankh has, in fact, pursued the option of becoming an UnDead herself. One must consider how Mr. Dancy got himself into such a condition—was it purposeful or accidental that he came upon the vampires? And how did it happen he was allowed to live and turn UnDead rather than be drained dry and left for dead as others have been? Is it a random happenstance, or a plan? Did he *choose* it or was it foisted upon him? That, my dear Evaline, is why I am so quiet. There are many things to consider at this time."

She nodded, and appeared to be slightly mollified. "That's true."

"I don't suppose you engaged him in any sort of conversation before—er—dispatching him?"

"Do you mean did I ask him how and when he became UnDead? And by whom? No, I did not. I was too busy attempting to stay alive."

This was a sore point for Miss Stoker—my suggestion that she should attempt to engage the UnDead in some sort of meaningful discourse before staking them. I felt as if she should take any opportunity to interrogate them, and she was too impatient to do so. "Very well, then. But it would have been helpful to know where the vampires are congregating and how they are finding their prey . . . and even how many of them there are in London."

I thought I heard the sound of teeth grinding from my partner. Instead of responding to my reasonable suggestion, she said, "In regards to her desire to become immortal . . . the chess queen is exactly the sort of object the Ankh would be keen to obtain, don't you think? If there are ancient secrets hidden in that chessboard, she would want them."

"Indubitably. Even if there weren't ancient secrets or any treasure to be found in the base of the chess table, the very idea of owning the chess queen—a symbol of feminine power, as well as being an artifact possessed by so many other powerful women of history . . . Most definitely the Ankh would want to obtain the chess queen. And that is precisely why we must hasten to locate it—before she does."

"I agree."

"Now, I must ask whether you've any news about the

note you submitted through that false Domesday Book. Have you had any response?"

Evaline and I had spent some time discussing the best way to keep her identity safe, and the most expedient and convenient location through which communication from Mr. Pix would come. In the order, which I'd asked Mrs. Raskill's nephew Ben to write for us, we'd indicated any messages should be affixed under the last pew in the last row on the right in St. Sequestrian's Church in St. James.

"Pepper's cousin's neighbor's daughter prayed in the church this morning, and there was no message yet."

I nodded. "That cannot come as any surprise, considering the events of last night. And no one would be able to connect you or me to your maid's cousin's neighbor's daughter, even if she were to be seen."

"Yes. I asked for Callie to check again later today. Perhaps there will be a message then," said Miss Stoker. "But for now, would you have any objection to making a stop at Scotland Yard?"

My heart gave a funny little jump. "Whyever for?" I asked, admittedly a trifle sharply.

"Inspector Grayling was injured last night, and I simply wish to ensure he's had the wound properly seen to. And to thank him for his assistance."

I owed Grayling my gratitude as well, and I had certainly intended to express it at my earliest convenience. In writing;

not in person. I was not looking forward to the lecture he was bound to inflict upon me.

"Very well," I said, unable to manufacture a reason for declining that Evaline wouldn't immediately ridicule and discard.

If I had hoped Providence would smile down upon me and arrange for Inspector Grayling to be absent from the offices of the Metropolitan Police, I was bound to be severely disappointed. We found him in his office, along with Angus—who was vocally delighted to see me—and, interestingly enough, Inspector Lestrade.

"You're a hard-lined cognoggin, Brose. If you can't figure out what it is, I don't know who can. Aside from Holmes, that is, and the bloke can be such a bloody—" Lestrade started when he saw Evaline and me being accosted by an enthusiastic Angus, who was acting as if I had appeared solely to deliver more Stuff'n Muffins to him.

"Down, doggie, good doggie," I said, unable to keep a hint of crooning from my voice. I also found my hand—still gloved of course—straying down to pat the little beast on his white and chestnut-brown head. It was at a most convenient height, for he was jumping up on Evaline's skirts in an effort to determine whether *she* had brought him a muffin-flavored bribe.

I was more than a little irritated when she produced a bit of wrapped cheese from the depths of her reticule. She could have a piece of cheddar in her bag, but forget to pack money for the street-lifts?

"Erm . . . good day, Miss Holmes," said Inspector Lestrade. His cheeks were slightly pink. "And . . . ?"

"Miss Evaline Stoker," I said.

"Well . . . erm . . . give my best to your uncle," he said, taking his leave so abruptly he nearly stepped on one of Angus's ears. "Brose, will you take a look at that today and give me something so at least Holmes—er—right, then. I'd like to have something to tell him for once, since he . . ."

"Yes, of course," Grayling said as he put something on his desk. Then he turned to greet us, and I observed his left arm was injured. Not because it was bandaged—although it likely was, for there was extra bulk beneath his coat sleeve—but because of the way he was holding it, unmoving, against his torso and the fact that his shave on the left side of his face wasn't as clean. "Miss Holmes. Miss Stoker. To what do I owe this pleasure?"

I was quite certain he wouldn't have greeted me so cordially if Evaline hadn't accompanied me. In fact, I was fairly certain his greeting would have been something rather loud in volume and vehement in tone.

"How is your arm, Inspector?" asked Evaline. "I hope you've taken the time to have it looked at by a doctor."

"It's naught but a scratch, but I thank you for your concern. And also for your—er—assistance last evening." The tone of his voice was something I had heard only rarely, and never directed at me. "I don't believe . . . well, it was not at all what I expected when I was called to the club." Now he turned to fasten that arrogant gaze on me. "There were, in fact, several unexpected discoveries last night. Might I inquire, Miss Holmes, what on this blooming earth you were doing there?"

I found it rather offensive that he would pose such a question to me, and not to Evaline. Was she not there with me? Was she not also party to the Princess Lurelia debacle? And dressed in men's clothing as well?

"I had business to attend to," was all I could think of to reply.

"I cannot begin to imagine what business—"

"Excellent, then. You shouldn't waste your brain power attempting the impossible." I leveled my gaze at him, and he returned the favor. His gray-green eyes sparkled with fury. I decided that disarming him might be the best option. "Regardless, I owe you a debt of gratitude, Inspector Grayling, for your discretion last evening. I'm certain you're aware of how disastrous the outcome could have been—on many levels. I am truly in your debt."

The ire in his gaze eased. "You're too kind, Miss Holmes. I did only what any gentleman would do."

"Except for Mr. Richard Dancy," said Miss Stoker. She'd sidled over behind Grayling and sat at his desk chair, petting a wriggling Angus. The creature appeared ready to bolt into her lap. I thought of warning her about the volume of hair the beast would leave on her skirt, but lost the opportunity when she continued. "It was he who—um—murdered Lord Wexfeld."

"Am I to assume Mr. Dancy will never be called to task for it?"

"No, he will never been seen again. Unfortunately." She gave Grayling a hopeful glance. "Is there any way to notify his family that he . . . er . . . is . . . won't be back? Ever? So they needn't always wonder—and hope?"

He nodded gravely. "I'm certain there's a way to do so effectively. Thank you for suggesting it. I'll see that it's done immediately." He returned his attention to me. "And I do thank you for providing me with the information I needed to find Miss Stoker and help her find her way out as well. I . . ." He looked as if he wanted to say something more, for his gaze went from me to Evaline and back again. I suspected he wanted to know more about how *we'd* known of the presence—or even existence—of the UnDead. But he did not. "I . . . suppose I now have several notes to add to a—er—particular file of mine."

He looked meaningfully at me.

Oh. Drat! How had he known?

It was Angus's fault for startling me. I'd dropped the file and things must have gone out of order.

I felt my cheeks flush, but I made no comment.

"Right, then. Mina, we should allow Inspector Grayling to return to his work. Oh, I'm so sorry." These last words were spoken after the soft clunk of something heavy landing on the floor. "I didn't mean to knock that off your desk. I do hope I didn't break it."

She lunged under the piece of furniture before Grayling was able to do so, and when she emerged, she was holding the object Lestrade had given him. It took her longer than it should have, due to Angus's delight that someone had ventured down to his level.

"Why, thank you Miss Stoker. And I don't believe it's broken at all." He accepted it with the hand of his uninjured arm, and looked down at the small mechanical device. "Hmm. I've never seen anything quite like it."

"What is it? Where did it come from?" asked my companion.

"I'm not quite certain myself. Inspector Lestrade—whom you just met—asked me to look at it. Apparently, Holmes—er, Mr. Holmes—is assisting with a case over on Magpie-alley, and this was found on the site of the crime." Grayling turned the small object over in his hands, clearly favoring one over the injured other. "It appears to be some sort of . . . well, I don't know, but perhaps it provides some sort of power? But that's . . . hmm." He squinted at it more closely, making interesting sounds as he examined it.

He looked as if he'd just realized we were still there. "Right, then. Miss Stoker, it was a pleasure to see you again. And Miss Holmes, do attempt to keep yourself from the vicinity of any other dead bodies for . . . oh, perhaps at least a month?"

I sniffed and stooped to take my leave from Angus. His ears were so ridiculously long and soft. He flopped one of them on my shoe as he pawed on my foot in an effort to keep me from leaving. I would have to remember to bring more Stuff'n Muffins the next time I visited.

"Good day, Inspector," Evaline said. All of a sudden, she seemed to be in a great hurry.

"Good day," I managed to say as she fairly dragged me out of the office.

"Mina! Do you know what that was?" she hissed as soon as we were out of earshot.

"That small metal device? Based on your enthusiasm, I can only assume it is the very same mechanism your Mr. Pix is so secretive about."

Evaline's face flattened comically. "Oh. Well, you're correct."

"Of course I'm correct. I'm a Holmes."

"Well, since you're a Holmes, you can take advantage of that fact and find out from your uncle exactly what the case is and where that device was found. Then I'm going to learn once and for all what Pix is up to."

Miss Stoker

*In Which Our Heroine Is Enlightened
About a Number of Things*

I had Middy drop Mina off at her Uncle Sherlock's home on Baker-street to discover what she could about the Magpie-alley case. Then she planned to settle into her father's library to begin researching in which bower Queen Elizabeth had likely hidden the chess queen.

When I walked into the foyer of Grantworth House, I glanced at the stack of mail sitting on the front table. My sister-in-law, Florence, had recently instituted a new rule that all invitations were to be kept aside for her to peruse *with* me. This was due to the fact that, given the choice, I would decline them all. And also because only a few months ago, I'd gone to the Event of the Season without her knowledge—an event Florence claimed she would have killed to attend.

Though any invitations that might have arrived had already been taken away, there was a folded note on the table that bore my name. It was sealed with a simple blob of black wax. And it looked familiar. My heart thudded down to my belly.

Disbelieving, I broke the seal. Sure enough: it was the very same note I'd put in the Domesday Book last night—the order for one of Pix's devices. I stared down at it with chagrin and saw that someone—likely Pix himself, for the writing was a dark scrawl—had added a note at the bottom:

10 o'clock. St. Sequestrian's.

Ugh! How had he known it was me?

That *blasted* Pix. Had he been at Bridge & Stokes last night? How could I have missed him? And if he had been there, why had he not come to anyone's aid during the vampire attack?

I crumpled up the note and shoved it in my reticule, then thought better of it. I fished it out and called for Brentwood, our butler.

"Can you please tell me how this was delivered, and by whom, and when?" I showed him the note with its black wax still partially intact.

"Of course," he said. "It was delivered only a short time after you left this morning, my lady, by a young gentleman on one of those air-bicycles. Dangerous things, if you ask me, my lady, with the wings protruding as they do."

"A young gentleman? How young? What did he look like?"

If Brentwood thought my questions odd, he showed no sign of it. But his description of the young man—slight, no more than twelve, blond hair, and—the clincher—a twisted foot, made it clear Pix himself hadn't delivered the note.

Hmph.

Yes, I would meet him at St. Sequestrian's. And I might use the information Mina was sure to provide me by then as a bartering tool to get one of those devices. Blast it. If Inspector Grayling hadn't been in his office when we were there, I would have taken the device that was on his desk.

Florence didn't appear to be home, which meant I would have the opportunity to practice my fighting skills. I generally used the Mr. Jackson's Mechanized-Mentor, which my sister-in-law believed was so I could perfect my waltzing ability. She was in favor of anything related to me getting on successfully in Society. However, the machine had been altered so I could instead use it to practice my vampire-slaying technique.

Last night's battle with Dancy had been more difficult than it should have been, and I was determined not to be caught so unprepared again. That meant getting back to a regular practice schedule like Siri had demanded, and always carrying a stake with me. Pepper was going to have to find new and creative ways of hiding them on my person.

I was drenched with perspiration by the time Pepper knocked at the door to let me know I'd received a message from Mina, and that Florence had returned home. *Blast!* My sister-in-law didn't need to see me in the loose tunic and trousers I wore to practice. Thus, I'd have to sneak up the servants' stairs to my bedchamber so I could freshen up.

I read the note from Mina—which was long and overly detailed. I was able to summarize the two-page message into four sentences: There had been an unusual number of bodies found near Fleet-street that couldn't be attributed to normal factors such as disease or poverty. In the vicinity was an old Carmelite monastery, built during the thirteenth century for the Whitefriar monks. Most of the area had long been covered up by walls and hills and buildings but was accessible through the sewers near Magpie-alley and Bouverie-street. The mechanical device of Pix's had been found near one of the bodies and may or may not have anything to do with the series of deaths.

Not a lot of information, but enough that I knew I would be paying a visit to Fleet-street to see what else I could learn.

After a bath and clean clothing, I made my way down to have dinner. I had to figure out a way to avoid attending any social engagements with Florence this evening.

I loved my brother's wife. I truly did. She was more of a mother to me than my own—who was quite elderly now, and still living in Ireland. But Florence was also like an older sister. And, she had one thing on her mind for me, and that was marriage.

"I heard the most dreadful news today!" was how she greeted me at the dinner table.

It was just the two of us, for Bram rarely dined at home in the evening due to his obligations at the theater, and my nephew, Noel, was still visiting Florence's cousins in the country.

"What was that?" I said, eyeing the roasted beef tips and gravy and fresh applesauce with interest. I'd worked up more than the usual "feminine" appetite and couldn't wait to dive in. But my sister-in-law would be scandalized if I scooped up a huge portion to begin with; I had learned to pace myself so she didn't notice how much I ate.

"Apparently there was some sort of accident at a gentlemen's club last night, and Lord Wexfeld was killed . . . and so was your nice Mr. Richard Dancy." Her eyes, usually sparkling with life, were filled with grief. "They say his body was . . . well, unrecognizable."

My insides lurched a little. "That *is* terrible news," I said sincerely. And I didn't even correct her assertion that he was "my" Mr. Dancy. What was the point? "I can't believe Mr. Dancy is dead. That's just . . . awful."

"I'm so sorry, Evaline."

I nodded, and to my surprise, tears burned my eyes. She had no idea.

"Tonight we must call on the Dancys and pay our respects. His sister and mother will be devastated." Florence gave me a look that brooked no disagreement.

But for once, I had no desire to sidestep an outing. In fact, I knew it was my duty to attend. Just as it had been my duty to kill Mr. Dancy.

All of a sudden, the beef tips didn't look quite as appealing.

⤙⦁⤚

Florence and I arrived at the Dancy household in Mayfair just before nine o'clock—late for a social call, but when a family was in mourning, those sorts of rules tended to be ignored. I would make up some excuse to leave so I could meet Pix at ten.

"What do I say to them?" I asked Florence as our carriage rolled to a halt. "I don't have any idea what to say to make them feel better." I realized I was nervous. What if I said the wrong thing and made things worse? I didn't know what to do around people who'd lost a loved one. Would everyone be crying? Sobbing constantly? I couldn't imagine a more awkward situation.

She patted my hand and looked at me with sympathetic eyes. "I understand your worries, Evvie. But the main thing is to show you care simply by visiting. You don't even have to say much. People who are grieving often just need someone to *be* there. Just to listen and be present for them. There isn't anything you can do to change the situation. All you can do is let them talk."

I nodded, still uncomfortable. I would do my best.

The Dancys' home was, as expected, shrouded in black: curtains at the windows, crape over the door. The butler wore a black armband, as did the rest of the servants. Inside we found a number of visitors. Most of them were sitting in the parlor with the grieving family, who was also dressed in black.

Florence had brought a large meat pie and two loaves of fresh bread, for even though the Dancys had servants to cook and clean, they too would be mourning for the loss of their young master. Aside from that, food and drink must be offered to all the visitors and be on hand for the funeral.

I expressed my condolences to Priscilla, the sister, as well as her parents. All of them had red-rimmed eyes and wore expressions of shock. I couldn't help but feel responsible, even though *I* hadn't made Richard Dancy become UnDead.

But the fact remained, if I'd been patrolling the streets of London regularly instead of ignoring my duty, I might have killed off the vampires. Then Mr. Dancy would never have met them. And he would still be here—making sweet jests about my *eau de limone* scent and whirling young ladies around the dance floor.

This realization put me in a foul mood, and I went into the dining room where the refreshments had been laid out for visitors.

I opted for a piece of cheese and some slices of apple, simply to appear occupied. Back in the parlor, Florence remained sitting next to Mrs. Dancy and they were speaking intently, but I had no desire to talk to anyone.

Frustration and rage burbled inside me as I stood in a corner and nibbled on the apple, trying to appear unmoved.

"Why, Miss Stoker, what a pleasant surprise to see you here. Not that the reason for our visit is pleasant, of course, but it's nice to see you again."

Lady Cosgrove-Pitt. She held a cup of tea separate from its saucer, as if she were just preparing to sip. I gave an automatic curtsy, mildly surprised to see someone of her social stature present. "Good evening, my lady. It is a shame the reason we're here, but I'm certain the family appreciates all of the support."

"Of course. And please, call me Lady Bella. There's no need for such formality." She smiled—she was very pretty, about Miss Adler's age with gray eyes and soft brown hair that was pulled smoothly over her ears. Then she cocked her head inquiringly. "I understand you and Richard were quite friendly, and I see from your expression you are taking this quite hard."

"It's a terrible shame. Mr. Dancy was a very charming gentleman. I can't imagine what sort of accident happened."

"No, indeed. Nor can I. I understand whatever it was occurred at his gentlemen's club." Lady Bella gave a little shiver. "Of course, being a woman, I would have no idea what happens in a gentlemen's club, but one would think they were relatively safe. One never really hears of such tragedies taking place there."

"No. Not at all." I nibbled on my apple. "You've heard nothing about what happened? Surely Lord Cosgrove-Pitt would know something . . ."

"Oh, Belmont hates to sully my tender ears with unpleasantries." Lady Bella lowered her voice conspiratorially. "But I do hear some things from others who aren't quite as restrained. Miss Southerby—just over there—was saying she heard from her brother that Mr. Dancy had been frequenting another gentlemen's club as of late. I can't imagine that had anything to do with what happened, but one never knows." She shrugged. Then, as if ready to change the subject, she looked around and said, "Why, there's Irene Adler. How curious that she would take time from her position at the museum to come here."

I was just as startled as Lady Bella to see Miss Adler making her way toward us. My mentor sported the same grave expression everyone else did.

"Hello, Evaline. Isabella, how good to see you." Not for the first time, I noticed a definite chill whenever Miss Adler and Lady Bella were together.

"Irene. I see you've torn yourself away from your . . . er . . . employment to make a social call. How very kind of you."

Oh, yes. Definite frostiness. And from both parties.

Both were smiling the cool, false smiles that are common in Society when one is really gritting her teeth.

"Oh, and there is Lady Griffen. If you'll excuse me, please, Miss Stoker, Irene . . . I've been meaning to ask her and her husband to dinner. Politics, you know," Lady Bella added with a winsome smile. "They're discussing a new bill in Parliament next week, and Belmont wants to ensure Lord Griffen's support. Don't ask me what the bill is, though . . . I haven't a clue!" She tinkled a pretty laugh.

With that, Lady Bella took herself off, leaving Miss Adler and me in the corner. I was torn between wanting to ask my mentor about their history and finding out what I could from Miss Southerby about Mr. Dancy's recent social activities.

I opted for the simplest approach. "I get the impression you and Lady Cosgrove-Pitt don't care much for each other."

Miss Adler looked startled for a moment, then her expression turned sheepish. "I suppose it is a little obvious. Isabella and I have known each other for a long time. We actually lived in Paris at the same time, oh, goodness—has it been two decades already? Before you were born, at any rate. There was a crowd of us who socialized together—some English, a few French and Betrovians. I was the only American in our little group. Even though I was in the theater business, singing and doing a little bit of acting, I was well connected and we all moved in the same circles. And, well . . . there was a *gentleman*." Her eyes twinkled a bit, crinkling at the corners.

"A gentleman? Do you mean the case you were involved in that Mr. Holmes investigated?" I remembered Mina telling me about it shortly after we began working with Miss Adler. It was remarkable because apparently Miss Adler had actually outsmarted Mr. Holmes.

"Oh, yes, there *was* that matter with the King of Bohemia . . . a 'scandal,' I believe Holmes's friend Dr. Watson called it. But it was the handsome young prince of Betrovia who nearly was my undoing." She blushed. "I was young and we were in Paris . . . but it so happened he was Isabella's cousin."

"Lady Bella is Betrovian?" That must be why she'd known how to dance the *kelva*.

"Half Betrovian. Her mother was Betrovian, but her father is English, of course. Her aunt had married a Betrovian prince."

"And she didn't care for you being involved with her cousin—who was royalty."

"Indeed not. Not only was I American and not a member of the gentry, but I was also an *actress*, and had to work for a living—and therefore of dubious character." Her lips twitched. "She might have been correct about that last bit."

How very interesting. But now it all made sense—the tension between them, and the snide comments Lady Bella always made about Miss Adler's work for the British Museum. "And your Prince of Betrovia . . . surely he wasn't the one who ran off to Gretna Green with a servant girl?"

Miss Adler laughed heartily. "My word, Evaline, how old do you think I am?" She was clearly not offended, but simply amused. "No, that particular incident happened more than fifty years ago—when the chessboard was finally being delivered to London. As for *my* Betrovian prince . . ." Her humor vanished. "Hugh, unfortunately, died much too young. And in very much the same way your Mr. Dancy did."

I opened my mouth, then closed it again. "How . . . awful. Who . . . er . . . how . . . ?"

Miss Adler shook her head; she clearly did not want to discuss details. "I do believe he was my one true love. The King of Bohemia and Godfrey Norton and the others—even Emmet Oligary—were all merely distractions."

I hid my surprise. She had just given me a fascinating bit of information. "You know Mr. Oligary?"

"Of course. He was a bit older than the rest of us, but he was in our circle in Paris in the early seventies as well." Then she said briskly, "I can only conclude you had a hand in the . . . ahem . . . dispatching of the problems from last night? Which is why there are no remains belonging to Mr. Dancy?"

"Yes, unfortunately."

Just then, the clock struck half-past nine. If I were going to meet Pix, it was time for me to make my excuses. "Miss Adler, I need to leave . . . and I need a good reason to do so . . ." I glanced toward Florence, who was still sitting with Mrs. Dancy and Priscilla. I felt a pang of guilt that I wasn't doing the same—after all, if it weren't for me . . .

"Understood. Leave it to me."

Miss Adler moved smoothly across the room and at that moment I saw Miss Southerby—and even more importantly, her brother. I pushed through the small throng of people with the same intent as Miss Adler, and moments later was "accidentally" bumping into Mr. Southerby's elbow.

"Oh, pardon me!" I said, pretending to blush as I ducked my face. "I'm so ridiculously clumsy."

"Miss Stoker . . . never say such a thing. You are one of the most graceful ladies I've ever had the pleasure of dancing with." He smiled, his buck teeth taking up a good portion of his face. His cheeks had pinkened. He didn't seem to know where to look and kept his eyes bashfully downcast.

"You're very kind, Mr. Southerby." I didn't have much time, so I launched right into the conversation—but not without looking up at him as if he were the most fascinating man in the room. "It's just terrible about Mr. Dancy! I cannot believe what happened. Though no one really knows, do they?" I dropped my voice to a whisper, and noticed him lean closer to me. "I heard it happened at his club . . . but didn't he belong to two clubs? Surely you know all about those sorts of things."

"I don't know what happened either, Miss Stoker. But I do know whatever accident it was happened at a place called Bridge & Stokes." He remained unable to find a place for his gaze to rest, and his cheeks were even more pink.

I pressed my advantage and changed my expression to one of confusion. "Oh. That's odd. When we were dancing at the Midnight Palace—wasn't that a lovely ball?—I was sure he mentioned a different club. The name escapes me, however."

I was standing very close to Mr. Southerby, and I noticed he smelled of basil and starch. Not unpleasant, but certainly not cinnamon and clove and some other pleasant scent, like someone else I knew.

Blast and *drat*!

"You must be speaking of the Goose & the Pearl," Mr. Southerby replied. "Dancy had just begun visiting the place. He seemed rather taken by it. It's more of a public house than a gentlemen's club, you know, and I was surprised he would want to spend his time there." Clearly Mr. Southerby would not.

"Miss Stoker, there you are."

I turned to see Miss Adler standing beside us with a meaningful look in her eye. "Your sister-in-law, Florence, has agreed to allow you to return to the museum with me—you left your cloak there last week?"

"Right. Of course. I'm so glad you were able to find it." I turned to Mr. Southerby. He hadn't given me as much information as I'd hoped, but it was a start. The Goose & the Pearl would bear some investigation. "Good evening, Mr. Southerby. It was a pleasure speaking with you."

Before he could muster up the wherewithal to ask me to go for a ride in the park or to the theater or some other event, I gave a little curtsy and turned to follow Miss Adler.

Once we were outside, however, she indicated I should take her carriage. When I protested, she merely smiled mysteriously and said, "In fact, you are doing me a kindness, for now I can send my coach away without inviting comment. I have made other arrangements for the evening."

As she said this, an unmarked carriage pulled to the curb and the driver climbed down to open the door. Miss Adler gave me a smile, then stepped in . . . with the help of a gentleman's gloved hand from the inside.

Very well, then. I shrugged and did as she bid, heading toward the vehicle she'd called up to the door. "St. Sequestrian's Church," I told the driver. We started off as Big Ben struck three-quarters past the hour. I should arrive just in time.

I'd never been to the church, but had chosen the place because of Pepper's cousin's neighbor. When the carriage stopped in front of the building, I saw it was on an older block, where there were no street-levels except for the ground.

Inside, the church was shadowy and still—as to be expected at ten o'clock at night. There was one long aisle with two columns of pews on either side. Unlike many churches, this one's nave was not in the shape of a cross, but designed as one long rectangle with the altar on one end, and the entrance through which I'd come on the other.

Candles flickered in the front and in a bank of two or three dozen on the left side. A statue of some saint—presumably St. Sequestrian—looked down on the collection of flickering flames. I smelled the faint scent of incense and beeswax candles. And of course the ever-present pungency of smoke.

I stepped in and listened, closing the door softly behind me. The only sound was the faint trickle of water, as if someone hadn't turned off the holy water font all the way.

Speaking of holy water . . .

I went to one of the covered metal bowls at the back of the church and filled a tiny vial with the water. It was always good to have extra on hand when one might encounter an UnDead. As well, when salted, holy water was the best cure for vampire bites.

Thus far, I'd heard and seen no sign of life. But the clock hadn't tolled ten yet, so I was early. Unless . . .

I went and sat in the last pew on the right-hand side and felt under the seat. No message.

Silence reigned. Nothing moved . . . not even a whisper of air. I knew Pix was as noiseless and slick as a shadow, and I braced myself, waiting for him to make his appearance. Likely, he would sneak up behind me. He'd whisper in my ear from behind, stirring my hair, his breath warm upon my bare skin . . .

When something finally happened, however, it was not what I'd expected. Just as all the clocks in the vicinity struck ten, with Big Ben tolling the loudest, a side door right next to the St. Sequestrian statue opened.

Moonlight spilled in, along with a silhouette that was definitely not Pix . . . unless he'd taken to wearing female clothing. Which, while I wouldn't put it past him, didn't seem to be appropriate for tonight's meeting.

Someone coming in to pray, then, perhaps.

I remained silent and still in my pew back in the corner, waiting to see what happened next.

To my surprise, the female figure walked purposefully through the row of pews to the center aisle, then down toward the back of the church where I sat. As she came closer, the flickering candlelight illuminated her blond hair . . . and then eventually, more of her face.

She turned into my pew and when she saw me, she froze. "You aren't Pix."

I stood. "No, I'm not. But clearly you were expecting him, Miss Babbage."

Olympia Babbage peered at me in the drassy light. She obviously was too vain to wear spectacles. "Is that you, Miss Stoker? What on earth are you doing here?"

Before I could respond, the back door of the church opened. More moonlight spilled in, along with another figure. There was a clatter as something fell onto the ground, then rolled in a noisy circle before coming to a shivering silence. Likely it had been the silver top to one of the small holy water basins.

"I might ask you both the same question," said the new arrival.

Miss Stoker

Our Heroines' Endgame Begins

"Mina? You too?" I said, coming out of my pew near the side wall of the church to stand in the back. "What are you both doing here?"

"Obviously, I received a message," said my partner, as if it were the most logical answer in the world. "I'm not terribly surprised to see you here, Evaline. But Miss Babbage . . . would you care to explain how you came to be present as well?"

"Pix sent me a message to meet him here at ten o'clock unless I received word otherwise," she replied. And for once, she seemed to be focused on what was happening around her, and not on some invention she was mentally designing.

The way Miss Babbage spoke of Pix—so casually and with such familiarity—annoyed me. Did they meet often? Did he send her messages regularly? Did he call her *luv*? "Well, he seems to have asked all of us to be here and hasn't bothered to show himself. I see no reason to wait around any longer."

I brushed past Miss Babbage, who was just a little bit taller than me and a little more curvy in certain areas, and started for the door.

"Oh, don't get your gloves all in a knot, Evaline," said Mina. "I think it would be prudent to wait for a few moments in the event he does arrive."

I glowered into the darkness. He was probably already here, lurking about, watching and listening to us. Blast the man!

"I'm not waiting for more than a few minutes," I announced. "I have other things to do. Including a visit to the Goose & the Pearl."

"Is that where Mr. Dancy was spending his time as of late?" asked Mina, infuriatingly correct, as usual.

I gritted my teeth. "Yes."

"Excellent work, Miss Stoker. I shall go with you—"

"I think you're wrong."

Mina and I swiveled to Miss Babbage. "Excuse me?" Miss Holmes sounded as if she were choking. "Wrong?"

"I'm not certain Pix is planning to be here. Or ever was."

"Please explain," I said, my jaw still tight.

"The message I got from him was perhaps a little more detailed than the ones you must have received. He told me he was investigating something near Bouverie-street today, and if all went well, he would be in communication. But his message stated that if I didn't hear from him by nine o'clock, then I should come to St. Sequestrian's at ten."

"What did your message say, Mina?" I asked, growing more annoyed by the minute.

"There was no signature, but the author was clearly a male—and appeared well-educated too, to my surprise—and in a hurry. The message said I should be here at ten o'clock if I wanted to learn more about a situation my uncle was investigating." Mina looked at me. "I suspected Mr. Pix might be involved simply because of the locale of the meeting place, knowing you had chosen it for your communications center. Naturally, I had no way of knowing you would be here as well." She looked around the high-ceilinged chamber. "The fact that he isn't present, but has collected all of us here, leads me to believe he meant for us to meet in his absence. And his absence is obviously a sign something has gone wrong."

"Why do you think that?" My irritation faded.

"He indicated Miss Babbage should be here unless he told her otherwise, and he also told her he was going to investigate at the very same area as a case my uncle is investigating. That can't be a coincidence. The fact that he isn't here tells me something went wrong, and he wants the three of us to determine what to do next. Each of us must know something that will contribute to the solution."

That sounded like Pix. Never tell any one person everything.

I looked at Miss Babbage. "I assume you are the one who supplies Pix with those mechanisms. The devices Pix sells. What are they?"

"I've invented countless devices—and some for Pix, yes—but nothing that he sells. He recently asked me to work on something special . . . but I haven't completed the project."

Now she had an odd look in her eye, as if she knew something I didn't.

I wanted to stamp my foot. "Well, maybe you invented this device *once* and now he has someone else manufacturing it. It's about the size of my palm, and it—"

"It looks like this." Mina produced one of the devices.

I opened my mouth to ask from where she'd obtained it, then closed it. Even I could figure out she'd either borrowed it from Inspector Grayling, or, more likely, her uncle had come into possession of another one.

Despite the dimness, Miss Babbage examined the device closely. She made a sound of irritation as she turned it over and over, and Mina responded wordlessly by shining a beam of light on it.

"Fascinating. I'm not fully certain, but I believe it might be a sort of portable, miniature source of power. I've not seen anything like this, but I have heard about the concept. I believe they call it a battery. The only ones I've heard of were much larger than this—such as the size of a butter churn." Miss Babbage focused on me with an odd expression. "And, no, I did not create this. If I had, I would most certainly take the credit. It's ingenious. And it's also highly illegal, for it appears to conduct electrical power."

"And so we have learned several things," announced Mina unnecessarily. "Mr. Pix is dealing in an illicit trade, which is not particularly startling news. Today or this evening, he went to investigate near a location where two or more of these devices have been found, along with an unusual number of corpses. He has been concerned about a new customer of his, who, Miss Babbage, for your edification, had apparently placed a rather large order of these items. It's quite simple to connect the dots. Mr. Pix believes this customer intends to use this large number of portable—batteries?—for some nefarious purpose, and he went to determine what it is."

"And now something bad has happened." They both turned to me. I might have sounded a little upset. "We have to find him."

"Naturally. That's why he wanted us here. So we could determine how to locate him. But we are *not* going to go haring off without a plan, Evaline." Mina glared at me.

I opened my mouth to argue, but she spoke over me. "I'm sure you consider Mr. Pix a relatively capable and intelligent young man—disregarding his reputation, of course. One must assume if someone with his wiles and skills found himself captured—or worse—then it would behoove us to be as prepared as possible. Especially in the event we find ourselves encountering the very person whom I believe is this mysterious client of his. You and I have personally experienced this cunning and dangerous individual. It will not do to underestimate the Ankh."

It took much too long for the preparations Mina insisted upon, and more than once I tried to storm off on my own.

But she was right. If someone had managed to capture or otherwise detain the slick, sneaky, wily Pix, we needed to be prepared.

However, *I* needed no preparation other than a variety of weapons. I was faster, stronger, and more physically agile than most any other person in London—mortal person, anyway. It was Mina and Miss Babbage—who'd somehow, to my increasing annoyance, remained involved—who felt they needed a complete arsenal of weapons and gadgets.

And not only that, more manpower. So we had to wait not only for Dylan to arrive, but also Inspector Grayling. Of all people!

We'd gone to Miss Babbage's workshop because it was closer, and because she claimed she had things we might need. I was wandering around restlessly when I came upon something in the corner that looked interesting. Like a miniature crossbow with finger-sized arrows. Hmm. I was much more of a handmaker than a cognoggin, but this looked like something even I would want to use.

Miss Babbage noticed me poking around and immediately came over, draping a cloth over the project. "People aren't allow to look at my work until it's done," she said.

Fine. I marched back over to a stool near a table cluttered with cogs and dials and pipes. I didn't care that I'd accidentally-on-purpose knocked over a container of nuts and bolts. Miss Pretty Blond Inventor Girl didn't seem to notice or care.

Dylan arrived first, to Mina's obvious relief. "You said it was urgent," he said, shrugging off her thanks. "Of course I came."

"But you've been so busy at the hospital, I didn't know if you could get away."

He got very serious, stepping close to look at her. She was nearly as tall as he, and he put his hand on her shoulder. "Mina. If you ever need me, you know I'll be there. *Always.* You've done so much for me, and I . . ."

I had to look away because the moment seemed so private and personal, as if the two of them had forgotten anyone else was there. For once, Mina seemed to have nothing to say. And when I turned, I saw Inspector Grayling standing in the doorway of the workshop with Miss Babbage. She was watching with interest. He had an odd expression on his face.

When no one spoke, Grayling cleared his throat loudly. Mina jolted, then spun away from Dylan. "Oh—er—excellent, Inspector Grayling. You've arrived."

"Obviously." Grayling seemed rather stiff as he and Miss Babbage walked over to join the rest of us. "Indeed. And what—no dead bodies in the vicinity? What have you gotten yourself into this time, Miss Holmes?"

Mina explained briefly—for her. She included the fact that this was related to a case her uncle was working on with Lestrade in order, I assumed, to give credibility to the situation. The only thing she did not mention was her belief the

Ankh was involved. And, surprisingly, she also gave no details about Pix and who he was. Or wasn't.

Grayling absorbed the information quickly. "Very well. I can only suppose you have a plan, then, Miss Holmes?"

"Naturally." She went on to describe what she had in mind while I paced and grumbled.

"Let's *go*," I finally snapped. "We can prepare forever, but if we don't *get to it*, nothing will get done." I started for the door, not caring whether anyone followed me.

But Grayling, Dylan, and Mina were right on my heels—with my partner still giving directions and making suggestions. Miss Babbage had been elected to remain behind in case of the worst happening—she would notify Mr. Holmes and Sir Mycroft if she didn't hear from us by dawn.

One could only hope she'd remember to do so and not get distracted by one of her private inventions.

Mina refused to ride on Grayling's steamcycle, but I was more than happy to climb on. Thanks to the split skirts I'd donned in anticipation of a meeting with Pix, I was able to ride astride very easily. I felt Grayling wince as he leveled his arms on either side of me to take the handlebars, and I wondered if the vampire gouges were bothering him.

But then we were off in an exciting burst of speed, leaving Dylan and Mina to ride in a taxi. That was part of the plan, for us to arrive separately in case someone was watching. We would also do what Dylan called "covering" each other. Apparently that meant for one set of us (Mina and Dylan) to watch as another set (Grayling and I) went in first, in case there were problems.

I was still a little surprised Mina even *wanted* to go after Pix. But I remembered how determined she was to capture and reveal the Ankh and realized that desire must take precedence over her dislike of dark, underground places and dangerous escapades.

No matter to me. I was born to do this sort of thing.

❖

Access to the subterranean monastery was through the sewers that were part of the network around the River Fleet. The river traveled north and south through London, but because it had become so clogged and filled with waste over the past centuries, buildings had been erected around and on top of it. Most of the river, therefore, was underground. The avenue above it was, of course, called Fleet-street.

Grayling and I left his steamcycle hidden inside the entrance to the sewers. We were hardly a few yards inside but already the stench was overwhelming. My eyes stung and the inside of my nose felt as if it were on fire.

"Aren't you afraid someone will take it?" I asked, handing him the aviator hat and goggles he'd loaned me. "And incidentally, I don't care what Mina says—I'll ride on that cycle any time."

He flashed me a brief smile, then glanced toward the tunnel entrance as if to check whether Mina and Dylan had arrived. "No one will take it, Miss Stoker." He leaned forward and pushed a button, then stepped back.

As I watched in astonishment, the vehicle seemed to cave in on itself. It sighed and groaned, then sank down—for it had been hovering just above the ground—and when it was finished, the cycle looked like nothing more than a jumble of junk. He whipped something out from beneath his coat and a black cloth settled down over the lump of misshapen steamcycle. "Shall we wait or go on?" he asked after the cover was in place.

Of course I wanted to go on, but I sensed he preferred to wait. So I compromised. "Let's take a look around first."

I was able to stand upright in the tunnel, but Grayling was too tall and had to stoop a little. Along the edge of the sewer canal were narrow walkways that kept us mostly out of the disgusting muck; although there were many places where it overflowed when the path dipped. The tunnel was dark as night, and the only illumination was from the small head-lamps we each had strapped on like hats. Rats darted about, slipping into the putrid sewage with soft splashes. There were other creatures I didn't care to identify that splashed and surged in the oily water. I had a walking stick that also dou-bled as a knife blade, and I used that to assist in keeping my balance when I came across something slippery or uneven.

It would be a miracle if Mina didn't end up in the sewer canal.

I could hardly imagine what it must be like for the toshermen who made their living by trudging through the sewers, day after day in the dark and disgusting filth. They skimmed through the muck in search of anything valuable: coins, buttons, keys, objects made of metal or ivory . . . even bones—human or otherwise—which apparently were used to make glue.

Suddenly, my stick probed something too soft, heavy, and large to be ignored. My heart lurched into my throat.

"Grayling."

He joined me as we knelt next to the body, and from somewhere on his person, he pulled out a larger, more powerful light.

I reared back at the sight of the white face, smeared with grime and already being nibbled upon by a horde of maggots and who knew what else. But *it wasn't Pix.* I exhaled with relief and looked away, but Grayling didn't seem to have any qualms about shifting the body.

"Hold this." He handed me the light as he bent closer to the victim, lifting arms and legs, and turning it onto its side. He was, fortunately, wearing gloves.

I couldn't watch as he examined the white, maggoty body, which was why I saw the two shadows as they approached. They were accompanied by small circles of light. The soft splash followed by a muttered cry confirmed it was Mina and Dylan.

I looked toward them so my headlamp would light their way, and when they got close enough I called out softly, my words echoing quietly in the cavern. "Hurry up, Mina. There's a dead body here for you!"

Grayling choked back a laugh, but whatever bit of humor he had expressed was gone by the time Mina and Dylan joined us.

"Take a look here, Miss Holmes," Grayling said as Mina crouched unsteadily next to him. I could smell a bit of sewage clinging to her hems and saw that she, too, was wearing heavy gloves. "There are no marks on the body that I can find . . . except this here. What do you make of it?"

I obligingly shone the light down, but was beginning to get impatient. Pix was in here somewhere—I thought—and the longer we waited, the more of a chance . . .

Well, the more of a chance something awful had happened to him.

Or was happening.

"Two small marks. Not a vampire bite," Mina said. She sounded very nasally, and I realized she was breathing through her mouth so as not to inhale the stench of the sewers. I wondered how long that would last.

"A vampire bite?" I said. I should probably take a look. But I didn't really want to. The memory of a maggot crawling out of the dead man's nose still haunted me.

"I agree. The marks are too far apart, and too small. And the position is wrong," Grayling said. "But it's like the others they found."

"Let me see." Dylan pushed his way in, and so the four of us were thus crouched around the corpse. "Where—oh. In the back of the neck. One on either side of the nape. That's an odd place. There is a little bit of red around each of them. Like a burn?"

"Indeed." Grayling pushed to his feet, his movements stiff.

"I observe your arm is still bothering you, Inspector," Mina said, also standing. Her hatless head was dangerously close to brushing the top of the tunnel. "Have you had it seen to? Vampire gouges are nothing to be trifled with."

"You've been clawed by a vampire?" asked Dylan, also standing. "That can be very seri—"

"I'm fine." Grayling's voice was flat and nixed any further comment. "Now, shall we be on with this?"

"Yes. Let's be off."

Mina hesitated, but Dylan spoke softly to her. I knew from the first time we'd encountered the Ankh that she had a fear of dark, underground places. But she'd made it this far—and apparently the possibility of encountering and capturing the Ankh, as well as the calming presence of Dylan Eckhert, helped.

Grayling strode on ahead without a backward glance, and I was more than happy to catch up to him. Mina and Dylan could plod along at their own pace.

We went on for some time, picking our way carefully along the edge of the canal. In order to maintain an element of surprise—if indeed we found anyone or anything worth surprising—we turned our headlamps off and made do with a small, handheld device that Grayling shone on the ground in front of his feet. I walked close behind so I could see where to step.

At last, we came to a widening of the tunnel. The walkway veered to the left, and the sewage canal continued straight on. The roof of the tunnel over the pathway became a pointed arch, and I could make out the columns carved into the wall here and beyond.

And just beyond, I could see a faint spill of light. I heard voices. And saw shadows moving about.

We were here.

We'd found the crypt of the monastery.

And as Grayling and I paused, edging into the shadows, I heard a cry of agony.

A man's cry.

Pix.

MISS HOLMES

Into the Depths of Hell

I could do this. I *had* to do this.

But I closed my eyes, gripping the back of Dylan's coat with both hands as he navigated our way through the dark, close, terrifying tunnel.

If I closed my eyes, I couldn't see how the walls and ceiling pressed down upon me. I couldn't feel how narrow the space was, how near the sewage canal was to my feet . . . ready to swallow me up in its darkness.

And so as we made our way along, tediously slow, I allowed my mind to click through what I'd observed and experienced in the last week. What I thought I knew, and what I had been led to believe. It was an organized, mental process, paging through everything I knew or deduced since Evaline gave me the note from Mr. Pix's client.

About the chess queen and the letter from Queen Elizabeth. About Lurelia and her blackmailer, about who could be terrorizing a young princess and why . . . and who had the opportunity to do so. About why she'd lied about being attacked at the Welcome Ball, and what had happened instead. About the vanilla-scented face powder that matched the residue on the note to Pix—which he and I were both certain came from the Ankh. About the fact that Lady Cosgrove-Pitt had been present both times I believed the Ankh had shown up, and that no one seemed to recognize the Ankh at Bridge & Stokes. There was also the fact that Lurelia had actually *seen* the Ankh, and noticed the tiny diamond stud.

There were many things that made sense . . . and yet some of my observations didn't quite fall into place. Clearly the Betrovian princess was attempting to hide a love *affaire*—or at least an infatuation of hers. I had several suspicions as to whom it could be—none of which were ideal candidates. Particularly for a princess who was already engaged to be married. I'd suspected all along she was hiding something, particularly when she sneaked off to Westminster Abbey under the guise of pretending to be abducted. One could assume she was meeting her lover. Likely that, too, was the excuse for her so-called attack at the ball. Perhaps she made up the attack not only to gain my assistance in finding the chess queen, but also to explain a disappearance so she could meet her lover. If she loved someone else, that was yet another reason not to want to marry as her father ordered.

The question was what she intended to do about this presumed lover, and how it would reflect upon the English nation. If she bolted, as her ancestor had done fifty years ago, that would be quite the diplomatic upset.

And then there was the question of who would benefit if she *did* run off and create a scandal, thus upsetting our relationship with Betrovia. The English? Someone in Betrovia? The French?

As we trudged along, I also thought about what those two marks on the back of the dead man's neck could mean. Two of the other bodies found in this area, both of which were part of the investigation Lestrade was leading and my uncle was consulting upon, also had tiny marks like that. In the same position, at the back of the neck.

And no other noticeable injuries on the body.

And then there was the museum guard, who'd also been found with the same markings.

I had no doubt Grayling had already made the connection.

I shivered and fought the urge to bury my face in the back of Dylan's coat. Even though my eyes were closed, I could still feel the darkness. And the closeness.

If it hadn't been for him, I wouldn't have stepped foot inside this tunnel. I was very grateful Dylan was with me, and not Grayling . . . for the last thing I wanted was for the inspector to see me in a moment of weakness.

And yet . . . I was certain I'd seen him in a moment of weakness. He was clearly favoring one arm, and the pallor of his skin wasn't quite right. He seemed to move less gracefully, more carefully, more slowly. There were beads of perspiration along his temples and hairline.

I admitted to myself I was concerned for his health. Dylan's tales about patients dying from infected vampires wounds had made a strong impression on me. If I had been aware of Grayling's worsening condition, I would never have sent word for him to come to our aid tonight.

If something happened to Grayling, then . . . well, who would find out who'd killed his mother?

Just then, I heard the sound of a long, keening cry in the distance. It sounded as if someone was being tortured.

My eyes flew open and I stumbled around Dylan, trying to listen even as he continued to edge along.

"Careful," he whispered, taking my arm.

I could see the dim filter of illumination ahead, and that emboldened me enough that I no longer squeezed my eyes closed. Two dark shadows ahead of us, one exceedingly tall, and the other slighter and much shorter, told me Evaline and Grayling had paused as well.

When Dylan and I approached, she gestured for us to move in more closely.

"Vampires," Evaline said into my ear. "Somewhere ahead."

Then the four of us held a whispered argument for a moment in which the suggestion was raised that Dylan and I remain here while Grayling and Evaline went on ahead and investigated, but I immediately declined. Regardless of what was ahead, I preferred to find out rather than to wait here in the close, enveloping darkness.

I was prepared. We were all armed. We had the element of surprise. And we had a vampire hunter in our midst.

For the first time, I was quite relieved to leave Evaline in the lead.

My opinion prevailed, and the four of us inched along through the dim light. The pointed stone arches resembled nothing so much as a church, and the passageway led around a corner. There were two other branches leading off into dimness, but by now, flaming sconces lit the way very nicely.

I held my uncle's Steam-Stream gun at the ready, and noted that my companions had also armed themselves. Grayling gripped the fascinating firearm I'd noticed the night he brought me home and we encountered Dylan trying to get into my house. Evaline, of course, brandished a stake along with her knife-blade walking stick. Dylan had also been outfitted with a gentleman's walking stick that doubled as a sword.

The tortured cries echoed more loudly . . . but the victim was becoming weaker. I shivered, but pressed on until Evaline held out her arm in a silent, sudden gesture to halt. She curled her fingers around the edge of an entrance and turned to look back at us with shocked eyes.

A spill of light poured onto the uneven dirt floor just beyond the wall where we'd paused. I edged forward, pushing past Grayling to peer around the corner.

What I saw made me catch my breath audibly. The chamber was low-ceilinged and quite large. It was punctuated by a series of pointed archways that led into the darkness, and

I deduced the space might originally have been a chapel or even a small church for the friars. It smelled musty and damp, but there was a lingering scent of something burning . . . something unfamiliar and ghastly. I feared I knew what it was. Gas lamps studded the walls, lighting the space as brightly as a parlor in Mayfair, but the rest of the furnishings were rudimentary: stone walls, uncovered floors, crude tables, chairs, and benches.

Except for the scene in the center of the chamber.

It was a laboratory; that was the only way to describe it. Machinery, wires, lights, and a variety of tools filled the space. At the far end was a tall glass enclosure with an opening on one side. In the center were three long tables. And on each of the long tables and in the glass enclosure was a figure. Captives—all men as far as I could tell, held in place by straps and cuffs.

Moving between the three tables was the perpetrator of the torture. I say this because the individual would stop next to a table, move a lever, and there would be a white spark that traveled from a wire to the man on the corresponding table. He would arch and shriek and writhe as sparks zipped over the wire. Thus, the scent of burnt flesh.

But what caught my attention most horrifically was that when the victims arched and cried out, their eyes turned blazing red. Fangs burst from their gums, and tendons and muscles bulged as they writhed helplessly against their bindings.

Vampire torture.

But even knowing they were malevolent beings, I couldn't bear to watch . . . I couldn't excuse the ongoing torture.

And while I *wanted* and *expected* the torturer to be the Ankh, I immediately recognized it wasn't. However, when she—yes, indeed, a female—moved away from the line of tables to adjust some settings on a panel, I saw her face and recognized her as one of the Ankh's assistants during the Sekhmet ordeal. I couldn't tell which of the two nearly identical women known as Amunet and Bastet she was, but at the moment, it didn't matter.

Evaline gripped my arm, pulling my attention away. Her eyes shone wide in a face of dead white. *Pix*, she mouthed, but I had already noticed the dark-haired man at the far end of the row of tables. Unlike the others, he wasn't strapped to a table, but was affixed upright in the glass enclosure, sagging in some sort of bindings. His condition didn't appear promising.

Then the horrible thought struck me. Good gad . . . was Mr. Pix an UnDead now? Though he was a miscreant and a thief, I didn't want to see him like that. Being vampiric was a death sentence . . . and despite the inadvisability of it, Evaline seemed to care somewhat for him.

Thus it was my turn to grab Evaline's arm, and she seemed to read my mind. Face taut, eyes dark pits, she shook her head in sharp negation—whether it was to tell me he wasn't an UnDead, or whether he *was* and she was writing him off, or whether she didn't know wasn't at all obvious.

But before I could insist on clarification, a different sound filled the chamber. A number of new arrivals made themselves known: three burly men, one of whom I was certain was Hathor—another unpleasant individual from the affair of the clockwork scarab—as well as two more females (one being Amunet or Bastet's counterpart, and the other unfamiliar to me) . . . and the Ankh. The lower half of her face was covered, but her mode of dress and the gloves on her hands told me everything I needed to know.

I tensed, vibrating with fury and triumph. She was here. I'd *known* she would be.

Strong fingers closed over me from behind, and I struggled, then realized it was Grayling and Dylan, both of whom had clamped hands on my arms to hold me back. As if I would have rushed forward willy-nilly. That was Evaline's style, not mine.

Still, I could feel myself itching to go boldly forth and take that evil villainess by surprise.

"What have you to report, Bastet? Any progress with these gentlemen here?" The Ankh spoke in a deep voice as she gestured to the row of three beds.

"They don't seem to be responding properly to the treatment, master."

The Ankh's demeanor portrayed displeasure. She gestured to Hathor and the other two burly men. "Free one of them. Let us see whether they have learned to respond appropriately."

I was quivering with fascination, even as I felt Evaline gather herself up to burst forth. *No*, I thought silently. *Wait*. We had to see what she meant to do . . .

As her men went about doing her bidding, the Ankh retrieved a small metal device from near the table and spoke intently to Bastet. The mechanism was larger than the one Mr. Pix dealt in, and even from my position I could see it was not the same. It was less elegant and more bulky. Additionally, there were dials and levers on it, as well as a curling wire that dangled like a tail. The Ankh held the mechanism in her hand as one of the vampires was freed from his bindings. He stumbled off the table, looked around, and then lunged toward the nearest individual—Amunet. No, it was the scientist/torturer Bastet.

The Ankh did something with the device—turned a knob—and the vampire jolted, pausing for a moment . . . but he did not release Bastet.

He plunged his fangs into her throat, and the woman shuddered and arched, clawing ineffectually at him as he drank deeply, roughly and violently. I could not look away from the horror of the tableau. The rich, iron scent of too much blood filled the air, and the other two vampires began to struggle, fighting desperately against their bonds. They wanted the blood too. They wanted to drink.

Evaline shivered next to me and I felt her body as it grew taut and ready.

Not yet, I thought hard, trying to send her a mental message. *Not now.*

Our other companions seemed to agree, for I felt them move closer to hold on to Evaline this time.

To my disgust, the Ankh merely watched as the vampire gulped from his helpless victim. She seemed to be fiddling with the device in her hand, but whatever her intent, nothing appeared to change. Was she trying to somehow control the vampire?

The UnDead fed on, desperately and roughly, and the jolting of Bastet's body slowed and her twitches became further and further apart as her struggles waned.

At last, the vampire pulled away and released the woman. She slumped to the ground and lay there unmoving. The Ankh stepped over her as her three male assistants grabbed the sated vampire and held him by his arms. The UnDead struggled, but the Ankh ignored the vampire as she walked around behind him.

Though she didn't speak, her movements were filled with anger and frustration. Clearly, whatever she'd hoped to happen had not come to pass.

I couldn't see precisely what she was doing behind the UnDead, who, despite having fed, was still too weak to shake free from his captors. The Ankh appeared to have raised her arms and was doing something at the back of his neck. When she at last came around from behind him, she was holding a small palm-sized object. I could see two wires protruding from it at one end.

Pix's device.

My eyes widened and I turned to Grayling, who had been watching with the same horrified expression I knew I wore. He looked at me at the same moment, recognizing precisely what I'd just realized. Had she just detached the device from the back of the vampire's neck? Even from here, I was certain it was the same sort of device Mr. Pix had been selling.

Was that what had caused the creature to buck and writhe during the torture, somehow controlled by the other mechanism the Ankh had been using?

"Restrain him again," said the Ankh in her deep, fake male voice. "I don't wish to have any distractions while I deal with this one."

I felt Evaline go utterly still as the villainess moved toward Mr. Pix's glass enclosure. She stood in front of the opening, tilting her head as she faced him.

"Still alive, I see. Excellent. I'd hate to lose you so quickly, my clever friend. You have kept me on the chase for quite some time now . . . and I confess I wasn't quite certain it actually was you until you made your appearance here. But now I have the opportunity not only to find out precisely what you know, but also to engage you in some of my own experimentation. You are the perfect candidate—and how ironic that you should be the one to supply the tool for that which seals your own destiny. Hasn't anyone ever explained the dangers of dealing in illicit business, my dear Mr. Smith?"

To my surprise, and Evaline's obvious relief, Pix moved. He lifted his dark, matted head and must have said something to the Ankh, for she reared back a little in surprise.

"Indeed. Well, we shall see about that. I suspect with a little more convincing, you'll be more than happy to tell me everything you know about Emmet Oligary. And then after you've confessed everything, we shall move on to more amusing things."

She stepped back and moved a lever. Evaline's muscles tightened, but nothing violent occurred. Inside the glass enclosure, Pix revolved, spinning slowly around until he faced the opposite direction.

The Ankh picked up a familiar metal device in her gloved hands. The same two wires protruded from it like the one she'd removed from the vampire. They looked like the antennae on an insect, but this was no insect. I watched in fascinated horror as she moved inside the glass enclosure behind Pix. I had an awful suspicion I knew what she was about to do.

Apparently so did Evaline, for I felt her gather herself up.

"Now, keep very still, my dear," warned the villainess. "It will hurt less . . ." When the Ankh's arm moved sharply near the back of his neck and Pix jolted, then shuddered violently, I knew my suspicions about how she was using Pix's devices had been correct.

There was no holding Evaline back any longer.

She shrugged easily from the grip of our companions and burst wordlessly onto the scene. The trio of hulking men spun in surprise and roared toward her even as the Ankh turned to see.

"Why, Miss Stoker. How good of you to join us. And—oh, you've brought reinforcements!" Even as she greeted us, the villainess positioned the second wire into the back of Pix's neck. He cried out as she jammed it in place, and for the first time he began to struggle against his bindings.

Evaline hadn't paused in her attack; nor did she waste energy or effort with the social nicety of speech. She flew sleekly at the first of the men who came toward her, swinging her stake and slamming it into his flesh as she ducked under his beefy arm. He wasn't an UnDead, but he did cry out and stagger back under the onslaught of the infuriated vampire hunter. Blood spurted from the wound in his chest, but he dove after her anyway.

Grayling, Dylan, and I were right in her wake, and in a matter of moments, the melee was on. I trained my Steam-Stream gun at one of the burly men, pulling back sharply on the trigger. The blast of steam roared forth with such force that I flew backward and nearly landed on my posterior.

"What on earth are you doing? Free them!" the Ankh shrieked, forgetting to keep her voice deep and masculine. She'd turned from her position behind Pix, and watched in fury even as she continued with her work behind him.

Amunet, who'd been slinking off toward one of the arched hallways, started and rushed back to untie the three vampires.

I didn't see what happened next, for I'd tripped over the body of Bastet and stumbled to my knees. Fortunately, I kept a good grip on my firearm and blasted it at the back of one of the men as he lunged toward Dylan. The hulk cried out as the shot of steam seared through his trousers, and he crashed to the ground.

Exhilarated by that small victory, I rushed past Grayling, who was facing off with one of the guards, his cognog firearm shooting streams of something blue and green in turns. He seemed to have that combat well in hand, and I headed toward the Ankh. I needed to pull that mask from her face . . . or better yet, steam her with a stream from my gun.

But I misjudged the corner of a table and slammed into it, which knocked me off my path and sent tools and equipment flying. Someone grabbed me from behind and I smelled the stench of death and blood as the face of an UnDead swooped toward me.

Just as the fangs scraped my skin, the vampire froze, then jolted against me. *Poof!* He was gone in a cloud of thick ash. Coughing, I spun to see Grayling stagger away. Even in that moment, I saw he was seriously favoring his wounded arm, and I watched in horror as one of the vampires grabbed him up and flung him onto a recently vacated table.

Grayling's weapon spun from his grip and clattered to the ground. I dove for it, just missing being stepped upon by one of the hulking men.

I didn't know what button did what on Grayling's device, but I began pushing them and pulling on the trigger as I roared up with the weapon in hand, aiming it randomly. A stream of green blazed out, shocking me with its violence—and slicing the skin off Amunet's arm.

I staggered away, spinning to see the vampire holding Grayling on the table with one large hand as he lunged toward his shoulder with gleaming fangs. Grayling's free arm swung away and up, then shot forward, fingers gouging into the UnDead's eyes.

The vampire shrieked and reared back, then lunged again toward Grayling as I sprinted toward them. I used all my strength to clock the UnDead on the back of the head with the firearm, then stumbled away as I dug furiously around my skirt for the wooden stake I'd stuck in there.

As I slammed backward into someone behind me, I found the stake with my fingers. The vampire flew toward me, and I fumbled the wooden pike into an awkward grip . . .

Poof!

The vampire couldn't stop himself in time and impaled himself directly on the stake. The force of his movement was so strong, my arm snapped back painfully, and my whole body swung around. I skittered to the ground with a thunk.

As I pulled myself to my feet, I heard a furious cry from the direction of the Ankh, then immediately the sounds of sparking and an ugly zapping noise.

"No!" screamed Evaline, flying through the air toward the glass enclosure, the Ankh, and Pix.

Pix gave a roar of pain, then one massive jolt and collapsed bonelessly, hanging there by the restraints around his wrists.

I warded off another attack by one of the hulking men, who slung me violently to the ground by the back of my bodice. My breath was knocked out of me, and I hit my head so hard black spots danced in my vision. I reached weakly for the weapon I'd just dropped, but a large boot kicked it away.

Then someone slammed into the back of the man's head. I caught a glimpse of Dylan as he jabbed behind him with the blade of his walking stick as he barreled past, stabbing the man with his knife. The man roared and lumbered up after him, flinging blood everywhere.

I shook my head, and after a moment pulled shakily to my feet, aware that the sounds of the melee had eased. I looked around.

Ash wafted through the air, thick and smelling like death. Bastet lay on the ground, and one of the hulking men was hobbling out of the chamber as quickly as he could on his injured leg. Something heavy rolled down after him, blocking his exit . . . and that of the others as well.

The Ankh was gone, and so were the rest of her assistants. Presumably, all three vampires were dead.

Evaline was at the glass enclosure, tearing at the bonds that held Pix in place. Dylan was there with her, and together they freed him quickly. His muscular body sagged to the ground, and Evaline put her hand at his throat in a position to feel for a pulse.

She looked up at me, her eyes wide and terrified. *No,* she mouthed, and dropped her ear to his chest. "No!" she cried. "*No!*"

"Move." Dylan shoved her out of the way and put his head to Pix's chest as well. "Heart's stopped beating."

"No," breathed Evaline. She didn't seem to care that the Ankh—who'd murdered Pix and whomever else—had gotten away. I wanted to rush after them, but stopped. There was a stone impediment where the doorway had been, and Pix was . . . well . . .

"Heart's stopped beating," Dylan said again. "He's dead."

Miss Holmes

Wherein an Evil Device Redeems Itself

"H e . . . he can't be dead," Evaline breathed. "He *can't* be."
I started to pull her away. I didn't truly understand her
attachment to the man, but clearly she had one. "It was that
device. It shocked him, all the way to his heart and stopped it."

"That's it!" Dylan shrieked suddenly and surged up,
then lunged back down. He began tearing at Pix's filthy,
blood-and-sweat-soaked clothing, pulling it away to bare his
chest and throat. "Get me one of those things. Not this one, a
different one. A new one. Now! Make the wires long. Inspector,
do you know how to work it? Can you make it work?"

"I believe so," said Grayling, sliding away the one that
had been attached to the back of Pix's neck. He settled down
to examine it, his long fingers nimble and quick.

I stumbled away to find one of the devices. When I
turned back with one in my hand, I saw the most curious thing.

Dylan had tilted Pix's head back, lifting his chin as high as possible. And he knelt next to him, with his hands clasped together, back-to-palm. As I watched, he thrust them sharply against Pix's sternum.

"Where . . . is . . . the . . . de . . . vice," he said between thrusts. I heard him counting under his breath, then to my shock and surprise, he bent and *blew air into Pix's mouth.*

Then he returned to the same process of pumping against Pix's chest. "Hurry . . ." he puffed. "Not . . . much . . . *time* . . ."

"Let me," said Evaline, pushing at him impatiently. "Show me."

"Here," said Dylan, positioning her hands. They switched places with an ease and speed that startled me. She picked up the rhythm almost perfectly, and I watched in fascination as I handed the new device to Dylan.

"Can you make it work?" He demanded as he gave it to Grayling. "We don't have much time, and even then . . . well, I'm not sure if it'll work as a defibrillator or not."

I didn't know what he was talking about, of course, but the possibility of saving a life had me asking, "What can I do?"

"Find another one. Find wires. Find something like . . . like tape if you can. Something to hold it to him. Mina, *quickly.* I want a backup, in case . . . We have maybe one more minute. Grayling, do you have it?"

"Yes. It's ready. What do you want—where do you want it?"

Dylan didn't respond, just yanked the device from Grayling's grip. I found another of the devices, but I couldn't find anything like adhesive.

I started to tell Dylan, but he interrupted me. "We don't have time. Move, Evaline."

He fairly pushed her away, utterly rude and focused in the process, but under the circumstances, no one cared. I know I was watching with abject fascination and careful hope as he took the two wires, looked at them briefly, then drew in a deep breath.

"I don't know any other way. But I have to try."

I jolted when he jabbed one of the wires just beneath the skin of Pix's bare chest near the sternum. Evaline made a sound of dismay and argument, but Grayling stopped her when she would have reached for Dylan.

"Let him do it."

"I need the strongest surge of power possible. In one shot, okay? When I say. Don't hold back," Dylan said to Grayling as he inserted the second wire. "I'm not even sure exactly where to put these," he muttered, then sat back on his haunches. He looked terrified, and he captured my gaze with his, then turned back to the bare-chested man with two wires protruding from his flesh.

"I guess it can't make matters any worse," he said to himself. "Here goes. Have the backup ready, Mina." Then he looked at Grayling. "Go. *Now*."

The Inspector hesitated a mere moment, then, face tight and wet with perspiration, he pushed a button.

I *felt* the surge of power as it jolted through to Pix, who arched up and then fell back to the ground with an ugly, dead-sounding thud. Evaline made a sound of distress, but Dylan was already turning to me. "The other one. *Now.*"

He yanked away the device and snatched the other one from me. Grayling assisted this time, jamming one of the wires into skin while Dylan did the other.

"This is it," Dylan said. "Give me all you've got. *Now.*"

Grayling moved the switch and the same fierce jolt blasted through, shocking Pix so hard his body lurched off the ground even higher this time.

Dylan dropped his ear to the other man's chest once more and we all held our breaths . . . waiting.

Waiting.

Then a smile curved on his handsome face and his eyes lit. He remained in position for another minute, then rose slowly. His breath was shaky as he whispered, "We did it."

Just as he spoke, Pix drew in a deep, shuddering, violent breath. Then he began to cough and tremble, but his heart was beating and he was breathing.

He opened his eyes and looked around. Blankly for a moment; then, somehow, he focused on me, then Grayling, Dylan . . . and finally Evaline.

"Blast . . . ," he murmured. "I told Bilbo not to send the messages . . . until . . . tomorrow."

"Never mind that . . . you're alive, you fool!" said Evaline. Her voice sounded odd to my ears. Tight and high.

"Where . . . is . . . *she*?" he managed to whisper.

"She's gone," I told him. "That way." I pointed toward the doorway that was now blocked by a heavy stone door. "They all got away."

I pulled to my feet. I wasn't angry that I'd helped with Pix, of course, while the Ankh and her assistants escaped . . . but blast and blots! I'd nearly had her in my grasp, and she was gone.

Again.

"Let's take a look around," said Grayling. "They might come back."

I turned to agree, then really looked at him for the first time.

"Good gad, Inspector. You look as if you're about to fall over at any moment. And from my observations, it's not from a new injury." His face was bone-white, nearly gray, and an unhealthy amount of perspiration trickled down his temples and jaw. He trembled faintly as he stood, and he kept his arm clutched to his side. He was panting for no discernible reason.

He winced, then tried to cover it up. "I'm just fi—"

"Don't be ridiculous. Do you know how many people have died from vampire gouges? What will happen to—to Angus if you do? And what about your unsolved cases? What then?" I glared at him. "And who on *earth* would want that dratted steamcycle of yours?"

My voice echoed in the cavernous chamber, and I realized everyone was staring at me. Even the newly resurrected Mr. Pix. Was he *laughing*?

"Gad knows *you* wouldn't want it," Grayling said. "But now is not the time. I want to look around some before we leave."

I considered stamping my foot at the imbecility of the male gender—sometimes they could be so stubborn—but that would have been such a female action that I resisted the urge to do so. "Very well. But—"

"Do be silent, Miss Holmes."

I had no choice but to chalk up his rudeness to the immense pain and discomfort he appeared to be under.

The others and I joined him in poking around the large chamber. There was little to see other than a number of Mr. Pix's mysterious devices, as well as the tools and equipment that had been scattered during the melee: wires, levers, cogwheels, and the like.

"Do you know what she is doing here?" Grayling swung around to ask Mr. Pix. "What all this is?" Then he stopped and looked closely at him. "Do I know you?"

The pickpocket met his eyes boldly, his demeanor languid and calm. Perhaps too calm. "I don't know who ye know, Inspector, but I can't say as I recall the pleasure of meeting ye." Surely I wasn't the only one who noticed his Cockney accent was almost non-existent.

Grayling stared at him for a moment, then made a thoughtful noise. Without another word, he pivoted back to a wall he was examining. "I believe there is a . . . yes. Here we go." With a grunt of exertion, he shifted something heavy, and the wall moved with a dull, grating slide. When he stepped back, he was breathing heavily and his complexion appeared even more gray. I noticed, too, that something ugly and dark was oozing from beneath his sleeve—for his coat was long gone during the battle.

However, he'd made his opinion clear and I decided the sooner we vacated this place, the sooner he would consent to having Dylan examine him. I squelched the sudden fear that nothing could be done, that the injury was too far gone, and followed Grayling into the adjoining chamber.

I didn't know the first thing about taking care of dogs, anyway.

"*Mina!*"

Dylan's excited shout had me spinning out of my thoughts and toward him. He pointed at a display on the wall in the room Grayling had revealed. It appeared to be a shrine to Sekhmet, the goddess the Ankh had tried to resurrect—or at least, resurrect her powers—only a few months ago.

In the center of the ornate display was an image of Sekhmet hanging on the wall. Embedded in her chest was a real Egyptian scarab about the length of my thumb, and twice the width.

"Could that be what I think it is?" Dylan whispered. "It looks . . . it looks just like it!"

I reached for it, and managed to free it easily from its moorings. I flipped it around in my fingers, certain he was correct. I even felt a buzz of energy from it . . . something inherent in the tiny object that bespoke of its power.

It was the same beetle—it had to be; I'd seen the place for it in the base of the Sekhmet statue—that had yanked Dylan unwittingly through time to land in my world. I was certain of it. Why else would the Ankh still have it—and on display in such a manner? She must know its power.

I looked up at him. Something inside me shifted unpleasantly, painfully . . . but at the same time, I was flooded with hope for him. "It appears to be."

"Then maybe I can go home now." His beautiful blue eyes filled with tears of joy, and the next thing I knew, I was in his arms, enveloped in a strong embrace.

"Yes . . . surely you can," I whispered into his shoulder.

Miss Holmes

In Which the Inspector Is Decisively Overruled

When we at last vacated the Ankh's lair, it was just before dawn. We'd found nothing else of interest, and weren't able to determine how to open the doorway through which she and her minions had escaped.

As we slogged our way out, we passed several toshermen just beginning their day's work in the tunnels. At first, they seemed threatened by our presence—for we certainly looked as if we'd been digging around in the sewage—but once I explained we had no interest in "poaching" on their territory, they went back to their work and ignored us.

I wondered, as we passed the dead body we'd seen on our way in, whether Mr. Pix would have been discovered in the same position if we—if *Dylan*—had not been there. The thought sent a sharp twinge through my chest. Whatever would we do without him?

But I couldn't dwell on what-might-have-beens, or what-might-bes—there were more pressing matters to which we must attend.

"Dylan, you must first attend to the inspector's injury, if you will," I said briskly in an attempt to keep my tones nonchalant and businesslike. "And we must send word immediately to Miss Babbage that there's no need to raise the alarm."

"I'll see to that," said Mr. Pix.

Evaline didn't appear to appreciate his offer, but she said nothing as she climbed onto Grayling's steamcycle. Without even being invited. Her face was grim as she yanked the aviator cap down over her face.

"I'll meet you at Charing Cross Hospital," Dylan said over the rumble of the cycle. "I believe time is of the essence, Inspector. Do not delay."

When the infernally stubborn ginger-haired detective opened his mouth to argue, I glared at him. "I will be there as well. If you do not appear in a timely manner, I will be forced to take extreme measures, Inspector Grayling. I have no desire to see Angus trundling about on his own again."

He muttered something that was lost beneath the sound of the engine. Then, with a sharp nod of acquiescence, he and Evaline roared off in a great puff of steam.

"You're going to put *moldy bread* on his injuries?" I exclaimed, eyeing the blue-green fungus that had long taken over a piece of bread.

Grayling looked even less pleased with Dylan's preparations than I. Maybe it had been a mistake insisting as I had done. Perhaps a real doctor would be better suited to treating the situation.

But when I looked at the inspector, I realized the situation had become desperate. His color was as dingy as his name suggested, and his skin shone with a thin layer of perspiration. Except for a spark of shock when he realized Dylan's intent, his eyes were dull and unfocused. And his movements were clumsy and slow.

And then there were the injuries themselves: four long marks on the back of his forearm. They were open, revealing shiny red insides, and the crusty skin was peeling back at the edges. An unpleasant stench had emanated from the wounds when Dylan unwrapped the bandages, and ugly green pus oozed from each opening.

Even after Dylan had carefully cleaned the area, as Grayling gritted his teeth against the obvious discomfort, it was clear the injuries were beyond the help of normal medical assistance. He would die if something wasn't done. But *bread mold*? It seemed so strange.

But I had seen Dylan do miracles.

"Not the bread, Mina. Just the mold. It's called penicillin, and although it won't be discovered for more than twenty years from now, there is a chance we can use it today. I don't have everything I'd need to completely isolate it from any other bacterium that might be growing with it, but I did the best I could, keeping things sterile and using some rudimentary methods. At this point," he said, his face grim, "nothing will make things worse. But this could make it better."

Grayling, who'd succumbed to the need to lie prone, made a sound of irritation and possibly protest, but we ignored him.

"What about—what about adding some of this?" Evaline pushed her way closer. "It's good for vampire bites, but maybe it will help vampire scratches too." She offered a small vial of what I assumed was salted holy water. "I gave him some the other day—did you use it, Inspector? I told you to try it."

Grayling nodded. "Helped . . . a little." But clearly not enough.

"Perhaps it will help more, in conjunction with the—er—mold," I suggested, looking at Dylan.

"Again. It cannot hurt. Nothing can hurt. Inspector, you're going to die of sepsis if we don't do something. Do I have your permission to try?" Dylan spoke calmly and quietly.

Grayling's eyes slid to me, and then back to Dylan. There was a flare of determination in his expression. "Yes."

We watched as Dylan—after washing everything thoroughly and wearing gloves made of some thin, rubbery material—applied the bright blue-green mold to the ugly wounds. When he was finished, he sprinkled the salted holy water over it for good measure. While loosely bandaging the injuries, he instructed his patient to return late in the day to be checked and for a reapplication.

There was nothing else to do but wait and see whether it worked.

Since everything that could be done had been, it was time to take my leave.

"I have several things to attend to," I said briskly, "but I shall see you all in three days' time." I looked pointedly at Inspector Grayling to let him know I would accept no excuses. I desperately hoped he would not need one.

"Where and why?" asked Evaline.

"I shall inform you of the specifics shortly, for I have solved the puzzle of where the chess queen is hidden. I suspect there are a number of people who will be interested in seeing it revealed—including our friend the Ankh."

MISS HOLMES

Wherein Mina Explains Herself

As planned, three days after our emergence from the Ankh's monastery-lair, a group was gathered at my behest at the Tower of London.

Included among the attendees were Princess Alix and Princess Lurelia, of course, as well as the Lord Regent of Betrovia and Sir Mycroft. Also in attendance were Sir Franks (the manager of the British Museum), Miss Adler, Dylan, Evaline, Inspector Grayling (who appeared to have regained his color and full movement of his arm, thanks to Dylan's bread-mold treatment), the Cosgrove-Pitts, the Bentley-Hugheses, and several other important and powerful members of Society. Mr. Oligary was also present, and our group just barely fit inside one of the bedchambers inside the Tower. In fact, it was the bedchamber in which Queen Elizabeth had slept when she was imprisoned in the Tower.

Being a tourist stop, the bower was now furnished in the manner in which it had presumably been done during her captivity.

I collected everyone around me and gathered their full attention, then I began to speak.

"In solving the puzzle about where she'd hidden the elusive chess queen, I did a significant amount of research about Queen Elizabeth's favorite bedchambers—that is, the places she slept in the residences she preferred to visit. She was, of course, raised at Hatfield and it was there—while sitting under a large oak tree one day—that she learned she was to be queen.

"One would think that was the day of her most 'glorious' moment. After all, she became known as Gloriana—the glorious queen. Therefore, at first, I was certain her bedchamber at Hatfield must be the location of which she spoke in her letter. But I realized in order to be thorough, I must consider other options as well: Nonsuch, her favorite residence; Whitehall, her largest home and the one she used most often; and even Windsor Castle, where she would be in a stronghold should England ever be threatened.

"None of them seemed to make as much sense as Hatfield, but I still wasn't completely convinced. There was nothing obvious about Hatfield that fit with the 'nightmare' and 'triumph' element of her letter.

"And then . . . I realized I had been wrong. It wasn't Hatfield. Where had Elizabeth had the most nightmarish existence of her life? When she was imprisoned here, in the Tower of London, suspected of plotting treason against her half-sister, Mary the Queen. She was held for two months, having entered through the River Gate of the Tower in the shadow of where her own mother had been executed.

"Indeed, she literally walked past the place Anne Boleyn had been beheaded. Most likely, the scaffolding from Lady Jane Grey's recent execution was still in place when Elizabeth was brought there, and it's said she refused to walk through the gate into the Tower until she became so cold and wet she had no choice but to go inside.

"While she lived here for the two months, she must have feared every single day she would be called to the hangman's stage. It was the most real and immediate threat of her life, for Elizabeth *was* likely guilty of treason. If any scrap of evidence had come forth, she would have followed in the way of her mother. She must have known it could happen at any moment."

"Right, then," Miss Adler said. "But how could it be her most triumphant moment if it was also the place of her nightmares? She was at Hatfield when she learned she was to be queen; I agree that would have been her triumphant, glorious moment. And she lived at Woodstock and Hatfield under house arrest for several months after being released from the Tower, so she was still in some danger then."

I nodded at my mentor. I couldn't have planned for her to ask any more suitable question. "Indeed. And that was where I was stopped in my thought process . . . until I remembered the details of our coronation ceremony—an often forgotten task that is instrumental to the crowning of a new monarch. The first thing the new monarch must do is to 'take' the Tower of London. In our modern times, it's merely a symbolic gesture—by 'taking' the Tower of London, the new queen or king is asserting his or her sovereignty over the land. And Queen Elizabeth did indeed 'take' over the Tower of London on the thirteenth of January in the year 1559. That was, incidentally, the last time she visited the Tower of London—at least publicly. I am quite certain she visited this location once more in her lifetime . . . and that was to hide the chess queen."

"Brilliant," murmured someone in the small crowd.

I smiled modestly. "It does make quite logical sense. And then when one considers the element of soldiers and sailors . . ."

"Quite! For the Tower of London overlooks the Thames, and there are sailors there, guiding barges along the river. There would have been a great number of soldiers standing guard over the prisoners as well," said the director of the museum, Sir Franks.

"Yes, of course, and perhaps that is what one would think . . . if one didn't realize that soldiers and sailors have another more pertinent meaning in this case." I swept my hand to encompass the chamber. "This is the bower where then Princess Elizabeth would have slept. Note well the brickwork on the walls. It's quite ornate and interesting, is it not? And if one were seeking a hidden chess queen, one might look for a loose brick around the fireplace, or in the floor . . . or anywhere else.

"But if one were a bit more thoughtful about soldiers and sailors, one would know that this"—I gestured to a brick that had been set vertically, narrow-side out—"is known in bricklaying terms as a soldier. And these"—I ran my fingers over a row of wide-side-out, vertically arranged bricks—"are known as sailors." I smiled as murmurs of comprehension and admiration swept the room. "And so from this point, it was quite simple to find the only location in the chamber whereby there are four soldiers arranged above three sailors . . . *et voila!* The chess queen is located, slipped inside a hollow brick."

I demonstrated, using a small mechanical tool to quickly and easily cut through the mortar surrounding the piece of masonry. As the small blade buzzed softly, I daresay I appeared calm—but in reality my heart thudded and my palms were mildly damp. I was utterly certain about my con-clusions . . . but this would be the telling moment.

Inspector Grayling gallantly stepped forward, assisting me to ease the brick from its position. The dull scraping noise was the only sound in the chamber, and I felt a surge of excite-ment when I confirmed the brick was indeed hollow . . . and *there was a cloth-wrapped item inside.*

My fingers were calm and steady as I dug out the bundle and unrolled its protective leather covering. I caught my breath and heard the soft intake of others doing the same. *She was beautiful.*

And I had been right. Of course.

"I now present to you all, for the first time in more than three centuries: the Theophanine Chess Queen." I held it aloft for all to see.

It was a lovely piece on its own merit, carved of pure white marble with only a single vein of rose. The piece was nearly translucent it was so pearly. Her Majesty was tall and elegant with sweeping curves that resembled a long flowing gown. The symbol of her royalty was nothing more than a copper crown set atop her head. She was positioned on a lacy copper base that appeared almost modern, and with a little twist, I found I was able to remove the bottom. There were numbers carved into the top of the base, now revealed by the removal of the queen—likely the combination that would enable the chess table to be opened.

Everyone in the chamber broke out into applause and murmurs of congratulations and admiration. I couldn't have been more pleased with the reaction, and I blushed modestly as I wrapped the queen back in her protective cloth.

"Excellent work, Alvermina," said my father as he approached. "I am delighted—"

He cut off his words as a strange figure appeared in the doorway of the chamber. He . . . or she . . . was dressed in sleek black clothing and a white shirtwaist. His gloved hand held the knob of a walking stick, and he wore a tall, formal hat over slicked-back hair. He . . . *she* . . . had no facial hair, but the lower part of her face was obstructed by a sort of mask made of metal. On the front of the mask was a familiar image.

An ankh.

A hush fell across the room. Evaline and Grayling—both of whom were near me—tensed, as if preparing to move, but the figure held her other hand aloft and looked directly at them. She had something in her fingers—a small black object.

"Please don't make me use this."

Everyone stilled and all was very quiet except for the sound of her breathing behind the mask. In the distance outside, the sounds of voices and chatter wafted up from below. But no one would bother us here in this private meeting.

The Ankh walked in casually and continued speaking. "If anyone moves, I will detonate this device. The gas inside will be released into the chamber. When you inhale it—and you will, without the protection of a mask—you'll have only a few short moments left of your life."

My heart was pounding, but I had been expecting *something* like this to happen. Not necessarily this—no, not precisely this—but *something*. This was why I'd planned such a public unveiling.

Therefore, I was prepared. I shifted carefully to the side, using Grayling's body and my skirt to hide my deft movements.

Everyone's eyes were on the Ankh as she strolled over to Princess Lurelia. I felt a rush of anxiety shudder through the chamber as she approached the younger woman. She gestured with her walking stick. "Get the chess queen. Now."

Lurelia paused only a moment before making her way toward me. She was frightened out of her wits and would not look directly at me.

Without hesitation, I gave up the chess queen and placed the wrapped object carefully in the princess's hand. "Be brave," I whispered.

She closed her fingers around it and then she looked up at me for the first time. "Thank you, Mina Holmes. We would never have been able to do this without your assistance." The princess smiled coolly at me, and for almost the first time, I saw true emotion in her eyes. Triumph, excitement, and *life*.

This I had not expected.

I was so stunned I could hardly breathe, and yet as I stared at her, all my observations and deductions metamorphosed into a new perspective. It was as if I was peering through a kaleidoscope and had turned the dial . . . and everything looked different.

And yet still made sense.

She'd fooled us all.

She'd lied about everything.

"I see you're beginning to understand." Lurelia turned and fairly skipped back over to the Ankh, who watched her with smiling eyes.

"Yes, Miss Holmes has indeed been quite an asset during this entire adventure, hasn't she?" said the Ankh.

"But . . . why? What is happening?" Trust Evaline to seize the bull by the horns and charge in without thinking.

Princess Lurelia turned to the Lord Regent. "I have no intention of marrying Sparling's son. You can deliver that message to my father. I will never return to Betrovia, and now that we have this"—she brandished the slender bundle of fabric—"we will have whatever treasure it unlocks."

"You lied to us, then," Evaline said. I could tell she was gritting her teeth and trying to figure out a way to attack them.

I moved closer, curling my fingers around her arm—and was relieved to see Grayling do the same from the other side. It would be just like Miss Stoker to leap into the fray, causing the Ankh to set off that ugly black explosive.

"I did what I had to do in order to get your assistance," said Lurelia. She and the Ankh had begun to edge toward the door. "There was no blackmailer, of course. Ever. Nor, though I tried to make you believe otherwise, did I have a lover. And I stole the letter during the Welcome Event because I didn't want anyone else to find the chess queen. I slipped it beneath my skirt when the lights went out."

"I heard you crackling when you moved!" Evaline said. "I thought you just had too much starch in your clothing."

Lurelia laughed merrily. "Of course, for no one would dare to search a princess, would they? If only you'd investigated further, Miss Stoker, and paid attention to your observations . . . like your friend Miss Holmes here." She shook her head. "But you'd already realized there was no attack on me during the

Midnight Palace ball. I hoped you'd believe I was attempting to hide a love *affaire*, sneaking off by myself and making up an *obvious* lie about being attacked. But I had to meet with my mentor while at the ball," she said, smiling at the Ankh. "We had no other way to finalize our plans. And then I needed another excuse so we could meet again. That was the day I went to Westminster Abbey.

"And then," Lurelia turned to look coolly at me, "there was the fact that you were stupidly released from your duty to entertain me, and I knew I would need you to locate the chess queen. So I wrote that letter and threw it in the waste can, knowing you'd be called back to assist. I dropped hints and clues about seeing the Ankh so you would be certain to put it all together. It was all very simple, and it was all so that I could be *free*."

My vision swam red and my face was so hot I thought it might explode. I knew something was off, I had *known* Lurelia was hiding something . . . but, as she'd clearly planned, I'd attributed her secrecy and lies to wanting to hide a love *affaire*.

And despite the fact that the Ankh was here, making her first public appearance and in doing so, proving to everyone my theory that she wasn't dead, I was infuriated and even a little frightened. Why was the villainess doing this? Why expose herself, revealing that she was indeed still alive? Why be so *public*?

What did she have planned that made her so bold?

What we'd found in her lair didn't appear to be finished, or ready . . . Was there something else?

I couldn't understand it. And at the same time, I wanted nothing more than to launch myself forward and tear the mask free from the Ankh's face, exposing her identity to everyone.

Lady Cosgrove-Pitt had been here only moments earlier. I'd seen her standing in the corner. It would have been so easy for her to slip off and change into the Ankh while I was explaining how I'd come to determine the location of the bower. No one would have noticed her absence during the time it took to remove the brick.

But now was my chance to at least unmask her, even if I couldn't apprehend her. I'd prove without a doubt that the Ankh was the wife of one of the most important political figures in London.

I rose on my toes and met the eyes of the Ankh over the crowd for the first time. She looked at me, but I didn't feel the same shiver of connection I had felt in the past. Her gaze was blank, as if she were attempting to hide any sense of recognition.

"I knew you weren't dead," I announced, drawing everyone's attention. "I knew you were still alive, and I know your true identity!" My voice carried and I cast my glance over those present in the chamber, all of whom stared at me. "And now, I shall—"

My words choked off. I couldn't believe my eyes.

There was Lady Cosgrove-Pitt. In the same place she had been standing only moments before—and, apparently, all along. Our eyes met across the chamber and I felt a rush of shock, then confusion . . . and then fury.

For as she met my eyes, steady and knowing, she laughed at me with her gaze. And her mouth twitched up at the corners as she lifted her chin in acknowledgment.

She *knew*.

And then she mouthed a word at me—an unmistakable word that told me everything I needed to know.

Checkmate.

Miss Stoker

The Final Checkmate

Though Mina had stopped talking abruptly, the chamber remained quiet.

But despite everyone looking at her, she merely shook her head and pressed her lips together. Her face was white and drawn. I heard her swallow hard, and had no idea what had just happened . . . but I didn't care. Mina being speechless was a novelty, but I didn't have time to enjoy it.

Apparently the Ankh didn't either, for she handed Lurelia a mask similar to hers and raised the small black device in her hand. "Farewell, all! Until we meet again!"

She yanked off a pin-like item from the black object, then lobbed the black ball into the center of the chamber. It landed on the brick floor in front of us. A spark crackled from it, and smoke began to stream from the device as the door slammed closed behind our captor.

Someone shrieked and someone else gasped, but I had no hesitation. I dove for the floor, bringing one of the metal suits of armor with me in hopes of smothering whatever was coming from the device.

I was a little too late, however, for Dylan—who was closest to the object—had lunged just a moment before me. He kicked the device sharply and it flew straight into the large fireplace as the suit of armor I'd grabbed clanked onto him with a dull rattle.

Inspector Grayling was already moving too, and so was Mina. They wrestled bedclothes from the mattress and yanked tapestries from the walls, stuffing them into the fireplace.

We found as many heavy pieces of fabric as quickly as we could and flung them over the smoking device, trying to choke out whatever it was spewing. Meanwhile, Sir Mycroft and the Lord Regent struggled to open the door, which had been bolted from the other side. The gas filtered into the chamber—sweet and heavy—but the cloths seemed to be doing their job. The windows were hardly more than arrow slits, but the smoke didn't get much stronger. I felt no ill effects.

Of course, at any moment, I could tumble to the floor, dead, but . . .

Mina grabbed my arm. Her face was tense and white. Her eyes were furious. "It's not poison. It's a harmless gas."

I didn't ask how she knew, but when no one collapsed, and the men—with the help of Dylan and Grayling, and without my flimsy feminine strength—finally broke through the door, I knew whatever danger there was was over.

"We have to get to the museum . . . *now*," Mina said as everyone streamed out, suddenly babbling and chattering with relief. Her eyes were wild and determined. "It's the only chance we have to catch them . . . They'll want to try . . . and get the treasure." She looked at Grayling, still panting from her exertions. "I am exercising . . . my prerogative."

"To change your mind?" He almost smiled, but his eyes flickered warily to Dylan, then back to Mina. "Right, then. Let's go."

That left Dylan and me, along with Princess Alix, Miss Adler, the Lord Regent, and Sir Mycroft—as well as the rest of those in the chamber—to find our own speedy way to the museum.

Apparently, Mina *was* in fact going to ride on the steam-cycle again.

⤖

Fortunately, Princess Alix's royal carriage provided us a very quick journey to the museum. Traffic was forced to make way for the carriage marked with her seal, and in a record amount of time, Dylan, Miss Adler, and I were rushing up the steps to the museum.

The sight of a parked steamcycle told me Mina and Grayling had already arrived. But the rest of us were right on their heels, with the princess, Lord Regent, and Sir Mycroft traveling by another carriage.

We hurried to the Arched Room and found Mina and Grayling there, along with three of the museum guards, who'd been assigned to watch over the chess table since the letter was stolen.

But despite Mina's theory, there was no sign of the Ankh or Princess Lurelia. According to the guards, no one had attempted entry to the Arched Room all morning.

She seemed to read my mind. "The Ankh is very canny. She must have realized it was a fool's errand to come here immediately. I suspect they will attempt to gain access to the chess table sometime when we least expect it. But when they do, they shall be stymied. For . . ." With a flourish, Mina pulled a slender white object from her skirts.

"The chess queen!" said Miss Adler. "Excellent, Miss Holmes! I can only surmise you did a brilliant sleight-of-hand whilst everyone was watching the Ankh."

"Indeed. What I gave the Ankh was a crude stone copy I had made of what I imagined the chess queen would look like. I bundled it up in the original wrappings while everyone was distracted during her speech. My experience with the mediums and séances during the spiritglass debacle made me realize what a helpful skill learning sleight-of-hand would be. Miss Louisa Fenley, the medium, was more than happy to assist me with some of the basics when I pointed out that the Met might be *quite* interested in how she made her living." She glanced at Grayling. "And now . . . shall we play chess?"

They settled across from each other at the table. "Of course, I shall play white," Mina said.

Grayling gave her a reproachful look. "As if there were any other option."

She sniffed, but she didn't seem annoyed. In fact, Mina was in her element as she arranged the white pieces on her side, and Grayling did the same with the black ones on his.

Once they were in place, she removed her hands from the table and leaned back to admire the staging. "This is the first time in more than four centuries that the entire collection is together."

"Excellent work," said Miss Adler warmly. "It is a beautiful scene."

I couldn't help but agree. Perhaps it was the handmaker in me, but I did admire the simplicity and beauty of the chess set and its platform in a world of so many devices and mechanisms. I'd seen it before, during the Welcome Event, but only from a distance, and of course I had been underwhelmed by the thought of an antiquated chess set.

But now I could appreciate it: the huge pedestal that made up the base of the table and its elegant "feet" that jutted out in three directions from the bottom. The top was round, with the chessboard square set into the marble. And each square was indented in the marble, and inset with rose-pink and black marble squares. The outline of each square was made from some metal—bronze, I thought, which gave the table itself an almost modern feel.

Each chess piece itself was mounted on a small metal base that fit perfectly inside the indented squares of the board. The metal bases also reminded me of a modern cogworked design, for the black pieces sat upon bronze bases, and the white pieces were staged on copper bases. The metal designs were lacy, ornate metalworks that clicked as each piece was placed in its starting location.

The game pieces themselves were carved of marble with long, sweeping curves and little ornamentation. And the one and only chess queen on the board—for the black side sported a vizier piece in place of the female royal figure—was the tallest piece, and had a beautiful vein of rose threading through the marble.

"I shall read to you the movements," Mina said to Grayling as they faced each other to play. "There are only six of them per side, and the combination will unlock the chess table."

"So this isn't to be a true battle of strategy?" he asked.

"Not at this time. But . . . perhaps in the future." Her cheeks were slightly pink. "Very well, then. King's pawn to E-three is my move . . . and now you, Inspector: King's pawn three to D-six . . . Then White King's knight to F-three . . . And now, Black Queen's—er, *Vizier's* knight to D-seven. Do make certain not to touch any other squares, and to fit the base in perfectly or I fear the combination won't work."

"Of course, Miss Holmes," said Grayling. Patience oozed from his tones.

I watched, not completely following the directions. But apparently Grayling understood and he moved as indicated. Each time a piece was settled into place, there was a soft click, as if a magnet snapped to the bottom of the pieces.

"The combination presumably works because of the weight of the pieces, and the order in which they are placed—do you notice how each one feels different?" said Mina.

"Indeed. Although one would expect since the chess *queen* is the one which is the most important element, it is the heaviest—or lightest, perhaps—of them all."

"Precisely. Which is why simply replicating the piece wouldn't work for the combination. There must be a certain weight built in to the bottom . . . I can hear something moving inside the base when I tilt it."

"Indeed. That slight tilting, in combination with the magnetization, is the key. So to speak."

When it came time for the last move, the entire room seemed to hold its breath. "And now . . . White King's bishop to G-six, and *checkmate* . . ." Mina moved her piece, setting it into its square.

There was silence for a moment, and then a soft *click*, followed by a *whirr* from beneath. The top of the chess table began to slide off with a low, mechanized grinding.

As it rolled to the side, we crowded around and looked down into the large round base. It was an open cavity, and there was something inside.

"Miss Holmes." Grayling gestured courteously for her to do the honors. "Unless you'd prefer not to slide your hand into parts unknown."

"Definitely not." Mina stood and bent to thrust her hand into the base. She pulled out a thick white envelope that was certainly *not* hundreds of years old. "What . . . ?"

Staring at the packet, her cheeks turning white and then flaming red, she made a soft, furious noise. I saw over her shoulder that the envelope was addressed to *Miss Holmes*.

What?

Mina tore open the packet and yanked out a single sheet of paper, spinning away from the rest of us to read it. We waited in tense, confused silence until she turned back.

"It was a ruse." Her movements were stiff with anger. Her cheeks were circles of bright red. Her eyes flashed with green-brown fury. "All of it. Every last *bit* of it."

"What are you talking about?" I took the paper and envelope she handed me. I recognized the writing as the same—or similar—to the penmanship on the paper from Pix.

The letter said:

Miss Holmes,

You are indeed a formidable opponent. But if you are reading this, then it means I have in fact outwitted and out-smarted you . . . and in fact have checkmated you in this little game of ours.

You did precisely what I hoped and planned, including locating the chess queen . . . and clearly substituting or some-how exchanging the original at the last moment. Brava!

You are a worthy opponent . . . but not quite skilled enough.

What you cannot have realized until this very moment is that the chess queen was in my possession first, and I have already relieved the chess table of its contents. Then I returned the queen to her original hiding place so you would have the pleasure of solving the puzzle on your own. Again, congratulations! Only two of us have been clever enough to do so, and how fitting that we are both of the "lesser" gender.

Incidentally, you may at some day in the future learn what was secreted inside this table . . . but then again you may not.

That shall depend upon whether you are able to keep up with me.

Until we meet again.

And the letter was signed with the familiar symbol of the Ankh.

MISS HOLMES

In Which Our Heroine Is Thoroughly Rooked

"The entire thing was staged," I raged. "Everything!"

It was the day after we found the letter inside the chess table, and I hadn't slept nor given up my ire since then.

"Do you mean there was no letter from Queen Elizabeth?" asked Evaline.

"There was a letter, of course—but if you recall, it was conveniently 'stolen' before anyone had the opportunity to read it. Or at least, before *I* had the opportunity. And then Lurelia, also conveniently, had made a copy of it. Which she shared in order to lead me on the chase to find the chess queen."

"But when did the Ankh actually obtain the chess queen?"

"I don't know. We might never know. Possibly she used the original letter—provided to her by Lurelia at the Midnight Palace, or possibly even long before Lurelia came to London— to find the queen. Or perhaps she somehow found it without the letter. Surely Queen Elizabeth was intelligent enough not to leave only a single document explaining its location."

"And so Princess Lurelia never had a lover?"

"I don't believe so. I believe her partner in crime, so to speak, was not a man she loved, but a woman she admired—that is, the Ankh." I could not keep the note of bitterness from my voice. I had been outsmarted by *two* of them. "And now that the princess has disappeared, who knows what will happen between England and Betrova. You may no longer be able to buy Betrovian silks, Evaline." The jest fell flat, as indeed, it should have. This was not the time to be witty.

"But why would the Ankh go through so much trouble? Did she want the chess queen or not?"

I gritted my teeth. "Of course she wanted the chess queen—but what was more important was whatever might have been in the table. But there was more to it than that."

I knew precisely why the Ankh had done what she did. And the villainess was correct—I had blindly followed the path she laid out, ending up precisely where she wanted me: mortified, and utterly—as one might say—rooked.

But I couldn't explain it all to Evaline. She wouldn't understand. She wouldn't *believe* me.

No one would believe Lady Cosgrove-Pitt was the Ankh. Everyone who mattered had been present when the Ankh made her appearance, and had seen Lady Cosgrove-Pitt also in attendance.

I could never prove she and the Ankh were one and the same, even though I now knew for certain they were. Lady Cosgrove-Pitt had made sure of that.

That was the real reason for this elaborate ruse. She could continue to create and execute any nefarious scheme she wished, and no one would ever suspect the wife of the Parliamentary leader of being the Ankh.

There *was* a silver lining—a small, slender, gossamer one— to this cloud. Clearly, Lady Cosgrove-Pitt saw me as a serious threat and a great adversary—otherwise, why should she have have gone through all of this trouble?

The only person I'd confided in was Dylan. He'd believed me. Of course he had . . . but now he was going to be leaving. My heart wrenched a little, and all of a sudden I felt very alone. More solitary than I had in a long time.

These last few months, partnering with Evaline and getting to know Dylan . . . learning to care for him in a way I'd not cared for anyone before . . . and having a purpose by working for Miss Adler and Princess Alix . . . and even encountering and competing with Inspector Grayling— all had contributed to a life filled with comrades and activity, and even social engagements. A type of life I'd never thought possible for someone like me.

But now . . . I wasn't certain what the future held.

I returned my attention to Evaline. "Since we don't know for certain what was inside the chess table, I cannot surmise whether the Ankh—or Lurelia—truly wanted the chess queen. Or if the entire caper was simply a way for her to ruin my reputation."

It was my mistake that had brought me to this situation. It was my pride and boastfulness that had been my undoing, for when the Ankh had held Evaline and me captive in the opium den, I'd told her I knew who she was. I told her I recognized her.

And then, to prove my accusation, I appeared shortly thereafter at Lady Cosgrove-Pitt's residence. I was prepared to find her not at home, and to use that to prove she was the Ankh . . . But *she had been home.*

That was when *she* knew *I* knew.

Was that why she'd laid low—as the Ankh—for several months after the affair of the clockwork scarab? To plan this whole scheme? Had she traveled home to Betrovia during that time and conveniently met Lurelia, or had they known each other for some time? Who had sought out whom? And did Lurelia know the Ankh's true identity? I didn't know the answers to any of those questions.

But one day I would. I would give her her comeuppance for one-upping me in such a public manner, for the deaths of three young women, for the death of the museum security guard, for the death of Pix (short-lived as it had been) . . . and who knew what other terrible crimes she had committed.

I still didn't know for certain how she'd done it all . . . but I had several plausible theories. And although I didn't know why she was attempting to control vampires by using Pix's devices, whatever the reason was surely not a pleasant one.

I must be on my guard. The Ankh's gauntlet had been flung quite decisively in my direction, and the battle between us was on.

It would take all my cunning and cleverness and Holmesian abilities to match her . . . but I had no doubt I would come out the winner.

"We're here," Evaline said unnecessarily as the carriage came to a jerking halt. (I had a moment of regret that Middy was driving, and not one of Princess Alix's coachmen.)

I looked up at the colonnade of the British Museum—a building I had seen countless times, a structure I'd visited daily for the last quarter of a year. It was a place in which I felt at home, a place where I felt as if I belonged, surrounded by people who knew and respected and perhaps even liked me.

But today I would quite possibly be saying farewell to the first person who'd truly cared for me and accepted me just as I was. Was it because he was from the future, where women were seen differently?

I suspected that was at least part of the reason.

My eyes burned a little as I climbed out of the carriage with Middy's assistance. A Holmes did not cry, even during good-byes.

⊰•⊱

We gathered—Miss Adler, Evaline, Dylan, and I—in the small, dingy basement chamber in the museum where the large statue of Sekhmet had been stored after the affair of the clockwork scarab. Everything was arranged just as it had been when Dylan arrived from one hundred twenty-seven years in the future.

The only thing that had been missing was the scarab that fit in the base . . . and now it was present.

Dylan said his good-byes first to Evaline. She sniffled a little, and embraced him tightly. "Thank you for saving his life. Even if he didn't deserve it."

Dylan chuckled and pressed a kiss to her cheek. "He did deserve it. You know he did. Besides, everyone deserves to be saved."

He turned to Miss Adler. "Thank you for allowing me to stay here, for helping me to find a place to fit in and to find clothes, and a job . . ." His voice shivered a little, and her eyes glittered over his shoulder as she hugged him.

Finally, Dylan faced me. His eyes were suspiciously bright and for a moment he couldn't look right at me. "Now I know how Dorothy felt," he muttered.

"Good-bye, Dylan," I said bravely. "I'll miss you and your fascinating device." My laugh was rough and unsteady and I felt as if the world was crumbling away at my feet. The first person to care for me aside from my mother—who'd also abandoned me—was leaving.

"I want you to have this, Mina," he said. Something cool and solid was pressed into my hand, and I opened my eyes to see the little device he called a cell phone. "In case . . . well, there might be a time when we can . . . well, connect."

I closed my fingers around it, emotions I didn't care to name or examine swelling inside me. I knew he'd had odd moments when this device had "connected" to his world. I didn't know the first thing about doing so, but the fact that he wanted me to have it made my throat dry and rough and my eyes sting. I'd never forget him, of course . . . but now I had a small memento too.

"I wrote down some instructions," he said, and handed me a small packet of paper. "Just in case."

"Thank you, Dylan."

He looked down at me for a moment. I read grief in his eyes too, and yet also excitement and hope. Hope shined through, and my sadness began to ebb.

He had to leave. It was the right thing. He didn't belong here.

"Thank you for tending to Inspector Grayling. It truly was a miracle, you and your bread mold."

Dylan laughed, breaking the tension. "Yes. Who'd've thought bread mold could save the day!"

I nodded. I just wanted this to be over, so I could get on with my life. "Good-bye, Dylan. I don't know what we're going to do without you . . . You've been such a . . . miracle worker. Saving so many people . . ."

"Good-bye, Mina." He looked at me, trying to tell me something with his eyes, and then pulled me tight in a long, *long* embrace. Then . . . very softly: "Come with me."

My heart stopped. Had I heard him correctly? Surely not . . .

But he pulled back a little to meet my eyes. "You could come with me, Mina," he whispered, tightening his arms. "Just think of what you could learn! And it's so different there—like, you could wear pants whenever you wanted to."

My brain felt as if it had exploded. *Go with him. Go to the future.*

"I . . ." Words simply wouldn't form. I was . . . exhilarated by the thought, stunned, and curious. I could leave everything behind. I could be in a world where a woman didn't need to marry and bear children to be considered worthwhile. I could experience all of the things he'd told me about—voting, aeroplanes, electricity! Something called the Internet. I could leave this behind, forget about the Ankh and my father and my mother, and . . .

Miss Stoker would have to carry on by herself. With Inspector Grayling's help. And Miss Adler's. Likely Mr. Pix as well.

Perhaps they would be successful in capturing the Ankh.

I could leave this behind. This world. *My* world. A world where I'd just begun—with the help of Dylan, and Evaline and Miss Adler, and even Grayling—to fit in. To find a place.

No.

I was already shaking my head, despite the excitement and curiosity still rushing through me. "I . . . I can't," I whispered. "I couldn't . . . leave . . . them. Leave this. I . . . *drat* it, Dylan, I don't belong here . . . and yet somehow I do. I *do*. I've found my place."

He nodded, his eyes suspiciously bright. His laugh was a little strained. "That's my Mina. Tough and certain and, as usual, completely right. You're right. You *do* belong here. I'm just . . . really going to miss you." And then he pulled away, surreptitiously wiping his eyes. "I'm ready. Better go before I change my mind."

Miss Adler gave him the scarab and Dylan crouched in front of the statue of Sekhmet. With one final glance back up at us and a quick wink at me, he set the scarab in place and crawled beneath the statue.

I heard a sound . . . a soft *swoosh* . . . and felt a shiver of something in the chamber.

There was a crack of light, and when I opened my eyes, Dylan was gone.

Just like that.

MISS STOKER

A Thief in Priest's Clothing

St. Sequestrian's was silent as a grave and dark as the sea. Of course it was—for what time other than midnight would Pix want to meet?

I supposed we were making some progress, I thought, as I edged my way silently down the last pew on the right. He was sending me messages now, instead of merely lurking outside my bedchamber window.

Perhaps dying did that to a man.

I slipped into the seat, for it was a few minutes before midnight. I hadn't seen him since we left Magpie-alley, me riding off on Grayling's steamcycle, and Pix rushing off to Miss Babbage's without a backward glance.

I gritted my teeth, refusing to think about what sort of reunion the two of them might have had.

So why was I here?

I didn't know.

Yes, I did know. I had so many unanswered questions, and though I didn't really believe he would answer them—I supposed I hoped he would.

"I wasn't certain ye'd come."

The voice, though expected, startled me a little. It came from behind me, a whisper over the back of my neck, from where he'd silently appeared.

I didn't respond. My heart was thudding hard enough I could feel it pounding in my ears. He stirred the air as he moved to sit next to me, bringing with him that scent of cinnamon and spice and whatever else it was that was Pix. I choked on a laugh when I realized he was wearing priest's robes. Beneath the garment, his leg brushed against mine, warm and solid. It was hard to believe only four days ago, he'd been tortured, and then killed.

He held a parcel in his hands, which he placed on the bench next to him. I couldn't begin to guess what was in it—it was too large to be one of his special devices; and besides, I already had one.

"Bilbo wasn't supposed to give you three ladies the messages until the next day," he said, half-turning to face me in the pew. "I knew I'd either be gone from her lair, or dead by that time. Ye'd find my body in the sewers."

"Lucky for you he did," I spoke at last.

"Lucky for me . . . but dangerous for you, luv."

A spark of anger shot through me. I wasn't his *luv*. "What do you want? Why are we here?"

He was different tonight. His insouciant charm was gone, and so was his Cockney. He seemed . . . uncertain. Very unlike the Pix I knew.

Maybe dying *had* changed him.

"I'm sorry you had to see that."

"What was she doing there? Do you know?" As angry as I was, as hurt and confused, I could no longer keep the questions at bay. "Did you know?"

"Of course I didn't know what she was doing. I'm still not quite certain. But I have some ideas now."

"Is that why you ran off so quickly? So you didn't have to answer any of my questions? Or was it just that you wanted to see—" *Blooming Pete, shut up, Evaline!* I'd almost said something very stupid.

"Truth was, luv . . . I didn't want ye to see me puking my guts out. Apparently, dying does that to a bloke. I barely made it around the corner—I was holdin' it back for a long time. And trust me—it was a fearful an' ugly sight."

Blast him. I couldn't hold back a smile. Now that sounded more like Pix. "And it also gave you time to figure out how to answer some of the questions you knew I'd have."

"There are some things I can't tell ye, Evaline. I just can't." He looked at me steadily in the drassy light, and I realized with a start he wasn't wearing any elements of a facial disguise. "Not yet. I hope . . . someday, I hope."

That was something, I supposed.

"From what I could tell . . . from what I remember . . . she was torturing those vampires. Did ye recognize them?"

I realized with a start that I had, but somehow the knowledge hadn't been important in the face of everything else going on. "Lord Leiflett and Mr. Fernhill. They were friends of Mr. Dancy."

"They'd been frequenting an establishment called the Goose & the Pearl—where the UnDead's been known to prey. I heard . . . did ye truly stake your Mr. Dancy, luv?"

"I did. At Bridge & Stokes, your very own club, Mr. VanderBleeth. How did you know it was me who sent the message in the fake Domesday Book?"

He flashed a smile, his eyes dark and liquid in the dimness. "Did ye really think Bilbo wouldn't tell me ye were in Fenman's End?"

"So you knew it was from me. Did you also know Dancy was a vampire? Did you send him there?"

"I heard later about it. I didn't know . . . before. I didn't send the bloke to the Goose & the Pearl, if *that's* what yer thinking, Evaline. Or to Bridge & Stokes, where he might get attacked—well, bloody hell! I didn't like the bloke, but I wouldn't do *that*."

The possibility had occurred to me . . . but not seriously. Despite Pix's manipulative ways, even he wouldn't have tried to put Mr. Dancy—or anyone—purposely in the way of a vampire. "I didn't truly think you had. But were they—Lord Leiflett and Mr. Fernhill and the other one—were they vampires before or after the Ankh captured them? And what about the other bodies that were found—the ones Mr. Holmes was investigating with Scotland Yard? Don't pretend you don't know about them, Pix. You know about everything."

"Not everything, luv. I don't know who the Ankh is, but . . . to answer your question, I think they were already UnDead when she caught them. It appears she's trying to learn to control vampires. Maybe she wants them to be her minions or something."

"And what did she want with you . . . and the other men? The other mortals who were found dead?"

He shook his head. "I don't know. Truly, I don't, Evaline."

"She knows you. She recognized you."

"Yes. That is highly unfortunate."

"She was asking you about Mr. Oligary—why? And she called you Mr. Smith. I don't suppose that's your real name . . . is it?"

"Evaline . . . don't you understand? The more you know, the more danger you're in."

"Oh, right. Because I'm not in any bloody danger *hunting vampires* every night." I stood, disgusted, and began to stalk away.

He was right behind me, grabbing my arm. With a swift movement, he pulled me back to face him. "Yes."

"Yes, wha— Oh. Really? *Smith?* The most common, boring name in the world?"

"Why do you think I chose VanderBleeth when I had the chance?"

Blast him! He made me laugh again.

The next thing I knew, he was kissing me. Arms tight around me, bodies close, his mouth soft and sleek over mine. He tasted like spice and warmth, and I lost track of time and place until he pulled slowly away.

I was breathing heavily. So was he.

"Would you have done it to me?" His eyes bored down into mine as he gripped my shoulders. "Tell me, Evaline."

"Done what?" I tried to focus, but my body still tingled with shockwaves and heat.

"What ye did to Dancy."

I looked away.

There had been a moment . . . a few very long moments while we were in the Ankh's lair when I didn't *know* . . . I didn't know if Pix had been turned UnDead. And I wondered. I asked myself that very same question.

The truth was, I didn't know what I would have done. *Then.*

But I did know the answer. *Now.* "Yes."

He looked down at me, and one hand lifted to smooth the hair from my temple, then to slide his fingers gently along a loose curl. "Thank you."

He stepped back, turning toward the pew. When he faced me again, he was holding the parcel. "For you."

I took it. He slipped away into the shadows, robes fluttering like dark wings.

I waited until he was gone before removing the strings and unwrapping the package.

I recognized it immediately. It was the hand-sized, lethal crossbow device Olympia Babbage had been making in her workshop, complete with small, deadly wooden stakes.

A gift—a weapon, created and designed specially for me. From a man who understood.

ACKNOWLEDGMENTS

Once more, my heartfelt thanks to the entire team at Chronicle Books for making it such a pleasure and so exciting to write the Stoker & Holmes books. It's a joy to work with such a talented, devoted team. Thank you for all the support, from editorial to design to marketing and sales, and all the creative energies you've expended on behalf of Mina and Evaline: especially Kelli, Ariel, Jen, Lara, Stephanie, Sally, Jaime, and Taylor.

To Maura Kye-Casella, for steaming on with me through this series and other projects—thank you for talking me off the ledge when necessary, seeing things from every perspective, and your unflagging encouragement.

A big shout-out to Rachael and Renee Sanders and Bailey Kamp for bringing me much-needed sustenance while I was working on the first draft of this manuscript. I could not have survived that weekend in Vegas without your enthusiasm, support, and, of course, the chips and dip. You rock my world!

Thanks to talented author Kat Richardson for telling me how Betrovians take their tea, and to the supercool Karina Cooper for introducing us in New Orleans.

Gratitude to MaryAlice and Dennis Galloway for being so supportive of this series (and others), and especially to MaryAlice for creating Mrs. Hudson's Stuff'n Muffins for Mina and Evaline! I love those muffins even more than Angus does.

I owe Susan and Marcus Haight the biggest thanks of all for giving me a place to write this book when the rest of my world was filled with construction and noise. You have no idea what a difference it made! Thank you from the bottom of my heart.

Also, thanks to John Ditri who unwittingly helped me create the puzzle of the chess queen's hiding place when he pointed out a row of soldiered bricks!

Big hugs of gratitude to Dr. Gary March for helping me work out the medical issues in this and every book. Even though you might quirk an eyebrow and look at me as if I'm crazy, you always help me find a solution. You're da bomb!

And of course, always—love and hugs to my parents, husband, and children for listening, encouraging, understanding, and even plotting (I'm talking to you, StarWarsDude) when necessary. I couldn't do it without your love and support.

Book Club Discussion Guide

The following questions may be utilized with any/all of the novels as reflective writing prompts or, alternatively, they can be used as targeted questions for class discussion and reflection.

1. At the beginning of the series, Mina Holmes tells readers, "There are a limited number of excuses for a young, intelligent woman of seventeen to be traversing the fog-shrouded streets of London at midnight." What is the mood or atmosphere, and how is it conveyed?

2. Describe the setting of the series. How is the setting true to the historical era? In what ways does it differ?

3. Using evidence from the text, characterize the two protagonists, Mina Holmes and Evaline Stoker. How do they develop over the course of a single book, or the entire series?

4. How would you characterize Evaline and Mina's relationship at the beginning of the series? Discuss how it develops over the course of the three books.

5. Describe Mina's and Evaline's worldviews and values. How do they complement one another? How do they create tension?

6. The Stoker & Holmes series is told in first-person point of view, from the alternating perspectives of Mina and Evaline. How would this series be different if it were told in third person? Discuss what is gained by using alternating first-person point of view, or if it were told only from either Evaline's or Mina's perspective.

7. Research characteristics of steampunk fiction, and discuss how the series fits or does not fit with what you find. How would this series be different if it were not steampunk? Provide examples from the novel(s) as support.

8. How would you describe Dylan Eckhert? How do you think his being from the future affects his relationship with Mina? In what ways do you think they work well, or poorly, as a romantic couple?

9. How would you describe Pix? Is he a likeable character? Considering his actions over the course of the series, do you believe that he is a good match for Evaline? Why or why not?

10. What traits do Inspector Grayling and Mina Holmes have in common? Does their relationship remind you of any other pairings you have seen, in other books, television shows, or movies?

11. Both Mina and Evaline have famous relatives. Why don't they ask them for more assistance? What can be inferred about Mina's and Evaline's personalities by their choice not to do so? Do you agree with their decisions? Why or why not?

12. Consider the covers for each of the three novels. Discuss alternative design options for any one of the three, and explain why that cover would be appropriate.

13. In your opinion, what are the biggest challenges that Evaline and Mina face in each of these three novels? What further questions do you still have about the series?

14. The Ankh appears in two of the three Stoker & Holmes books. What makes the Ankh an interesting or compelling villain? What makes the Ankh a villain at all?

15. Discuss the ending of *The Chess Queen Enigma*. Is this ending satisfying or frustrating, and why? What possibilities exist at the end of the story? Discuss alternate endings to the story.

COLLEEN GLEASON is the award-winning, *New York Times* bestselling author of more than two dozen novels, including the Stoker & Holmes series and the international bestselling Gardella Vampire Chronicles. She currently lives in the Midwest with her family and loves to hear from readers. For updates and sneak peeks about her next project, visit her website at ColleenGleason.com.

Also by Colleen Gleason